PROM

As their kiss deep̲ ̲ ̲ ̲ ̲t account for his behavior. He ̲ ̲ ̲ ̲ ̲ ne couldn't deny this instant, this embrace.

But cursing himself, he drew back, summoning a stern frown. "I won't offer you an apology for that."

She touched her fingers to her lips.

"I never expected that you . . . we . . . would ever . . . kiss or . . ." She shook her head sadly and said firmly, "It isn't real. It's a trick of the night. Such . . . yearnings will vanish with the sunrise."

"Perhaps they will." He waited until she was nearly in the bedroom. "It won't happen again. The kisses, I mean."

She looked at him over her shoulder, her eyes dark with meaning. "I wouldn't be making any promises you don't intend to keep. . . ."

Books by Lisa Bingham

Silken Dreams
Eden Creek
Distant Thunder
Temptation's Kiss
The Bengal Rubies
Silken Promises

Published by POCKET BOOKS

SILKEN PROMISES

LISA BINGHAM

POCKET BOOKS

New York   London   Toronto   Sydney   Tokyo   Singapore

This book is a work of fiction. Names, characters, places and incidents either are products of the author's imagination or are used fictitiously. Any resemblance to actual events or locales or persons, living or dead, is entirely coincidental.

An *Original* Publication of POCKET BOOKS

POCKET BOOKS, a division of Simon & Schuster Inc.
1230 Avenue of the Americas, New York, NY 10020

ISBN: 978-1-4767-1576-6

First Pocket Books printing March 1994

10 9 8 7 6 5 4 3 2 1

POCKET and colophon are registered trademarks of Simon & Schuster Inc.

Cover art by Carla Sormanti/Dagwan

Printed in the U.S.A.

To Jane Jordan Browne,
Bill Peterson,
and the gang at Multimedia:
Thanks for your hospitality,
your support,
and your insight.

SILKEN PROMISES

Prologue

Illinois
Summer 1875

"Why aren't ye wearin' any clothes?"

Jacob Grey jerked awake, blinking against the omnipresent light that was determined to drill straight into his brain. Gradually his vision focused, leaving him peering, one-eyed, at the dry dust-caked grass beneath his cheek. As far as he could see, there was nothing ahead of him but foxtails. Miles and miles of silver-white foxtails that bobbed and shivered in the breeze.

He squirmed slightly, unsure of the validity of what he saw. When he felt the tickling of grass next to bare skin—skin that ought not to be bare at all—the last vestiges of sleep scattered.

Twisting so that he could glance over his shoulder, he squinted at the young girl who had hunkered in the dirt and inspected him with the same intensity a scientist might give a bug on a pin.

"What ye be doin' out here without any clothes?"

He heard the words. Heard them, processed them, and deliberated over an answer, but try as he might, he couldn't think of a thing to say. He could only feel a searing tide of embarrassment creep up his neck and into his cheeks.

Naked. Blast it all to hell, he was buck as a post and lying in a fallow pasture. He squeezed his lashes shut in the hopes that if he blocked out the sights, he would find this entire situation had been nothing more than a dream. A horrible, horrible dream.

When he dared to look again, nothing had changed. The foxtails still rustled in the sultry gusts of wind, the sun still hammered into his flesh, and that young, innocent imp still regarded him as if he were some sort of genie who'd popped from a bottle.

"Have ye lost yer wits then, an' can't make a proper answer?"

He shook his head. It wasn't much of a response, but it was the best he could do. The last thing he remembered with any clarity at all was finally cornering the thief known as the Gentleman Bandit in the Chicago Mortgage and Thrift. Then he'd heard an explosion, felt a stunning blow to the base of his skull, and . . .

Nothing.

Jacob's lips tightened and his hands knotted into fists below the ropes that held him. Damn the Bandit for having such a warped sense of humor. Instead of shooting Jacob or beating him black and blue, he'd tied him up and left him in the back-of-beyond somewhere. Jacob could only count his blessings that the thief had dumped him face-down, otherwise he'd have been suffering from far more indignities than he already was.

As if finding a naked man bound and deserted in a meadow were a normal occurrence, the girl settled onto the grass beside him. Plucking a foxtail from the dirt, she twirled the stem between her fingers, apparently content to sit and wait for his explanation.

Her hair, bright as sunshine and scraped into a thick braid over one shoulder, was coming loose from its moorings. The wind had tugged tiny tendrils free, and they sprang away from her face to be gilded by the startling afternoon light, affording her with a bedraggled halo. Her features, refined and dainty, were put at a disadvantage by smudges of dirt and too few meals. But her eyes were clear and bright and the most astonishing color of topaz and cinnamon.

She appeared unconcerned by her less than tidy appearance, unaware of the way the simple homespun blouse hung on her gawky frame, or how her bare shins and feet were exposed by the frayed hem of her skirt. She was dressed in the same ragtag collection of clothes worn by the urchins that thronged the poorer sections of Chicago, but her bright grin didn't have the hard edge brought by such a hand-to-mouth existence. Surprisingly enough on such a short acquaintance, Jacob had the impression that this child had the countenance of an angel and the mischievous bent of a hoodlum.

She touched the tip of the foxtail to her cheek and trailed it down the curve of her jaw. Her nose wrinkled beguilingly at the tickling sensation, then she sighed and tossed the weed away. Drawing her legs up to her chest, she wrapped her arms around her shins and rested her chin on her knees.

Not in the least bit shy, she examined him with overt interest, making Jacob acutely aware of what she must see. His hair, clipped short for his job, felt as if it were poking straight out and littered with all manner of leaves and twigs. He knew his face was probably dirty and stained with soot and smoke, while the rest of his body was a shade paler and covered in a score of assorted bruises. His wrists had been pulled behind his spine, then tied to a rope that also secured his knees and ankles.

"Y'appear a wee bit uncomfortable t' me."

He snorted at the understatement. The lilting brogue and odd juxtaposition of phrases identified her as a foreigner, but Jacob detected an Illinois flatness creeping into the vowels—as if time spent in such midwestern climes was beginning to have an effect.

Cocking her head, she offered, "Would y' be likin' me t'untie yer cords? 'Twouldn't be a trouble, I assure ye."

"Please." He managed to croak the word past cracked lips and a parched tongue.

She grinned, her gaze twinkling with unholy glee as she

purposely hesitated over her task. "Yer not a madman, are ye? Set free from an asylum? Or a robber? Or a murderer?"

An involuntary snort of laughter pushed from his throat. "No. I'm a lawman. A deputy."

No sooner had the words spilled from his lips than she scrambled to her feet and took a step away—not just physically, but emotionally as well. Jacob was astonished by the immediacy of the transformation. Gone was the teasing minx, and in her place was a suspicious stranger. Where once he had been able to read each thought as if it were tattooed on her forehead, her expression had now become as indecipherable as a sheet of glass.

"A deputy, ye say?" she questioned, obviously unsure whether she had heard him correctly. "And where would ye be pinnin' yer star, I'd like t' know?"

"Fiona? Fiona, dearlin', it's past time we were leavin'."

The call came from somewhere over the hill. It was followed by the jingling of traces and the rattle of a wagon.

"Over here, Papa." Without further ado, the girl brushed off her skirts and bolted in the direction of the road. She was several yards away when Jacob realized she meant to leave him there.

"Wait! Aren't you going to untie me?"

She turned to face him, walking backward. Those piercing topaz- and cinnamon-colored eyes raked a path from his ears to his toes with insulting thoroughness, effectively assigning him to a place deigned unworthy of her attention.

"No."

"Why not?"

"If ye were a madman, I'd do it. If ye were a thief, I'd do it. If ye were a killer, I might think twice. But a deputy? The world would be a lot better off if ye were left bound for good in a pasture."

Offering him a sweet smile worthy of the Madonna herself, she ran the rest of the way to the rutted dirt track and clambered aboard a peddler's wagon. A crudely

painted sign had been attached to the side and read: *Dr. McFee's Traveling Miracle Show.*

Groaning, Jacob fought to loosen his bindings. "Fiona? Fi-o-na!"

The girl didn't bother to turn in his direction. He could hear her speaking, but the snatches of words that floated to him sounded more like a poetry recitation than an explanation to her father.

Damn.

Damn, damn, *damn!*

Jacob kept a wary eye on the road. He had to free himself before someone else appeared. With the vein of ill luck he'd been having, some nearsighted shopkeeper would mistake him for a goose and string him up from the nearest tree.

It took him almost an hour of straining and grunting to escape. By then, his backside was an uncomfortable shade of pink and beginning to sting. Still muttering angrily to himself, Jacob began to pick his way, barefooted, toward a farmhouse on the distant horizon, knowing that he would never—*ever*—forget the little chit who had left him to burn his buttocks in the hot midday sun.

He would find her some day. By *heaven*, he would find her.

Then Fiona McFee—if that was her real name— would discover the true meaning of the phrase *the long arm of the law.*

1

FIONA WISHED THAT WHEN TROUBLE VISITED HER FAMILY, IT would come with some kind of warning. A shiver up the spine, gooseflesh. Any tangible signal that could have given her more time to think. To plan.

Stifling her own frustration, she twitched the heavy braid over her shoulder and hurried as quickly as she could down the boardwalk. Jefferson Boulevard teemed with people busy completing their noontime errands. Curses smattered the air like buckshot, commingling with the chatter of shoppers and passersby. Carriages and trolley cars struggled to make their way through the congested streets. Drays jammed the thoroughfares as drivers stopped the conveyances to unload their passengers or goods.

As far as Fiona was concerned, nothing could be worse than Chicago in mid-August on a sultry afternoon. The smells of summer-baked earth and humanity clashed with the muskier scents of livestock and manure. Everyone appeared intent upon some urgent business, causing the walkways to be crowded with more bodies than a person could count. Certainly more than Fiona found necessary to make a quick escape comfortable.

Her bootheels thumped on the weathered planks, beating out a hasty staccato rhythm that underscored her urgency. Glancing behind her from time to time, she tried to ensure that she was not being followed, but in the constant flow of people, the task was nearly impossible. She would have to rely upon her instincts, instincts that told her that she had a little time. Not much. But a little.

Her goal inched closer, from four blocks, to three, to two. Fiona's fingers itched to lift her skirts so that she could bolt that last slim distance, but she knew such an action would not only be foolhardy, but dangerous as well. Rushing pell-mell down a city street, petticoats flying, never failed to draw attention from the wrong sorts of people. People who had the power to make life difficult for the McFees: spies, interfering busybodies, or lawmen.

She clutched the basket she held more snugly to her waist. Since discovering the extent of her predicament, the hairs at the base of her neck had prickled as if a thousand sheriffs were watching her. Such fears were nonsense for the time being, she reassured herself. Utter nonsense. Although a deputy had come to find her at the laundry, she'd been able to duck away unseen. No one had followed her.

A gentleman wearing a bowler jostled her arm, and forgetting to consider the possible repercussions, Fiona muttered, "Mind where yer goin', y' big ox!" Fortunately, her words were lost in the noises of a hawker selling slippers on the corner. Fiona set her sights on her destination. One block. Only one block remained.

A trickle of sweat began to inch down the hollow of her spine. The tight ball of worry exploded in a flurry of silent accusations.

How could Papa have done this to her? *How?* She'd heard the deputy asking the manager at the laundry questions, so she had no doubts as to the current reason for their brush with the law. Drat it all! Mickaleen McFee had promised his daughter that he'd had enough of his capers. That he was going to be an honest businessman, settle down, retire.

Retire her foot! Not twenty minutes earlier, Fiona had discovered he was up to his old tricks again. Trying to pass himself off as the Duke of Buckingham. *Hmph!* As if anyone with the brains God gave a piss-ant wouldn't be able to fathom that a portly Irishman with a brogue as thick as clotted cream was in no way related to Her Majesty—or anyone else in the British hierarchy.

The Duke of Buckingham indeed. Didn't Mickaleen know that his escapades were beginning to wear a little thin? Didn't he know that nearly every lawman from Illinois to Virginia had locked the McFees in jail at least once and was determined to do so again? Papa was daft to put them both in such a position and endanger the first real job Fiona had managed to keep in over half a year. If he'd merely been content to stay out of his perpetual scrapes, she would have been collecting her pay come the end of the day. Instead, she was being forced to forfeit her hard-earned coins in order to arrange for the McFees to flee the law. Again.

Her stomach knotted in a fresh surge of panic. She knew who had sent that deputy after them. She'd heard rumors that Jacob Grey had been seen in town, and she had no doubts whatsoever that he was responsible for the search. If Fiona had known so many years before that abandoning Deputy Jacob Grey in a field of foxtails would have earned her more than her share of repercussions, she would have acted a little differently. She would still have left him lying in the pasture, that's for certain. But she wouldn't have approached him, wouldn't have spoken to him. Anything to avert a decade spent with that man tailing their every move, charting each indiscretion, documenting each fault.

Her heart sank as she remembered the last occasion the McFees had met up with the lawman: three years ago in the western territories. Her father had been masquerading as the Vicar of Doncashire, collecting monies for the heathens of the New Hebrides. Mickaleen McFee had gathered nearly seven hundred dollars. Then he'd been recognized by Jacob Grey. Shouting that the money was for the "charitable preservation of all things New Hebridian," he'd been dragged off to the nearest town. Discovering that the current sheriff had been shot in a barroom brawl and now refused to press charges, Grey had been forced to let the McFees go since they'd had the good fortune to be caught twenty miles outside Jacob's jurisdiction as a territorial marshal. But he'd warned them both that if Mickaleen McFee so much as dipped his little toe into a puddle of trouble in an area where Jacob Grey had any say, the lawman would lock her father in jail and throw away the key.

The week before, Fiona had heard that Grey had been made a U.S. marshal. Unless Chicago had seceded from the Union in the last twenty-four hours, she and her father stood smack in the middle of that particular jurisdiction.

The weathered stoop of the Honeycomb Hotel loomed in front of her. Fiona dodged inside and hurried up the front staircase, praying that her father was still napping. If so, it wouldn't take long to change into the disguises she'd managed to find, make their way to the railway station, then board the first train leading as far away from Illinois as she could afford to send them. Once she'd put a little distance between Jacob Grey and the McFees, she would formulate a more thorough plan.

Slipping the worn brass key into the lock, she moved into her own quarters. Studying the narrow cubical with its cot and wardrobe, she noted that the door leading into the adjoining room was ajar.

"Papa?"

The rustling of bedclothes and the squeak of the bedframe were her only answers.

"Papa, it's time ye were up." Dropping her basket on the floor, she yanked open the wardrobe and dragged out a faded carpetbag. Not bothering with niceties, she stuffed her few belongings inside, then began to strip off her clothes. She'd managed to steal some garments from the parochial school's washline across town. She would dress her father in one of the priest's flowing robes, then don a pair of overalls and a floppy jacket herself.

"Papa? Time's a-wastin'."

She reached for the buttons to her blouse, quickly pulling the fasteners from their holes. The minutes ticked in her head like a death knell. She was sure that since the deputy had appeared at MacGinnally's Laundry, Jacob Grey would soon be on her trail.

Hefting the carpetbag to a spot next to the door, she returned to the basket. Dumping the "borrowed" clothing onto the bed, she wormed out of her blouse and stepped from her skirt.

"Papa?" she called more loudly. Her haste added an edge of irritation and more than a touch of the Irish to her tone. "Papa, be gettin' yer shoes and stockings on quick as ye please. We'll be needin' to—"

"Leave?"

Fiona had just begun to release the closures of her corset cover when the deep male voice eased out of the shadows from the opposite room. One word. The man had only uttered one word, but she'd felt the gravel-toned growl to her toes.

Jacob Grey.

She didn't bother to retrieve her blouse or shield the bare skin of her shoulders with her hands. That would be the same as admitting that Grey disturbed her. He did. But she didn't have to admit it. Nor by any sign of discomfiture did she have to reveal the way she felt his gaze trailing down the hollow of her spine as if it were the touch of a bare finger.

"Well, if it isn't the high and mighty Jacob Grey." The words melted from her mouth in a slow drawl. One that clearly relayed her caution and the overwhelming disappointment she felt at having once again been bested by this man. Moving with great care and deliberation, she pivoted to face him.

The first thought that raced through her head upon

seeing her long-time nemesis was that Jacob had changed a great deal in the ten years she'd known him. Although she'd been just shy of thirteen the first time they'd met, she'd taken every advantage of that glimpse of a genuinely naked man. True, she hadn't seen Jacob without his clothes since, but she'd still been observant enough to mark the passage of the years. Each time she saw him, the cotton of his shirt stretched a little tauter over the width of his shoulders and the breadth of his chest. In the three years since she'd last encountered him, the most dramatic changes had occurred. He'd grown whipcord lean. Hard. His face had become blunter, all lines and angles.

She tried not to stare, tried not to let him see how much the mere sight of him sent a shot of adrenaline through her blood, but he must have sensed something.

"Fiona McFee, as I live and breathe. Has it only been three years?"

His coffee-colored eyes slid over her with an unwavering thoroughness, moving from the wisps of hair clinging to her damp forehead, to her neck, to the wedge of skin revealed by her corset cover. He held a revolver in her direction, the tip lazily pointed at her navel, but they both knew such a precaution was unnecessary. Fiona had done a lot of things in her life—on the right *and* the wrong side of the law. But she had never carried a gun.

His glance flicked to the carpetbag on the floor. "Going somewhere?"

There was no sense in denying her preparations. Not when he could see the evidence so clearly in front of him. But that didn't mean she had to kowtow to him either. "I thought I'd take tea with the Duke o' Wales," she retorted flippantly.

"Don't you mean the Duke of Buckingham?"

Seeing her guilty start, he chuckled, making a *tsking* sound of regret. "The two of you can't stay out of trouble, can you?"

He was toying with her, baiting her like a cat baited a mouse. Fiona knew it was a game, one they had indulged in often enough in the last few years when Grey invariably popped up during the most embarrassing moments. But he always played by the rules, never stepping beyond the bounds of his authority.

The thought that his authority had recently been extended caused a real fear to twine inside her. "What have ye done with him?" Her nervousness and her fear brought a thick brogue to her tongue. One she had nearly eradicated over the years. If he only knew how much her speech betrayed her, she would never hear the end of it.

"What have ye done with him?" she demanded again.

"Nothing that shouldn't be done. As far as most people are concerned, Mickaleen McFee should be strung up from the nearest tree—and I've a good mind to listen to them this time."

"No!" She flew forward, her hand upraised, but he caught her before she could scratch him, twisting her arm behind her and drawing her close.

"Is that any way to treat an old friend?"

"Friend?"

"Acquaintance, then."

"One I wish I'd never made."

"True as that may be, perhaps you should reconsider your position and adjust it accordingly."

Fiona knew he was speaking of her militant attitude, but the double entendre of the threat hit her about the same time as the realization that she was pressed intimately to this man, thigh meshed with thigh.

A bolt of iced lightning shot through her system. By all the saints, did Jacob Grey have to be so *big?* He towered over her, his chest broad, his stomach flat and hard, his legs ruthlessly fit.

Pushing at his ribs, Fiona tried to gain her release but only succeeded in bringing their bodies into even more intimate contact. Their hips ground together, making her succinctly aware that it was not just his gunbelt that nudged into her flesh.

Jacob Grey must have noted the same thing at about the same time, because his hold imperceptibly lessened and his eyes became a rich slumberous black.

13

"You've grown up, Fiona," he murmured. "Last time I saw you, there was still a bit of the child in you. Is that what they call a late bloom?"

She didn't bother to respond to such a question. His attitude had been irritating beyond belief, but comfortably familiar, like a pair of scuffed boots one had outgrown yet continued to use.

Unfortunately, that well-worn sense of familiarity had altered since the last time they'd clashed wills. She'd always been able to look upon this man as a bit of a pest, but today, Fiona felt his visual inspection as if it were a branding iron. With each pulsing second, she became overtly conscious of the scantiness of her attire. Her naked arms, the half-buttoned corset cover. The way her breasts pushed above the restraint of her stays and spilled into the tatted yoke of her camisole. Because of the heat of the day, she'd forgone her customary four petticoats and worn only two. The flimsiness of the fabric offered no resistance to the warmth of his legs and the buckles and ridges of his holster.

"When, Fiona?"

The words were barely distinguishable, more a gruff whisper than coherent speech.

"When *what?*" she ground out between clenched teeth, trying to deny the thundering sensations that spilled through her veins like the bubbles of a natural spring.

"When did you . . . blossom?"

The comment sounded as if the transformation was to be regarded as a miracle of gargantuan proportions. "Ye can go straight to bloody hell!" Her curse was punctuated by a hard kick to his shins.

Grey yelped in surprise, but his arms tightened rather than loosening. "You little wildcat!"

"Let . . . me . . . *go!*"

"Not until you promise to behave."

Wriggling, she fought to free herself as the scalding tide flooding her cheeks began to singe her hair. "As ye so plainly pointed out t' me, I am not a child t' be ordered about according to yer whims."

"No, you're the daughter of the man I've arrested."

Papa.

His statement effortlessly reminded her of what Fiona had so nearly forgotten. Papa had been here. Jacob Grey had probably stormed into his room, taken him captive —and who knew what else. Beaten him? Humiliated him? Dragged him off to some horrid prison?

"What have ye done?"

"Will you stay calm if I tell you?"

"Damn it, what have ye—"

He brought her flush against the cradle of his hips and a certain area of his anatomy with which she would rather remain a stranger. The heat in her face increased threefold. Since Fiona had a tendency to blush at the drop of a hat, she could only pray that Grey attributed her heightened color to the airless room and the fervidness of her protest.

"Not until you promise to remain calm."

Her teeth snapped together with an audible click, but she schooled her features into a concerted blandness.

"Fine."

He studied her suspiciously. "You will sit on the bed, arms folded, and listen."

Her lips pursed at his patronizing tone, but she nodded.

"Very well." He loosened his grip, bit by bit, as if expecting her to bolt at any moment. When she remained true to her agreement and didn't try to lash out at him, he gestured to the cot.

Whirling, she marched to her assigned place, sat stiffly on the edge, and folded her hands in her lap.

"What . . . have ye done with me father?"

Jacob propped his shoulders on the doorjamb, effectively cutting off her escape should she foolishly think to try such a thing. But Fiona was not a foolish woman. She knew the futility of such an attempt. Grey could outrun her should she try to dodge into the other room. Besides which, he had her father. Until she knew what Grey meant to do to him, she couldn't leave. Wouldn't leave.

15

"Mickaleen is safely tucked away."

"Which jail?"

Grey didn't immediately respond, and she glanced up. There was no softness in him, no hint of vulnerability. He could have been carved from stone.

"Well?"

"He's been taken into custody."

"At . . . which . . . jail?" she repeated.

"He's not in a jail."

Fiona could not have been more surprised had he burst into song. If there was one thing she knew about Grey, it was that he was true to his word. He believed that a man's actions were either black or white—there was no fuzzy area in between. If he said he would arrest Mickaleen McFee for breaking the law, it was only a matter of time. So if Mickaleen McFee had not been taken to prison, Grey must have . . .

The color suddenly bled from her face. Her heart clenched, then dropped to the base of her chest.

"Ye've killed him. Damn ye! Ye've *killed* him!"

2

"YE HUGE, OVERGROWN, BLOODY BASTARD!"

Jacob barely had the time to straighten from the door. Fiona launched herself in his direction, clawing and scratching, screaming a mixture of obscenities peppered with colorful Irish colloquialisms regarding his parentage. It wasn't until he caught the gist of what she was saying that he realized she'd misunderstood and thought her father was dead.

"Hold on now!"

She slammed him against the door panels and began to pummel him with blows. Swearing, he tried to restrain her, but she was possessed by some demon and wanted only to wreak her punishment for the hurt she imagined he'd inflicted.

The revolver tumbled from his grip and hit the floor, discharging into the wall. When she drew her knee up with an obvious aim in mind, Jacob hissed, wrapped his arms around her waist, and tackled her onto the cot, pinning her to the mattress.

"Hells bells, woman! Would you listen to me? Your father's not dead! He's at the Liberty Hotel!"

It took a full minute for his words to sink into her

brain. When they did, she didn't stop altogether but gradually calmed—a kick here, a punch there—losing her anger like a child's wind-up bauble uncoiling its spring.

"He's not dead?"

She panted beneath him, her chest rising and falling with the effort. Her hair, partially freed from its braid, spread wildly about her face, giving her an inexplicably wanton appearance.

"Ye haven't killed him? Ye really haven't killed him?"

"My word of honor."

His promise left her limp and suspiciously bright-eyed. She blinked at the telltale moisture, sniffed, then demanded, "So why didn't ye say so in the first place, lawman?"

His head dropped in weary resignation at her belligerent tone and he sighed, trying to regain his composure and his breath. He should have known better than to expect any show of gratitude or softness from this woman. He and Fiona McFee reacted as favorably to one another as a match to dried grass.

"Get up, ye big oaf."

She writhed beneath him, making him conscious of the way he sprawled upon her, his legs wrapped about her thighs. He'd stretched her arms overhead and grasped her wrists, causing her breasts to plump beneath the strictures of her undergarments.

"If I let you loose you'll emasculate me," Jacob stated after some time.

Without a word, she managed to relay that as far as she was concerned, such an idea would not be completely unwelcome. Jacob had to smother an unwilling grin. She had more fire and spirit than ten ladies combined.

"Let . . . me . . . *up!*"

"No."

Her glare could have set fire to his eyebrows, but Jacob ignored it. His fingers tightened around her wrists, absorbing the velvety texture of her skin. He knew she'd been working in a laundry, but he felt no evidence of such labor in the form of soap-roughened hands. No, not at all.

"Damn ye, stop gaping at me like I'm a peppermint stick in need o' tasting."

The very thought proved interesting, causing him to note the fullness of her lips, the ripe red color. Disgusted with the bent of his own thoughts, he pulled his wayward brain into line. True, he'd been away from the comforts of the city for quite some time. True, he'd been celibate as a monk for months and longed for a little bit of refined company. But this was not just any female. This was Fiona McFee. Tangling with her would be like tangling with barbed wire.

Clearing his throat to rid it of an annoying sense of dryness, he stated, "I want to talk to you, peacefully and rationally. If this is the way it has to be done in order to escape personal injury, then I'm willing."

"Get *off!*"

"No."

He waited until she realized he was not about to give in to her demands. Each involuntary emotional concession was plainly displayed on her face, first in the annoyed pursing of her lips, the jutting of her chin, then the shift of her shoulders. She took as deep a breath as she was capable of doing in her current position and asked, "What do ye want?"

"I'd like to make a deal."

"Do ye honestly expect me to take ye seriously? Everyone in the state of Illinois and beyond knows that Jacob Grey doesn't make deals."

"Perhaps I'm willing to learn."

She digested that comment, but obviously didn't like the hypothesis she'd formed after such ruminations. "So it's come to this. I dally with ye how many times . . . once? . . . twice? . . . and ye let my father go? Is that what ye mean to say?"

"Don't flatter yourself. I've got no designs on your body."

Rather than offering a sense of reassurance, his words

only insulted her. She fought with all her might, trying to release at least one hand to hit him, but he hastened to add, "I need a little of your time is all. Just your time."

"Get *off!*"

All her bucking had begun to exact a telling reaction from Jacob's body. Deciding he needed a bit of breathing room in order to best phrase his proposition, Jacob reluctantly slid off the bed and bent to retrieve his revolver.

Fiona scrambled backward, sitting with her shoulders to the wall and her legs drawn up to her chest in much the same position she'd adopted in the pasture on that day so long ago.

Turning the chair around, Jacob straddled it, resting his arms on the upper rung, his weapon once again pointing in her general direction.

Fiona attempted to repair the damage done to her hair as best as she could, buttoned the placket of her corset cover as high as it would allow, then rubbed her nose, sniffed, and asked, "What kind o' deal are ye proposing, an' what does it have t' do with m' sainted father?"

"Your father's a crook."

"Says ye."

"As well as the combined states of Illinois, Virginia, Missouri, Arkan—"

"Enough! If he's so blasted dangerous t' society, then why have ye put him in a hotel?"

Her brogue grew nearly as cloying as her father's, a sure sign that she was still angry enough to spit nails. It was a point he'd noticed about her long ago.

He grinned, stretching his legs in front of him. "As we both know, your father has racked up enough offenses that I could very well throw him into the nearest jailhouse and forget I ever put him there."

She didn't offer a retort but watched him with a steely gaze.

"Therefore, I find myself in the unusual position of being forced to make a trade."

"Forced? By whom?"

"The governor."

"D'ye mean t' tell me the governor himself is forcin' ye into this?" The idea caused her to chortle in delight. "The high and mighty Marshal Grey, bein' told t' fraternize with the lowly. Imagine that."

Her taunts had enough of a sting behind them to prick his pride, but Jacob refused to allow her the satisfaction of seeing that she'd struck a nerve. When the governor had been told the nature of their investigation and the methods that would have to be employed, the man had decided to extend the offer of a pardon to the McFees due to their unorthodox talents. Jacob had been the first to protest—but protest in vain. He had been requested—no, *ordered*—to put his personal feelings aside and enlist this woman's help.

"What kind of trade did ye have in mind, Grey?"

He stood, still keeping her well in the range of his sights. Beside the cot, a crate had been turned on its side and used as a makeshift nightstand. Fiona had topped it with a chipped china plate that was littered with all sorts of feminine frippery: hairpins, a needle, thread, brush, an empty bottle of scent, and a buttonhook. In the midst of it all lay a worn deck of cards.

Jacob collected the cards and extended them toward her. "You used to be a bit of a gambler."

"As far as I can recollect, such a skill's not a crime."

"Then you still play?"

She shrugged. "Now and then."

"Are you good?"

Her brows lifted with imperious pride. "I'm the best."

"Show me."

She took the deck. "What d' ye want me t' do?"

"Shuffle, cut the cards, and deal me a winning hand."

"Are ye an' the governor thinkin' of openin' a gamblin' hall, then?"

"Just do it."

She didn't bother to glance down. Her fingers, long, slender, and dexterous, shuffled, fanned, and cut the cards in a show of skill that would have made a saloonkeeper salivate. She then dealt a round for him and one for her. When Jacob showed his cards, his three of a kind bested her pair.

"Now deal another set that will beat both of us."

She grinned, flipping the cards onto the blanket. He was concentrating on her technique, trying to see how she would perform such a feat, but even to his discerning scrutiny, she appeared to be dealing fairly from the top of the deck.

"Turn them."

One by one, she exposed the cards. A royal flush.

"How do you do it?"

Her smile was leisurely and infinitely wicked. "I cheat."

"Has anyone ever caught you?"

"Nay."

"Do you think anyone ever will?"

She shook her head, her lips slipping into a slow, cocky grin—the tacit answer proving more emphatic than the most elaborate boast.

"Have you been gambling at all in Illinois for the last year or so?"

"Not that I can recall. It's more of a hobby than a vocation. As strange as it may appear t' ye, my father frowns on women playing cards in public."

Jacob settled into the chair. For the first time since cornering Fiona, he felt a slow thrum of satisfaction.

"I've been asked to offer a pardon—for you and your father—in exchange for six to eight weeks of your time, if you would be willing to play cards. In public."

"Why?"

"I have a little job I want you to do."

"Is it legal?"

He shot her a pithy glance, and she said, "I never thought ye'd make deals either. Why should I assume yer still on the right side of the law?"

"I've been made U.S. marshal."

"It hasn't stopped others from using such a title for their own gains."

Jacob had to concede that point. "I assure you that everything I plan to propose is completely above board." Seeing that he had her attention if not her agreement, he sheathed his revolver. "Recently the states of New York, Illinois, and several of the western territories have been plagued by a wave of counterfeit bills made with such skill and exact detail that they are nearly impossible to detect by anyone other than an expert. For two months, over a half-dozen lawmen have been trying to trace the source of the currency. We believe that we've narrowed the possible culprits down to one man, a Mr. Darby Kensington of New York."

"What does that have to do with me?"

"Our suspect is a gambler, working out of several cities and states by way of the tourist trains that travel from New York, Chicago, Denver, and finally San Francisco. I need someone to join the guests, get close to the man, and gain his confidence. That person should also have enough skill at poker to involve him in a lighthearted game of cards, then make him lose heavily enough to risk making more money to pay off his debts."

"That person being me."

"If you're agreeable."

She rose from the bed. Jacob stiffened, then relaxed when he saw she only meant to pace rather than run away. His idea had intrigued her enough to make her listen, but she obviously still had her doubts.

"I take it this man is a typical gambler—smooth, elegant, educated."

"Yes."

"Then how do ye propose that I snare him into yer little trap?" She gestured to her worn undergarments. "I'm not exactly a case for charity, but I'm not the Queen Mum, either."

"The governor has allotted a good sum of money to this cause. Whatever we need beyond that amount will come from other sources. I have some private connections with a banker who is willing to fund an appropriate wardrobe and whatever other expenses might occur. He's seen enough of the phony greenbacks coming through his establishment that he's willing to put his own stakes into having the man caught."

She stopped in midstride. "I'd be given new clothes?"

For the first time that Jacob could remember, Fiona McFee's mouth gaped. Suddenly he realized that her life had not been an easy one. She'd been dragged pillar to post by her father and forced to endure his never-ending flimflammery. Such a life wasn't apt to supply pretty things. The clothes she owned were probably stolen, castoffs, or cheap substitutions of the current fashions.

Standing, Jacob prowled toward her, mustering all of the charm he possessed. "Just think of it, Fiona," he commanded silkily. "New skirts and bonnets and shawls. Shoes and gloves and hair ribbons."

She bit her lip, obviously tempted. "What about the things for underneath?"

If Jacob didn't know better, he'd say a positive hunger gleamed in her eyes.

"We'll buy whatever you think you'll need. In silks and satins and laces, if you'd like."

He must have gone too far because she frowned. "Ye must want me badly enough t' promise all that."

"I need you."

"There are others who could do the job."

"But none with your talent for larceny."

He could see that she was weakening. Propping one hand on the wardrobe behind her, he leaned toward her, adopting his most conciliatory attitude. "We believe our suspect will be following his usual traveling patterns. If so, he'll be taking the train scheduled to leave in mid-September. We have four to six weeks to get you ready—but if he changes his plans we may need to adjust accordingly. The actual train excursion and ensuing card games should only take about a fortnight. In all, you'll be committing yourself to about six to eight weeks worth of work, but I need your answer today. If you say no"—he shrugged in obvious unconcern—"I won't try to change your mind. But if you agree, we'll begin preparing you for your part come morning."

"My part?"

"In order to add to your . . . mystique and whet his appetite, we'll attempt to pass you off as a British widow with a flare for cards."

"British?" She wrinkled her nose in distaste. She tried to brush past him, but he blocked her with the wall of his chest. "Ye've picked the wrong woman, Grey. I'm no Brit."

"No, but you *are* an actress." He leaned closer, his words becoming intense. "I've seen you, Fiona. For years you've been riding with your father, acting out schemes that would make most women blanch."

"If I'm with ye for six to eight weeks, where will my father be all that time? I don't want him taken to some jail. He hasn't been well of late."

"We both know Mickaleen is as healthy as pig, but I'll arrange for him to stay at the Liberty Hotel—with an armed guard, of course."

"Of course." Her lips pursed in thought. "What if ye haven't managed to catch yer counterfeiter by the end of the journey?"

"You and your father will be free to go."

"That's all I have to do for the pardons?"

Jacob hesitated, not wanting to lie, but knowing that Fiona would not be satisfied with anything less than the whole truth.

"For the most part."

"I don't like the sound of that. What do ye mean, 'for the most part'?"

"There is one final condition." He opened his mouth, choosing his words carefully. "I've been ordered to accompany you, every step of the way, come hell or high water, and never let you out of my sight. Therefore, I'll be boarding the train as your own personal bodyguard."

"Don't ye mean my 'warden'?" Fiona asked in a fit of pique.

His tone became as hard as a bar of iron. "Call it whatever you like, I'll be with you, morning, noon, and night."

"Damn."

"You didn't exactly expect us to supply you with a new wardrobe, a healthy stipend, and a ticket west, and then trust you to your own recognizance, did you?"

"Ye have my father."

"Touché."

"Two-what?"

"Never mind. Will you do it, Fiona?"

In his estimation, Fiona remained silent for an inordinate amount of time. He knew that her hesitation wasn't due to his failing to tempt her. She was merely a woman who had learned the value of caution. She'd been burned too many times in the past to simply snatch his offer at face value.

"Aye. I'll do it. Provided ye remember that the only thing I'm bargaining is my time and my talents—*not* my body."

He sighed. "How many times do I have to tell you that I have no designs upon your virtue? None whatsoever."

"Not yet, lawman." She stabbed him in the chest with a finger of warning. "But I know yer type, and I don't trust ye any farther than I can spit, do ye hear?"

He frowned in disgust but didn't choose to retaliate. "Go on back to the laundry. Finish your day's work, collect your pay, then tell them you've resigned."

"What fer?"

"We can't have anyone come looking for you." Striding back into her father's room, he retrieved his hat from the bed and planted it on his head. "I'll be here to pick you up tomorrow morning, early. Be ready."

She waited until he reached the door before asking, "What if I'm not?"

His jaw tightened. "I have your father. Don't forget that. And *don't* be forgetting who's in charge."

As soon as he'd slammed the door behind him, Jacob headed from the Honeycomb Hotel to a much seedier side of town. He took a tangled route in order to ascertain whether or not he was being followed, but by the time he reached the Liberty, he felt quite certain that no one had trailed him.

After entering through the servants' entrance and climbing the rear stairs, he knocked on a rough door on the second floor.

"Who's there?"

"Jacob."

The portal opened a crack, then he was admitted into the dim interior. As in Fiona's room, the curtains were closed, the air heated and stale, the mood oppressive.

"Where's McFee?" Jacob asked curtly.

One of the two deputies who was guarding the room nodded his head to one side, indicating the small bedroom that adjoined the sitting area. Looking inside, Jacob noted that Mickaleen McFee was fast asleep on the narrow cot, a handkerchief covering his face, the hem lifting and falling with each puff of air exhaled from his lungs.

"How's he been behaving?" Jacob silently closed the door to the room as he regarded his deputies.

"He yammered on about his daughter in the hands of heathens for about an hour, but once we brought in his meal and a bottle of whiskey, he settled right down."

"Good."

"This came for you a few minutes ago." The deputy lifted a heavy satchel and set it on one of the tables. Jacob crossed to examine the contents, and the two men whistled when they saw the stack of greenbacks inside.

"What the—"

"Our expense money," Jacob supplied before the man could finish his question.

"Where'd it come from?"

"A very wealthy banker. Ethan McGuire. And trust me: *This* stuff is real."

"McGuire . . . McGuire . . . where have I heard that name before?"

"He's married to my sister," Jacob reluctantly supplied. He was relieved when the simple answer satisfied the fellow. It wouldn't do for his deputies to divine that there was so much more to Jacob's relationship with McGuire than family ties. He and Ethan had a past together, and such information could get a little sticky if any of his men pieced it together and began drawing their own conclusions. Ethan's place in society depended on his keeping his past as quiet as possible.

"The man sent it over by messenger. I'd be bringing it myself, I should think," the older of the two deputies stated.

In ordinary circumstances, Jacob knew that Ethan would have done the same thing. But, Ethan was out of state, gathering evidence as to the extent of the counterfeiting ring among his banking associates. Jacob had discovered that the money lenders had a reluctance to talk about just how much they'd been burned by the phony greenbacks, lest rumors began seeping into the population causing a run on the bank. Ethan had been more than willing to volunteer to nose around a bit.

Jacob's lips twisted in a rueful smile. Who could have foreseen that the events of nearly a decade ago would come full circle in such a manner? It was Ethan McGuire who had been the Gentleman Bandit—the same thief who had stripped Jacob and left him in a field of foxtails to burn his backside in the midday sun. Then Ethan had retired from his career of wrongdoing, leaving Jacob thoroughly frustrated with the man because he had not been able to avenge the insult to his dignity—as well as to his modesty.

Much later, Jacob learned that Ethan had made every effort to become an honest man, disappearing from Jacob's life entirely until a copycat thief had begun to mimic the Gentleman Bandit's methods, forcing Ethan to return to Illinois to clear his own name. Upon his first hint of the man's return, Jacob had pursued Ethan like a bloodhound, only to discover that Ethan had sought sanctuary with Jacob's sister, Lettie.

What a mess that had all been. Robberies, murder, mayhem—and up to the very end, Jacob had believed Ethan responsible. Until fate had shown him that there was a far more sinister force at work. One created by a corrupt judge and his vigilante group, which he called the Star Council of Justice. After the true culprits had been uncovered, Jacob had been forced to make his peace with Ethan McGuire. A man now pardoned, a successful businessman, bank owner . . .

And Jacob's brother-in-law.

Jerking himself from his memories, Jacob took a small handful of greenbacks from the satchel, then snapped the bag closed and locked it. "I'm leaving this here with you. Hide it, guard it, and for heaven's sake, don't let Mickaleen McFee know it's here."

Shoving the money into his pocket, Jacob headed out again, this time in the direction of the railway yard. But he couldn't escape the irony of the whole situation—an irony that caused a heavy foreboding to settle into his chest. Ethan, Fiona, thievery, and pardons. The whole cycle seemed to have started again, this time with new players. In six or eight weeks, Fiona would have completed her end of the bargain, whether or not their man—Mr. Darby Kensington of New York—was caught. Then she would be on her way, to build a new life—just as Ethan had done.

But as he stepped from the curb and made his way through traffic, Jacob couldn't escape the knot that lodged in his midsection. One that warned him that such a process may not be so easily completed.

The barouche rattled over the rutted streets, causing the three occupants inside to gasp and grab for any sort of handhold they could find. Once they'd rolled to more solid ground, Alma Beasley pursed her lips, righted her bonnet, and jabbed her hatpin more firmly into her delicately blued hair.

"Lettie, my dear, you shouldn't have come to meet our

train," she scolded. It was obvious from the pasty color of Lettie's skin and the sweat dotting her lip that the outing had not been an entirely wise decision.

Lettie waved a dismissing hand. "Nonsense, Miss Alma. It's been so long since I've seen you both. I simply had to come."

Alma exchanged glances with her younger sister—although she supposed that Amelia's seventy-two years would not seem all that "young" to most folk.

Amelia, the smaller of the two, tried another tack, leaning forward to pat Lettie's hand. "But what about the . . . *b-a-b-y?* Shouldn't you be . . . incognito?"

Alma's brows jammed together. " 'Incognito?' What kind of nonsense is that?"

"You know, when a woman retires from society and . . . waits."

" 'Indisposed,' Amelia. A woman of breeding is 'indisposed.' "

"Whatever."

Alma rolled her eyes in disbelief, catching the way Lettie's lips twitched in amusement.

"I'm fine, Miss Amelia. Really," Lettie insisted. "I don't get out much these days."

She patted the roundness of her belly, shrouded in the all-encompassing cloak that was entirely unnecessary in the summer heat but that shielded her condition from anyone who might glance inside the carriage. A completely useless custom of society, in Alma's opinion.

"The baby can only enjoy the outing."

"Even if it makes you sick?" Alma demanded baldly. "You're pale as a ghost and shaking like a leaf."

"Indeed you are, dear," Amelia echoed.

Alma leaned her head out the window. "Driver! Head straight for home and don't spare the team! Miss Lettie isn't feeling well."

"Miss Alma, I—"

The old woman wagged a finger in her direction. "We came to help you, and help you we will—even if we have to confine you to your bed. You just sit back—and for heaven's sake, part that cape a bit. Give the baby some air."

Lettie reluctantly complied, but the relief in her gaze couldn't be disguised. Knowing she had to distract the girl from the jouncing of the carriage and the heated air that wallowed through the window, Alma sought another topic of conversation. "How's your family?"

"Wonderful. Ethan is in Saint Louis on business for another three days, or he would have been here to meet you. He asked me to give you both a kiss."

"Flatterer," Alma muttered.

Amelia blushed.

"The children?"

"Growing like weeds. They're so excited you agreed to come and visit again."

"We wouldn't miss this trip for the world," Amelia assured her. "And to time our holiday when you're about to have your baby—why, we couldn't be more pleased."

"You must let us use the time to help you," Alma stated firmly.

Lettie shook her head. "Nonsense. This is your vacation. I know you've been planning to visit the state garden exhibition for months. You're to enjoy yourselves, do you hear?"

Alma sniffed but didn't press. There would be time enough to change Lettie's mind. "What about Jacob?"

A definite pause hung in the humid air. Alma and Amelia exchanged cautious glances.

"Has something happened?" Amelia asked when the silence continued overlong.

Lettie grimaced. "I shouldn't worry. I'm sure he's fine, but . . ."

"He hasn't written?" Alma inserted.

"Or visited?" Amelia added.

"No."

"Hmph." Alma grasped her reticule more firmly in her lap and frowned.

"Oh, dear," Amelia breathed.

"I've heard that he's here, in Chicago, but . . . he hasn't . . ."

"The cad," Amelia grumbled.

Alma shot her a warning glance and rubbed Lettie's arm. As she leaned forward, she caught a slight movement from the curb, a man stepping into the street. Tall, dark-haired, dark-eyed. She couldn't be sure, but . . .

She straightened and tilted her chin at a determined angle. "Don't you worry, dear. I'm sure he'll be coming to see you soon." Very soon indeed, if she had anything to do about it. She wouldn't bet her money on that fleeting figure being Jacob Grey, but if he were in Chicago like Lettie had said, then Alma intended to find him. And once she did . . .

He'd be getting a piece of her mind concerning his neglect of his sister.

3

LIGHT WAS BARELY BEGINNING TO CREASE THE SKY THE NEXT morning when Jacob stomped into the Honeycomb Hotel and made his way up the stairs. For better or for worse, the time had come for him to collect Miss McFee.

Stopping in front of her door, he uttered a silent "Heaven help us all," then rapped twice on the panels. "You'd better be ready," he called as he unlocked the latch and threw open the door.

Fiona gasped and whirled to face him, clasping a rough shirt to her bosom.

"Good. You're dressed."

In fact, she wasn't. Not quite. She'd donned a pair of leather boots, cotton hose, and a skirt that was a little too short, judging by the amount of leg he saw. Above that, she wore little more than her underthings: a lace-edged camisole, a sturdy black corset, and a flour-sack corset cover.

"How dare ye! This is *my* room. How *dare* ye be enterin' it without my leave!"

"Let's go."

"But I'm not finished here yet! I've got me hair t' braid, and—"

33

"You look good enough to me." Suddenly aware of the golden hair spilling wantonly about her face and the bare shoulders gleaming velvetlike in the early morning light, he added, "For now, at least. Put your shirt on and we'll be going."

Fiona stared at him as if he'd spoken a foreign language.

"Put your shirt on, Fiona," he stated more firmly. "We've got to be leaving this place."

"Why?"

Why? *Why?* Because he said so, damn it.

The words raced through his head, but he didn't utter them aloud, knowing that nothing would cause Fiona to dig her heels in quicker than to issue a dare. Even so, it was time she discovered who was to be boss in this escapade.

Her chin tilted stubbornly. "I'll not be puttin' me shirt on 'til ye tell me what yer intendin' t' do."

"Fine. Have it your way." He caught Fiona's wrist and dragged her to the door. She balked, but she was no match for his own strength of will.

As he pulled her into the hall, she squealed, holding her shirtwaist to her bosom. "Where are ye taking me?"

"I thought I explained to you yesterday that we're going to make a real lady of you, Fiona. Judging by what I've seen so far, there's not a moment to waste."

After absorbing the blunt remark, she opened her mouth—no doubt to utter some scathing retort—but wisely reconsidered and used the time it took to travel downstairs to wriggle one-handed into her clothes. Jacob relented enough to pause at the main portal so that she could fasten the garment, then took her arm and pulled her outside.

"Blast it all, Jacob Grey! I'm not a pushcart t' be steered about, mind ye," she protested.

He ignored her, asking instead, "When was the last time you took a bath, Fiona?"

He saw the way she stiffened. How could he miss the

reaction? Especially when it caused her breasts to press against the well-worn fabric of her blouse.

"I'll have ye know I might not have more than a dozen coins to rub together, but I wash myself on a regular basis!"

"With what? Lye?"

"I get it free at the laundry, I'll have ye know. It does the job."

"It smells to high heaven. Especially in this heat."

She yanked free and, her hands propped on her hips, stood in the middle of the crowded walk, the tide of humanity swirling about them as if they were mere flotsam in a stream. He couldn't ignore the way her eyes sparkled and her skin adopted a becoming flush.

"When I agreed t' help, there was no mention made of any insulting remarks t' be coming with the position."

He didn't even pause but took her wrist again and tugged her after him. "Sheath your claws, Fiona. I merely meant that if we're to pass you off as a wealthy widow, we're going to have to start from the skin out. There are ways a man knows he's in the presence of a true lady. First, she's got to smell like one."

He took her to the Grand Estate Hotel on Michigan Avenue. As soon as Fiona had divined their destination, her steps slowed and her heart began a slow, thrumming beat. The Grand Estate. The first time she and her father had been to Chicago, she'd been about nine. Squeezing her hand, he'd led her to the opposite corner of Michigan Avenue so that she could watch the beautiful people who came and went through the revolving wooden door with its etched-glass insets. She'd stared in wonder, never having seen anything so wonderful, so elegant, as that stately sandstone facade. And the people! Women with feathers on their hats and bustled gowns dripping with ribbons. Men with bowlers, closely shaven beards, and black superfine suits.

"Jacob." She tried to protest, tried to wrench free from

his hold, but he'd been hauling her the length of several city blocks and wasn't about to be stopped now.

"You'll be staying at the Grand Estate where I can get you cleaned up a bit."

"But I—"

"Don't worry about your things at the Honeycomb. Your room is paid up until the end of the month."

Her things. Her *things.* Who cared about a paltry collection of mismatched belongings when he was about to take her through the front door of the Grand Estate—when she was wearing her work clothing and a dusty pair of boots, and her hair was spilling over her shoulders?

"I want you to—"

"No!"

Finally, a scant dozen yards from the front entrance, she tugged free.

"Fiona, what the hell—"

"I can't go in there!"

"Why in the blazes not?"

She stared at him in astonishment. Why had God made men so dense?

"Jacob Grey, *that* is the Grand Estate." She pointed distinctly at the building, then dropped her hand when the gesture caused people upon the brick walk to stare.

Jacob sighed and cast his gaze skyward as if his patience were severely taxed. "I'm quite aware of that fact. I made the arrangements for your suite."

A suite. Dear sweet Mary and all the Saints, he'd arranged for a *suite!* Her mouth fell open. She couldn't help it—she really couldn't—but snapped her jaws closed again when she realized she must look like a gasping fish.

"I can't go in there," she whispered, overtly conscious of the great chasm to be found between the classes, even here in the land of promise.

"It's been paid for already. I told you that someone else would be taking care of the bills."

"I'm not talking about bills!" She shot a nervous glance about her, feeling the curious stares by the well-dressed passersby as keenly as a marking brand. "Jacob . . . I can't go in there . . . like *this.*" She made a vague sweeping gesture to her simple blouse and skirt. When he continued to regard her blankly, she ground her teeth together. "If I go in that place with ye, looking like I do, they will think I'm a . . . a . . ."

"A what?"

He didn't know. He truly didn't know. How could a man spend so much time brushing elbows with an assortment of lawbreakers and remain so completely unaware of a few basic realities of life?

"Gaze about ye, man! Do y' see anyone dressed in anythin' but silks and satins?" she blurted. "Lord Almighty, even the servants here have got more finery than I do. If I go waltzin' through the lobby an' up t' one o' them rooms, they'll be thinkin' I'm yer fancy piece, they will."

His brows creased and he leaned forward as if he'd heard her incorrectly. "Fancy . . ."

"Piece. Fancy piece! A prossy." When he continued to squint at her she said, "A trollop, fer the love o' Mike."

A slow dawning spread over his face, softening the normally somber cast of his blunt features. "No one could possibly think that I would pay you money so that you and I . . . that we . . ."

She stamped her feet, her lips pursing. "Damn ye, I warned ye about the insults."

"Fiona, you're far from the sort of woman I would consider for such an afternoon of entertainment."

"Well, they won't be knowin' that, will they?"

At long last, her arguments bored through that thick skull of his. He frowned and eyed the smattering of hotel patrons as they went about their business, obviously noting for the first time that there was a distinct difference between the clientele's appearance and their own.

"Come with me."

He took her hand again. This time, instead of dragging her along like a toy on a string, he laced his fingers with hers and drew her around the block to a rear alley. They wound their way between drays unloading crates of exotic fruits, vegetables, iced fish, and flowers, and emerged at the entrance to the kitchen.

The door had been flung open in the muggy heat and the most tantalizing aromas permeated the air. Fiona would have been content to stop, close her eyes, and smell those exotic scents for the better part of the day, but Jacob didn't even allow her to pause.

Leading her inside, he ignored the curious glances they received, taking her directly to the servants' staircase.

"Good afternoon," he offered, touching his finger to his brow when a pair of startled chambermaids scrambled to get out of their way.

As they climbed the worn treads, Fiona bent close, whispering, "They're staring at me."

"What makes you think they aren't staring at me?"

She snorted at that unlikely idea. "Ye've got quite an opinion of yerself, don't ye?"

"No more than you seem to have."

She glared but refused to accept the bait he dangled, saying instead, "Ye might have avoided the gentry, but the hired help will still think I'm a fallen woman."

"Never you mind, Fiona. If by the end of six weeks you can play the lady as well as you play cards, they'll simply think you're eccentric."

"Eccentric, my arse. No one would ever be that daft."

His manner became serious, warning her in a way that caused her toes to curl in her boots. "They'd better, Fiona. Or we'll both be in a world of trouble."

Jacob directed Fiona to the landing on the third floor, then down a hall of gold-flocked paper. The walls were edged with a richly oiled oak wainscoting that reflected the bottom portions of their bodies as they walked past. A woolen runner stretched the length of the corridor, the intricate, intertwining colors of yellow, ocher, and brown appearing like crushed autumn leaves scattered beneath their feet. Mindful of her dusty boots, Fiona tried her best to walk on the extreme edge of the rug where it met the polished floorboards. But Jacob continued to tow her resolutely along, like a tug drawing a barge upstream, and she had no choice but to follow.

"You'll stay here," he said, stopping to withdraw a key from his vest pocket.

Fiona glanced about her, mindful of a man and woman who had exited their own room down the hall, beautiful people in beautiful clothes who stared at Fiona and Jacob in their simple street garb. The woman even went so far as to carefully hold her skirts aside so that her hems wouldn't brush Fiona's as she walked past.

Fiona felt a stinging heat seep into her cheeks. She'd lived on the streets long enough to recognize a tacit insult when she saw one.

"What's the matter?"

She started, knowing that Jacob had noted her discomfort. She couldn't bring herself to answer immediately, but when he continued to wait for a reply, she said, "I don't belong here."

"You will."

"No. People are born to places like these. If not, they can never truly belong."

He became quiet, still, as if this man, this *lawman,* knew that she felt a little too inferior, a little too rumpled, a little too alone.

He shifted closer—not in a way that threatened, but that somehow reassured. "You remind me of my sister, Lettie, sometimes," he remarked, hesitantly reaching out to tuck a thumb under her chin and tilting her face to the sunlight streaming through the window at the far end of the hall. "She used to give me fits, always getting into trouble, wearing her heart on her sleeve."

She stiffened. "I don't wear my heart on my bloody sleeve, lawman!"

At that remark, his brows rose as if he supremely doubted such a statement, but he didn't refute her comment. "Whatever you say, Fiona."

He twisted the cut-crystal doorknob and flung the door wide. "Welcome to your new home—at least your new home for a while."

"Dear Sweet Mary," Fiona whispered aloud.

Opulence. The room glittered with opulence, elegance, and a shimmering silver-studded stream of sunlight. Fiona was scarcely able to take all the sights in at once. And the colors! How had anyone ever conceived such a rich palette of colors?

"I take it your new quarters are satisfactory?"

"The Pope himself could live here—and quite happily, too."

She caught Jacob's quick smile but ignored it. Perhaps her enthusiasm betrayed her simple upbringing, but she couldn't dampen her excitement. The hotel suite beckoned to her, called to her in enchanted whispers, promised hours of untold delight. As she stepped onto the gray- and rose-patterned carpet, she felt a pang of unadulterated joy, an emotion so pure and strong it made her wonder if a person could go blind after catching a glimpse of such delightful surroundings.

The walls had been covered with a pink and black watered silk, interspersed with pastel flower studies. The furniture was fashioned of a rich mahogany that had been elaborately carved and upholstered in a burgundy sateen. There were graceful chairs and broad settees, a swooning couch, low marble-topped tables crowded with plants, dainty footstools, and an upright secretary carved in the shape of a ship's mast.

"This is where I'm t' stay? Ye aren't just pulling my leg, are ye?"

"No, Fiona. This is where you'll stay. After all, your surroundings should be appropriate for a wealthy British widow, don't you think?"

She didn't answer. She couldn't. A burgeoning exhilaration wriggled into her blood as she tiptoed over the rug as if it were a layer of goose down, so soft, so decadent, so genteel.

"Faith and begora, but a woman could grow accustomed t' this," she said with a sigh, the brogue thickening at her delight and excitement. Her fingers ran across the support of a chair, caressing the satiny texture of the wood, then spreading wide to test the cool sheen of the fabric cushion. "'Tis a room for a queen."

A cool shiver touched her spine at that thought. This entire situation weighed heavily to her advantage: a pardon, this room, new clothes. A voice within her kept muttering: *Trap, trap!*

Her gaze shot his way. Perhaps Jacob hadn't told her everything. Perhaps there was more to this bargain than he'd been willing to offer. "What will ye be askin' for next, Grey?" she asked, searching his features to judge whether he was secretly laughing.

His brow creased and she gestured wide to the room about her. "Ye can't possibly be meanin' t' give me this and the pardons, too. There's somethin' ye haven't told me yet."

"You are incredibly suspicious."

"I've a right t' be."

He sighed in frustration and strode toward her, taking her by the shoulders. Her eyes clashed with his, and something happened. A stinging excitement shot through her veins.

Jacob's lashes narrowed ever so slightly, his gaze dark and steady and filled with purpose. A hush settled over the room, that lovely, elegant room.

"Life has been a struggle for you, hasn't it, Fiona?"

Her gaze dropped then, fastening upon the scratched silver of his belt buckle, and she wondered where he'd hidden the silver of his star. The one she'd grown used to seeing pinned to the lapel of his vest.

"I've survived."

"At what cost?"

She lifted her chin to a proud angle. "I'm not a case for charity, mind ye."

"No, but you're past the age where you should have left your father to his own resources. You should have married by now and had children of your own."

His words stung more than he would ever know. "I'm happy," was the only response she could push through a throat tight with barely submerged regrets.

He followed the line of her jaw with his thumb. "Are you really?"

"No life is without its problems and its disappointments, Jacob Grey." Wanting to inflict an equal measure of hurt to this man who appeared so strong, so impenetrable, she added, "Even yers."

The strange bond that had formed in the last few minutes shivered, then dissolved as suddenly as it had come. Noises intruded: the clink of cutlery from the dining hall far below, the rattle of traffic, a shout, a muffled laugh.

Jacob drew his hands away, palms out, as if to show that her skin had suddenly become distasteful. In an instant, the gentle, sympathetic man she had so briefly encountered disappeared, leaving the professional lawman she was accustomed to encountering. "Come with me, Fiona," he ordered, striding to the far side of the chamber to throw open a connecting door. "This is where you will sleep, bathe, and dress."

Approaching him, she peered into the spacious room with its tall iron bedstead, mahogany wardrobe, and highboy.

"I know what a bedroom is for," she offered sardonically, but Jacob didn't even bat an eye.

"Let's hope you do." He marched inside to open another door, revealing a completely outfitted bathing room. "I also hope you know what you're to do in here."

She shot him a stern frown for his impertinence, but he was brushing past her and closing the draperies. In seconds, he'd cut out all but a sliver of light. Then he proceeded to do the same to the windows in the sitting room, leaving the warm, musky gloom of an artificial dusk to slip into the corners. With it came a rich heat caused by the damming of the window's meager breeze.

Fiona marched indignantly forward, intent upon drawing the window coverings again. "What did ye do that for? A body can barely breathe in here as it is."

His fingers closed around her wrist, preventing her

from sweeping the swags behind their brass hooks. "I don't want you standing at the windows where anyone can see you from the street. No one but a few of my own men are to catch a glimpse of you until you're ready to be introduced to the passengers of the tourist train."

Her lips thinned. "I don't see the need for such drastic precautions."

"I do."

"I suppose yer word is law on this point?"

He edged closer, his body taut. Grasping her chin, he forced her to peer up at him. "Yes, by all that is holy, my word *is* law. This isn't a game, Fiona. The next few weeks are to be treated as some of the most important days of your life. You won't be *given* your pardons; you'll *earn* them. This is work, plain and simple. Do you understand? Because if you don't, you may as well let me turn you over to the authorities right now."

Fiona caught more than the stern edge of a tone meant to discipline her. Buried deep in his words, she found a serrated edge of caution.

"Are ye telling me that this . . . adventure ye've planned could be dangerous?"

"You understood the risks when you agreed."

"I understood that I would go t' jail if I didn't join forces with ye, but ye made no mention of any kind o' danger."

"A man isn't accused of defrauding people of millions of dollars without becoming just a little bit mean about it. Once he knows he's being investigated, there's no telling what he may do."

"I see." She knew without asking that Jacob's blunt words were as much of an explanation as she was going to get. He wouldn't elaborate on the risks involved. It was up to her to see to her own safety. She couldn't trust anyone else with such a job. Not even Jacob Grey.

"I'll need a gun," she stated, breaking one of her own cardinal rules, which stated that, no matter how grim her surroundings, she would not carry a weapon.

"No."

"I *can* shoot one." She couldn't. But he didn't need to know that.

"Perhaps, but you won't be armed during this venture."

"Why not?"

"You're not exactly on the right side of the law yourself, if you'll remember."

"Are ye afraid I'll crash ye over the head, tie ye up, and go about my own designs?"

A slight stain of color touched his cheeks, and she was abruptly reminded of how they'd met. Of the way this man had been bound hand and foot and left in a field of foxtails.

"You'll have no need for a gun, Fiona."

"Ye've just told me I've reason t' fear for me life!"

"As long as you're careful, there's little likelihood of any trouble."

"But what if something *does* happen? I won't be walking into this situation like a lamb t' the slaughter."

He tucked his thumbs behind his gunbelt. "Have you forgotten that I'll be there with you, each step of the way? If you need any protection, you'll get it from me."

Her lips pursed at his obstinacy, but she didn't bother to argue. Not yet, anyhow. If there was one thing Fiona had learned in her twenty-three years, it was that there was a time to fight, a time to cajole, and a time to bide one's time. Now was the time for the latter. But she hadn't given up by any means. One way or another, she would find a weapon. She would walk onto that train prepared. Jacob Grey couldn't stay by her side every minute of the day. At some eventual point in time, she would be needing her own brand of protection.

"I've got to go and make a few arrangements for your stay," he said. "In the meantime, I want you to bathe and wash your hair with something other than lye. I'll return in an hour."

He strode to the door, paused there, and turned. "I

wouldn't be taking any unexpected trips if I were you, Fiona."

"Why would I be doing that when ye've got my father as a hostage?"

He eyed her, considering. "One never knows what to expect from you. I figure I'm a little safer if I keep warning you of the consequences of any foolish ideas."

"Fer yer information, I've got the memory of an elephant."

"Maybe. Nevertheless, I intend to remind you every chance I get."

With that parting remark, he closed the door behind him, leaving her in the humid, heated gloom of her palatial quarters.

Alone and unguarded.

Fiona stood still for a moment, waiting cautiously, carefully. Cocking her head, she listened to the heavy tread of his boots disappearing down the hall. Even though he'd told her he wouldn't return for an hour, she wouldn't put it past him to stop, tiptoe to the door, and open it, just to see if she meant to try and escape. But after she had waited for some time, her heart thumping, she realized he meant to trust her.

Trust *her*.

For some reason the idea of his faith in her discretion had her hurrying toward the window overlooking the street. From her vantage point several floors up, she feared she might not be able to recognize Jacob, but when he crossed the cobbled avenue, threading his way through the delivery vans and hired cabs, she noted his distinctive stride immediately. Even from this height, she could read the purpose of his gait, see the strength of his shoulders, the lithe rhythm of his legs.

Her brow furrowed in concentration. She didn't necessarily have to like him, but Fiona couldn't deny that Jacob Grey was a striking man. One who made more than a half-dozen female heads turn and watch his passage. He had a solid reputation and a reliable job.

So why hadn't some woman snapped him up long ago?

The very thought caused her frown to deepen into a scowl. What did she care? Even if he *had* managed to find a woman to marry him, Fiona would feel nothing more for the unfortunate female than pity. She could very well imagine the kind of ill treatment his spouse would have to suffer. He bullied women and told them what to do, when to bathe, what soap to use, and where to sleep.

But most of all, she thought with a quick note of panic, he was a man of his word. By the end of the hour he would have returned to see if his orders had been obeyed. If she wasn't washed, perfumed, and powdered, there would be all holy hell to pay, damn his hide.

Fiona marched into the bathing room, her arms folded, every muscle in her body resistant. She meant to remain strong, unmoved—truly she did. But the porcelain tub with its painted cherubs and honeysuckle called to her in silent temptation. Never in her life had she seen anything so rich, so beautiful, so . . . decadent.

A sigh of longing eased from her lips and Fiona felt suddenly gritty and ill-kempt. An hour. She had at least an hour until he returned. How lovely it would be to lie submerged beneath a tepid wash of water, to feel the dust being lifted free.

Infused with determination, she tugged her boots free, then her stockings, then reached her for the buttons to her blouse. As she stripped the fasteners free, she scanned the rest of the room, taking in the privacy screen, the fireplace, towel racks, commode, and dressing table. The only accoutrement she couldn't identify was a strange copper reservoir that had been bolted to the floor and connected to the tub with a peculiar tangle of pipes.

Fiona dropped her shirt to the floor, followed it with her skirt, then grew still, her heart making an odd sort of leap. No. It couldn't possibly be . . .

Touching a hand to her throat, she tiptoed forward with the reverence of a pilgrim paying homage to a holy shrine. Kneeling, she plugged the drain with a delicate piece of porcelain attached to a chain, then reached for the matches arranged in a cut-crystal cup. Striking the sulphur-coated tip of one on the floor, she held the flame beneath the copper tank, igniting the gas jet controlled by a valve to the side. When the mechanism ignited, wavered, then burned steady, she sat up in astonishment at having guessed the nature of the contraption correctly.

"Sweet heavenly angels, what a sight," she whispered to herself. Fiona had heard that the rich folk could heat their water right next to the tub, but she hadn't dreamed such an invention actually existed. Never had she imagined that *she* would ever see the benefit of such a contraption—let alone use it. However, as she listened to the liquid in the kettle begin to bubble and pop in a restless warming dance, she realized that she had somehow stumbled headfirst upon the gate to happiness.

While the water heated to a comfortable temperature, she stripped from her underclothes and wrapped herself in a towel. Moving to the dressing table, she examined the china washbasin, the stack of lace-edged linen towels, the jars of scented salts, and the pats of perfumed soaps. Unable to resist, she sniffed each container of scents in turn, delighted by the variety. Lemon verbena and lilac, rosehip and jasmine. There was even a pine bar, presumably provided for a man's needs, should one wash here—not that Fiona would allow Jacob to do such a thing. He could find his own blasted bathing room and his own blasted soap.

Filled with a niggling regret, Fiona returned the toiletries to their gaily-patterned boxes and the jars to their rows. She didn't dare use any of them. There must be a frightful charge added to a hotel bill if they were disturbed. And yet . . . Jacob Grey had *ordered* her to bathe, *ordered* her to wash her hair, and *ordered* her to smell like a rose. By jimmeny, she *would*. She would indeed.

While the water finished heating, Fiona dribbled a healthy measure of the lemon verbena bath salts into the tub. Then, upon second consideration of Jacob's order, she added half the jar, grinned to herself mischievously, then added half of the lilac, nearly all of the jasmine, and a wee bit of rosehip. Twisting the spigot, she tested the water, discovering that it had managed to heat to a tepid warmth. Not wanting her bath to grow much hotter on such a sultry day, she filled the tub midway and selected a floral-scented soap.

The aromas of the combined bath supplies filled the air in a pungent cloud of steam that could have cleared a person's lungs of the croup. Dropping the towel she wore, Fiona dipped one toe into the tub, sighed, then quickly clambered into the monstrous porcelain basin. Although the rising mist nearly seared her brain, she closed her eyes and leaned her head on the rim.

Lovely. Absolutely lovely.

Almost as wonderful as it would be to catch one glimpse of Jacob Grey's approving smile . . .

Her eyes popped open and she huffed in soft surprise. Whatever had possessed her to think such nonsense? Jacob Grey was nothing to her. Nothing but a means to an end. After she and her father had been given their pardons, she would be off in one direction while Grey took the other, and never the twain would meet.

Nodding emphatically, she sank beneath the water, dousing her head in the delicious depths. But as she rose and began to scrub her hair, she couldn't push away a nagging sense of sadness.

As well as a deep sense of regret.

4

Pattersonville, Illinois

DARBY KENSINGTON RAPPED HIS WALKING STICK ON THE RIM of the carriage. "Stop here."

The driver pulled to a halt in the middle of a rather unsavory section of town, one that in the past had been considered part of the more fashionable district but had now become the home of immigrants and thieves.

As accustomed as Darby had grown to such errands, he couldn't help sneaking a peek over his shoulder, searching to see if anyone recognized him, anyone had followed him. He saw no disturbances on the streets, no one that appeared overly interested in why a dapper gentleman would have come to this poverty-stricken area.

"Wait here."

The driver's brow furrowed in obvious misgiving. "Sir?"

"I'll be out in a few minutes."

"But sir . . ." He peered into the shadowy alleys.

"Just wait. I'll pay you handsomely for your trouble."

Darby jumped to the road before the man could offer any more objections. Moving quickly, he descended the chipped stone steps that led into the abandoned printer's shop in the basement of the sandstone building. After issuing a secret combination of knocks, he waited, his heart beating as quickly as if he were bluffing his way through a high-stakes card game.

The door eased open a crack, revealing one gray eye and a grizzled cheek, then he was allowed to enter.

Over the past few months, the cool, musky odors of the cellarlike room had been tainted by other smells. The stink of sweat and ink and whiskey had drowned out the fainter smells of dirt and decay.

Darby quickly surveyed the cramped cubicle. His gambling instincts served him well, allowing him to catalog the dozen men, all of them tired, dusty, mean, and just a little bit desperate. The number of henchmen had grown since he'd been here last, providing evidence that his employer was still gathering his forces—men who were wanted by the law in at least a half-dozen states.

He turned immediately to the man in charge. "Do you have it?"

One figure disengaged himself from the rest, tall and lean, his eyes gleaming in the semidarkness. Gerald Stone.

Darby had worked with the man off and on over the last few months. He'd heard a rumor that Stone had recently spent some time in jail, and Darby was inclined to believe it. The pallor of the man's skin and the gauntness of his features supported such a claim. But it wasn't those qualities that caused Darby to despise the man. No, Darby was close enough to the edge of the law to pity a man who'd been caught. What bothered him about Stone was the man's attitude of superiority. As if Darby were of no more importance than the dust on his shoes.

"You're very eager today, Kensington."

"I have things to do."

"More important than your errand here?"

Darby didn't answer, allowing the battle of wills to

intensify—longer than he should have done, he supposed, because Stone frowned.

"Take care how you proceed with me, Kensington."

"I'm not afraid of you."

One of Stone's brows lifted. "Maybe you should be." He turned away long enough to gesture to the shadowy person behind him, allowing Kensington a little breathing room. Not that he was able to do so comfortably. A potent air of menace lingered in the very air. He could only pray that Stone would give him his money so he could leave this place, these men. Then he'd be on a steamer to Europe.

Stone's assistant emerged again carrying a carpetbag. Kensington noted in satisfaction that he staggered slightly beneath the weight of the valise.

Darby took it from his hands, preparing to leave, but Stone stopped him.

"There's been a change in plans."

Darby stiffened. "I did what I was told to do. I've gambled heavily and lost, exchanging your counterfeit currency for legal tender. For that I was promised that I would be paid. Today."

Stone took a step toward him, subtly threatening him without saying a word. "There's been a change in plans," he repeated, more deliberately this time. "The currency in that bag is false."

A rage bubbled inside of Darby's chest. "Dammit! You promised I'd be paid *today.*"

"You *will* be paid. After one more run."

"The law is getting suspicious!"

"One more run."

Darby opened his mouth to argue, but when he saw the way Stone's men had subtly come to attention, their fingers stroking the hammers of their pistols, he thought better of it, saying instead, "I want twice the amount you offered as a reward for my services."

Stone's eyes narrowed.

"In *legal* tender—not that phony stuff. I can tell the difference, you know."

Stone thought for a moment, then nodded in agreement.

"I suppose you want me to take the train west again."

"Yes."

"Where do you want me to go this time?"

"There's a tourist excursion scheduled to leave Chicago in little more than a fortnight. It will travel via Denver to San Francisco. Book passage. In addition to your usual arrangements for a private car, you will also pay for the use of a boxcar. Once you've reached Chicago, I'll wire a list of supplies to load inside."

"I suppose I'm to use this to buy it all?" He indicated the counterfeit currency.

"Of course."

"What if I get caught? There are lawmen all over the Midwest looking for the source of that stuff!"

"Then you'd better be careful, hadn't you?" Stone's smile was cold. "A reservation has been made for you at the Grand Estate on Michigan Avenue. You have four days to put your affairs in order and check in."

Darby fought the urge to salute at the autocratic tone. Stone kept forgetting that Darby wasn't one of his thugs.

He hefted the satchel more securely into his grip. "This is it, Stone. After this, you either pay me or I go to the authorities."

Stone chuckled, a disturbing sound devoid of all amusement. Walking forward, he planted his dirty index finger into the snowy white folds of Darby's shirt.

"Don't make threats you can't carry out, Kensington. You and I both know you're so deep into this affair you can never dig yourself out."

"Fiona!"

The door to the main room slammed open and Fiona sat up with a start. Jacob was here.

Just the thought caused a surge of adrenaline. The last time she'd seen him, he'd promised to return in an hour. That had been over a day ago. Since then, she'd been left in the suite, wondering what had happened, whiling away her time by pacing the sitting room, exploring the bedroom, and bathing. She just couldn't seem to get enough of the porcelain tub with its heatable water tank. She'd had six baths, each with a different scent. Her skin was beginning to shrivel from all the water, but she didn't care. Especially when Jacob hadn't returned by nightfall and she feared he'd been killed or relieved of his duties and she'd be booted onto her ear in the streets at any moment.

"Fiona!"

Infused with energy, she scrambled to pull the plug. If she didn't hurry, Jacob Grey would most likely come storming into her quarters to see if she'd drowned. She rose to her feet in a rush of water. The stomping of Jacob's bootheels was followed by the pounding of a fist on the door. "Dammit all to hell, you'd better be in there, woman!"

"Of course I'm in here," she snapped, just as a heavy object smashed against the planks and the portal flew wide, whacking the opposite wall, then shuddering to a halt.

Fiona stood stunned. He'd broken down the door! Calm, controlled, implacable Jacob Grey had smashed the lock to smitherines. When he turned his attention in her direction, his untoward behavior fled from her mind, replaced by the immediate necessity of covering herself against the scalding heat of his eyes.

She whipped a damp bathsheet about her body, tossing him a scathing glance. "Ye could have knocked. Ye didn't have t' kick the blasted thing in!"

He took two steps into the room, then stopped, breathing hard, his muscles visibly relaxing. "You didn't leave."

"Of course I didn't leave! Have ye lost yer ever-lovin' mind? Ye told me t' stay, and I did. Ye told me t' bathe, and I did."

"I didn't think you'd listen to my instructions."

She snorted, and he obviously felt compelled to defend himself. "You've never followed my orders yet."

"Perhaps . . ." she drawled, brushing past him like a queen robed in wet linen, "that's because ye never had anything all that important t' say."

She opened her mouth to add an even more scathing remark but stopped in her tracks when she passed the threshold leading to the main room and caught sight of a little man with a valise cowering next to the door leading into the hallway. "Hello."

He started at her greeting, then smiled tremulously, adjusting the wire-rimmed spectacles that were perched upon the tip of his nose.

"This is Mr. Peebles," Jacob muttered, planting a hand in the hollow of her spine and pushing her into the room to confront the stranger. "Mr. Peebles is a tailor newly come to Chicago. I've hired him to help with your wardrobe, but he needs your measurements first."

Fiona grew still, a slow anger building within her. Not so much because of the shy man who stared her way, or because she stood in front of him wearing nothing but a bathsheet, but because of what he represented. "A tailor? Ye've hired a *tailor?* Damn ye, Jacob Grey, I—"

Jacob took her by the elbow and drew her into the bedroom, shutting the door behind them.

"Fiona, if this is going to work at all, you've got to guard your tongue. Especially in front of strangers!" He opened his mouth to speak, paused, then asked, "What smells in here?"

Fiona stamped her foot on the floor, but the gesture lost some of its power when muffled by the carpet. "Blast it all to hell, Grey, I told ye I wouldn't stand for yer insulting attitude!" She drew herself to a regal height but was still forced to look up at him. "Ye leave me here fer over a day! I've had nothin' t'eat but a bloomin' fruit basket, nothin' t' wear but a blasted sheet—"

"That's where I've been." He poked her in the chest. "Finding someone to clothe you."

She growled in frustration. "Blast it all, have ye no ken of what ye're doin' t' me? Regardless of my wishes, ye've brought a no-nothing man t' garb me. Not a woman, not a seamstress, not a couturier, but a man."

"I am not insulting you. I told you, this entire situation demands the utmost discretion—"

"A tailor?"

"—therefore we need someone who doesn't have a tendency to talk—"

"A *tailor!*"

"—such as a woman is prone to do. You know how they like to spread gossip."

After digesting his remark that women were no more capable of holding a secret than a sieve of storing water, Fiona stared at him in utter amazement. How had this man survived so far without having some woman crack him over the head with a skillet?

"Mr. Peebles will fashion some lovely clothes, I assure you. He's told me that he's made women's—Blast it all, Fiona, what is that smell?"

"He's made what? What has this man made?"

He waved a dismissing hand. "All that stuff and nonsense females use. He shouldn't find our order for garments too difficult to fill. After all, how different can women's wear be from fashioning a suit?"

"Jacob Grey, ye arc so . . . so . . . ." Refusing to bow to his level and sling a few insults of her own concerning the hardheaded stupidity of lawmen in general, she decided on a more direct form of protest. Drawing back her foot, she kicked him in the shins, then, without pause, opened the door and sailed into the sitting room.

Mr. Peebles jerked as if he'd been caught doing something he oughtn't be, when in fact he'd done nothing at all but stand by the door, hugging his valise to his torso as if it were a foundling child.

Realizing that this was her first contact with someone who would not know her as an Irish immigrant accustomed to living hand-to-mouth but as a wealthy British widow, Fiona paused, then summoned her most gracious airs. Haughty social graces were no trouble to assume after years of watching those who "had" from the position of one who "had not."

"Mr. Peebles, pardon our manners." She offered him a coy smile and the slightest of winks. Walking toward him, she extended a hand, bonelessly draped from the wrist. "How lovely t' meet you." Despite her attempts to speak like the queen herself, a wee bit of brogue escaped.

The stooped, curly-haired man had been steadily inching his way sideways to the door, but he stopped now and offered her a tremulous smile. When she did not chide, he reluctantly took her hand in a grip that was little more than a sandwiching of her fingers between his own.

Fiona waited, waited, until he'd summoned enough nerve to bend and kiss the delicate knuckles. Beaming, as much because it was expected of her as through sheer delight at having her role believed so readily, she said, "I understand you are going to make my wardrobe." There. That was better. One whole sentence without a trace of the Irish.

Peebles reluctantly released her and swept his bowler from his head, obviously embarrassed at not having done so earlier. "Yes, ma'am."

"Have you studied the current modes? I am a woman of fashion, you know."

If this little man with his receding hairline and corkscrew curls doubted her claim, he made no signs. Indeed, he appeared inordinately pleased to be in her company, despite her obvious *deshabille.*

Hiking his valise a little higher, he quickly said, "I shall endeavor to do my best to see that your new things meet your expectations, madam. In fact, I've taken the liberty of bringing my sample case with me, as well as some of the newer issues of the fashion gazettes loaned to me by the hotel. If you don't see what you need, I'd be happy to order whatever you require."

He believed her to be a wealthy British widow. Fiona couldn't prevent the smile that teased her lips. The next few weeks would be exciting indeed if everyone else proved to be so easily fooled.

"How very clever of you to think of everything in advance, Mr. Peebles." Relaxing in his company, she linked her arm through his and drew him to the settee. "Come and show me what you have."

As they settled upon the cushions, she offered little more than a glance at Jacob, who was limping into the room. But when he continued to stand just on the periphery of her vision, his features clouded in an ominous scowl, she realized that he was not about to disappear and leave her alone with Mr. Peebles to complete their orders.

Mr. Peebles touched the bridge of his nose, fiddled with his spectacles, and glanced nervously over the rims. Seeing his obvious distress and the evident confusion as to how to regard their relationship, Fiona asked, "Mr. Peebles, have you met me—*my* bodyguard, Mr. Grey?"

The tailor's keen eyes jumped from her bath-flushed cheeks to the man in question. It was obvious that he'd heard the way Jacob had forced his way into the bathing room, then their later scuffle of wills. "Yes, indeed. We have met. Earlier. That is to say, this afternoon."

"Mr. Grey was kind enough to arrange your services while I washed the grime of travel free." She met his gaze and bobbed her head encouragingly, hoping the funny little man would take her explanation at face value and not probe deeper for some kind of scandal.

"I see."

"*Do* y' see, Mr. Peebles?" she returned quickly, earnestly, then concentrated again on proper diction. Peebles appeared somewhat startled by her rejoinder, and she leaned closer as if confiding a secret. "I'm afraid you must excuse his brash behavior. Sometimes Mr. Grey grows a little overzealous in his job." She touched his hand, and the man's eyes widened. "My life is in danger."

"Really?" he breathed.

"Oh, yes. I've had threats—letters, telegrams—you know about that sort of thing."

It was obvious that Mr. Peebles had no idea about anything of the kind, but he whispered, "Oh, yes."

"I'm afraid I've been forced to take drastic measures."

"Oh, dear."

"I've left my country, my home, my family."

"Oh, my."

"I've come all the way to Chicago, and still . . . I'm being terrorized."

The little tailor blanched. "How awful."

"If not for Mr. Grey, I would be dead."

He gasped.

"Yes, Mr. Peebles, dead." Having obviously scared the man, she straightened and smiled. "So you see why I keep him on, despite his horrible manners. Mr. Grey might be a bit of a brute, and at times he displays the tact of a bull charging through a china-shop window, but he is very large, very strong, and carries a very big gun."

Mr. Peebles's eyes grew as round as a pair of goose eggs.

"A woman in my position, a stranger to this country, cannot be too careful. Wouldn't you agree?"

Mr. Peebles nodded emphatically.

"Even if Mr. Grey can be quite boorish at times."

She knew Jacob could hear each word she said, despite the confidential level of her voice. However, he gave no sign. No sign, that was, except for the slight glitter of his dark eyes. Unable to resist one last jibe, she sighed. "It is so difficult to find good help, don't you think?"

Mr. Peebles nodded as if he quite agreed and, moreover, he sympathized with every fiber of his being.

She grinned and patted his arm. "You're really quite sweet, Mr. Peebles."

The man positively blushed.

"I'm pleased you were able to help me during this distressing period of my life."

"Mr. Grey said your things were lost in transit to Chicago."

Fiona didn't even blink at the simple lie Jacob must have told him. "Yes. My trunks were clearly marked, but alas, they are probably on their way to China by now." She gestured to the sheet wrapped about her torso. "As you can see, I've nothing—literally nothing—to wear."

Mr. Peebles's chest puffed out in importance. "Then we must get to work right away." He hefted his sample case on the table in front of the settee and flicked the catches. "I borrowed a fabric book from a seamstress on Oak Street. We should be able to find something suitable that I can have sewn for you by morning. That will see you through until I can finish the rest of your wardrobe."

"How very clever of you to think of such a thing."

Mr. Peebles tried to smother a look of infinite pleasure but failed miserably in the task. Fiona took the opportunity to meet the gaze of the man who glowered at them from the corner. "Mr. Grey, since we'll have no need of you for the time being, would you be so kind as to arrange for a tea tray to be brought up to the suite? I'm frightfully thirsty, and I should think Mr. Peebles would care for some refreshment as well. Wouldn't you, Mr. Peebles?"

The cherubic tailor beamed. "If it's no trouble."

"No trouble at all." She met Jacob's gaze, read the flicker of irritation deep inside, but pursued nonetheless. "Be a dear fellow, Jacob, and ask for some sort of cakes or sandwiches as well."

Judging by the scowl creasing his features, Jacob had clearly intended to stay and mastermind the entire fitting session. But she'd effectively trapped him in his own web of lies. If he remained, Mr. Peebles would wonder why he had disobeyed her orders. If he left, he would have to trust her not to make a spectacle of herself. Amusement tickled her insides as she realized that Jacob thought such an occurrence a very real threat.

"We shall be fine for the few minutes you'll be gone, I assure you. The door will be locked, and if my assailant should try to murder me, Mr. Peebles will provide protection. Won't you, Mr. Peebles?"

"Oh, I don't—"

"There, you see? It's all settled."

She could see the way Jacob fairly seethed at her very clever manipulating, but he growled, "Very well," and charged to the door.

"Don't be gone too long, Mr. Grey."

He turned just before closing the panels.

"That is one thing, madam, upon which you can depend."

Jacob stormed from the room, barely restraining the urge to hurl the door closed behind him. He had the sudden, uncomfortable feeling that he'd just created a monster.

Blast Fiona's impudence, he thought as he stomped down the hall. Had she forgotten so soon that *he* was the man in charge? Had she forgotten that this wasn't some parlor game to be enacted, but a serious attempt to apprehend a dangerous criminal?

Trust her to adopt some Mary Queen of Scots attitude in an attempt to gain the upper hand. Mr. Peebles had taken one look at her tousled hair and damp, linen-wrapped body and melted into a spineless puddle of solicitude. By the time Jacob returned, she would have the man twined about her little finger and jumping through hoops.

He snorted aloud, startling a chambermaid who was leaving a room down the hall. Ignoring her wide-eyed stare, he marched past.

This wasn't the first time Jacob had seen a gentleman show this peculiar reaction to Fiona McFee. In the past few years, Jacob had been in contact with her father's marks enough to know that—despite what Mickaleen may have done—his daughter had always been held in the highest regard. She was considered to be a lovely girl, an angel, a dear.

Angel his ass, he thought bitterly, remembering the way she'd held out her hand to let the little tailor kiss her.

Kiss her. He hadn't been in the room more than a few seconds and she had him taking orders. How she did it, Jacob couldn't entirely fathom. He only knew that after a minute or two in her presence, people gravitated toward her, hung on her every word. That was one of the reasons the governor had decided she would be the woman to help in this matter. He'd met Fiona McFee twice at official soirees at which her father, masquerading as British royalty, had appeared, and he invariably referred to her as "that delightful child."

But she wasn't a child.

Jacob stopped short midway down the main staircase. His steps became slow, deliberate, as his attention turned inward, to analyze the complex swirl of emotions he had experienced in the past few hours.

Fiona had always irritated him. That fact was as constant as the sun that rose and set each day. But somehow, things had changed between them. Each time Jacob saw her, he couldn't squelch the erratic thoughts that wriggled into his head. Thoughts that were entirely inappropriate. Thoughts that were entirely . . .

Sensual.

"Was there something you needed, sir?"

Jacob started, realizing he'd made his way to the front desk without being aware of his own movements. Tapping his finger on the marble counter, he wondered what this man would think if he demanded to know what had occurred to change the Fiona McFee he'd once known inside and out. The one with scraggling braids and skinned knees. The impish minx with a flaring temper. What had happened to her—or to him—to suddenly complicate this entire situation?

"Sir?"

"Tea."

The man stared at him blankly, and Jacob scraped his thoughts together and frowned. "Could you please send some tea and refreshments to the Ambassador Suite?"

"Yes, sir!" At the mention of the hotel's most prestigious set of rooms, the clerk snapped to attention. Jacob glared at the man, realizing that here lay another conquest merely waiting for Fiona's attention.

"For how many, sir?"

"What?"

"The tea."

"Two—no, three!" Jacob quickly corrected. Bloody hell, he wasn't about to leave her alone with Mr. Peebles. If the two of them became too chummy, there was no telling what she might do. No telling at all. "Can you put something to eat on the tray as well?"

"Of course, sir. Sandwiches, cookies, tarts?"

"Yeah." He ignored the way the man's brow rose in confusion and wondered if there were some special protocol to ordering tea. His sister would know. Lettie had always concerned herself with learning the social graces, but Jacob hadn't the time for such nonsense. Didn't have the time for it now.

Lettie!

His mood instantly lightened. He had to get in touch with his sister. So far he hadn't even told her he was in town, but she would forgive him for that oversight. She would help him. She would know how to bring Fiona to heel. Moreover, she would know just how to turn that damp, Irish caterpillar upstairs into a genteel society butterfly. Fiona might have Peebles momentarily fooled, but a sophisticated gambler would prove another matter.

Jacob leaned close to the clerk, as if imparting a secret, and asked, "Do you have a boy I can hire to deliver a message?"

The clerk automatically lowered his tone to a discreet murmur. "Of course, sir."

Jacob took a sheet of hotel stationery and the gilt-tipped pen, dipped it in the ink provided on the swivel-based registration platform, and scrawled his note. After blowing on the ink so that it dried, he folded it in half.

"Have the boy take this to Mrs. Ethan McGuire at Twenty-Twenty Bunburry Cross."

This time both brows rose. "Mrs. McGuire? The poet?"

"Yes. Tell the lad that the message is urgent and must be delivered immediately."

The clerk snapped his heels together and offered a curt bow, obviously more impressed with Jacob's caliber since he had such a close association with someone so important to Chicago's influential literary world.

Jacob pivoted on his toes and strode a few feet away, then stopped again. "Oh, and see if they can't throw a steak onto that tea tray. Medium rare, the thickest you've got."

The man's mouth dropped ever so slightly at the odd request, but he quickly gathered his equilibrium. "Very good, sir."

Jacob paused only long enough to buy a newspaper from the gift stand, then headed for the stairs. It was not until he'd reached the landing that it suddenly occurred to him that he'd made an error in judgment. A horrible mistake. After all his years of protecting his sister's virtue, of ensuring that no man dared so much as glance at her cross-eyed, he'd left Fiona alone with a man. Unchaperoned. The chambermaid cleaning rooms just a little way down the hall would be more than willing to spread tales about the mysterious woman left alone in the Ambassador Suite with an unknown man. Hell. They couldn't afford gossip of any sort.

Seeing that the maid had stepped into the room across the hall, Jacob stormed forward and flung open the door to Fiona's rooms, sure that he would find her engaged in some sort of improper activity with the timid little tailor, if only to spite Jacob.

"Leave her be!"

Fiona and Mr. Peebles jumped slightly at the intrusion, the first glaring, the second shrinking into the squabs of the settee. But it soon became obvious to Jacob that, despite Fiona's less than proper mode of dress, a good yard of distance separated the two.

"Is something the matter?" Fiona asked dryly.

As she watched him, all knowing and slightly amused, Jacob felt sure they must both think him an ass. He'd come storming in, expecting the worst, only to discover that nothing had happened.

Nothing.

Still, there was a matter of explaining his odd behavior, so he closed the door muttering, "I thought I heard something."

Fiona didn't believe him. He could see it in the continued sparkle in her eyes, but her only comment was, "Maybe the Grand Estate has a problem with mice."

5

"OH, DEAR."

The comment came from Mr. Peebles, who stared at them both in evident discomfort. Hurriedly stuffing his things into his satchel, he took the opportunity to break the ensuing silence by stuttering, "I-if y-you're quite finished with your selections, Mrs. McFee."

"*Fiona.* Please."

The tailor's cheeks pinkened. "*Fiona,* then."

Jacob's teeth ground together slightly at their obvious familiarity, but he didn't comment. He couldn't. Not after Fiona had effectively tied his hands by spinning her pretty tale and relegating him to the role of petty servant.

"I'll begin your order right away and send these things to you as soon as possible."

"We need them by the end of the week. All of them."

Both Fiona and Mr. Peebles looked up at Jacob in surprise.

"A week!" Mr. Peebles grew instantly dismayed. "But I couldn't possibly have anything ready—"

"You may double your salary if you insist."

The tailor appeared momentarily stunned, then

grinned and hauled his valise to his chest. "In that case, I must start gathering accessories today."

"Accessories?" Jacob still stared at Fiona, measuring her strength, her will.

"For Mrs. Mc—Fiona."

This time Jacob's gaze did bounce in Mr. Peebles's direction.

"Accessories?" He couldn't resist the way the word slipped from his mouth much like an accusation. What had Fiona ordered while he'd been gone?

"There's no need to concern yourself, Mr. Grey."

No need? *No need?* His eyes narrowed suspiciously. Knowing her sense of taste, she'd probably ordered a wardrobe worthy of a saloon singer. He opened his mouth to question the tailor, but she was ushering Mr. Peebles to the door.

"Thank you for your help, Walter. We'll be notifying you at your shop with all of the arrangements."

Walter? *Walter?* Jacob felt the inexplicable urge to throttle the diminutive man.

"No trouble. No trouble at all." He cast a quick glance in Jacob's direction, then hurried into the hall.

Fiona closed the door behind him, then stood motionless, her back to Jacob. Waiting. Waiting.

"What in the hell have you done, Fiona?" he growled when it appeared she would not be the first to speak.

"Done?" She turned then, her brows lifting in feigned curiosity. "I've no idea what ye mean."

The Irish in her speech was back.

When she would have brushed past him, Jacob snagged her arm. "You're up to something."

"I merely followed yer orders, ye big oaf."

"In what way?"

"I ordered a selection o' clothing suitable for a British widow."

"I'll just bet."

Her lips pursed in irritation. "There is absolutely no call for yer sarcasm. Considerin' the way ye've been treatin' me, I'd say that I've been more than agreeable. Ye told me t' wait in this blasted suite—not fer a day, mind ye, but an hour."

"I had business to—"

"Ye told me t' bathe. I did. Ye told me t' play the British society matron. I did. Ye told me t'order a suitable wardrobe. I *did.*" She yanked her arm free. "Now, until ye're ready for me t' move on t' the next stage of the game, we've nothing more t' talk about."

Drawing the trailing ends of the bathsheet close to her hips, she sashayed into the bedroom with all the icy formality of a duchess in full snit, closing the door behind her.

Jacob's hands balled into fists and he inhaled, trying to calm the frustration he felt whenever this woman was around. But try as he might, he couldn't leave the situation well enough alone. He couldn't let her have the last word on the subject.

He marched after her, only to discover that she'd noiselessly flicked the latch. "Fiona," he growled in warning. "Fiona! Open this blasted door."

"I'll do nothing of the sort."

"Damn it all, Fiona!" His fist banged the panels. "I haven't finished with you yet."

"I should say ye have."

"You've got some explaining to do. Then we need to get to work."

There was a rattle, and the door flew wide open. "Explaining? Explaining! I've been the victim of yer harassment, yer insults, and yer anger. As far as I'm concerned, yer the one who needs to explain."

Her words took him by surprise, and she chose that opportunity to stab him in the chest with her finger. *"Why,* Jacob?"

He stared at her uncomprehendingly, seeing only the flush of her cheeks, the glistening of her eyes, and, buried somewhere deep inside, the hurt. The overwhelming hurt.

Jacob had always been a man who sided with the underdog. In his years as a lawman, he'd seen enough anger and misery to hate the sight of pain. He strongly believed in justice, but he'd also learned the hard way to believe in the necessity of mercy. Especially in regard to the young. The innocent.

Fiona McFee was not entirely innocent, but she was wounded. He didn't know why, he didn't know how, but the emotion lingered deep in her eyes.

Of its own volition, his hand lifted and his palm cupped her cheek. He needed to feel her velvety skin on his own. Just for a minute. Maybe two.

As if that single action had shattered something deep within her, Fiona blinked at the moisture gathering behind her lashes.

"Why, Jacob? Why must ye treat me this way?"

An unfamiliar tenderness crept into his heart. This was a grown woman. Complete in her own right. But lonely. Oh, so lonely. Just like him.

"We don't fit in, do we, Fiona?"

Her brow didn't crease, her gaze didn't falter. It was as if she'd taken the leap of subject at the same time and come to the same conclusion. In a world of conformists, they did not conform. In a world of blindness, they saw what occurred. In a world of pairs, they had been isolated.

The thought must have frightened her, because she took a sudden step away. "I don't know what ye mean, lawman," she said, pivoting on her toes and storming into the bedroom.

"Dammit, Fiona." But it was little more than a whisper.

When he stepped into the bedroom, she whirled to face him.

"What do ye want?"

He could have offered a teasing rejoinder, a sarcastic remark, but he found himself replying with utmost seriousness, "To understand you."

Her arms hugged her waist—unconsciously, he was sure. Fiona would never have willingly allowed him to see such vulnerability. She became incredibly brittle, incredibly wary of his mood.

"What's t'understand?" she offered flippantly, but he heard a different edge to her voice, like a chord played slightly off key.

"Why have you agreed to help us?"

She shrugged in patent dismissal. "Are ye daft? I wanted the pardons. And the clothing—I wanted that, too. Besides which, ye have me father. Despite what ye might think, he's a good man."

"He's a criminal."

"That doesn't detract from his goodness. Yer days must be completely without love for ye to find such a concept difficult to understand."

The remark was meant to wound him, to hurt him immeasurably, and Jacob was astonished to discover that it did sting. But Fiona hadn't finished yet. "I've seen the way ye live, cocooning yerself from every sort of bond. The closest thing ye have to a friend is yer horse—and that's because he's as cantankerous as ye are."

"I've got a sister—"

"That ye never see, from what the gossips say. That's no way t' live, without ties t' bind ye, t' hold ye in, make ye feel needed."

"My job takes care of that."

She prowled toward him. "What are ye going t' do twenty years from now? Snuggle up t'yer job on those long, empty nights?"

"Fiona!" He grasped her by the shoulders, shaking her slightly, wanting to keep her from saying anymore, wanting to keep the words from spilling from her lips. He didn't want to hear the truth he'd been avoiding for too long. But when he came in contact with those lithe shoulders, he found himself pulling her closer instead of pushing her away. His hands swept behind her back, drawing her to him, to that part of him that had been unaccountably awakened.

Her eyes widened, but he didn't wait for her to berate his actions. He didn't want her to stop him. He needed this. Needed to feel her hips grinding into his own, her breath short and labored. Forgetting all caution, all professionalism, his eyes fastened on her lips and he bent toward her.

As his mouth brushed her own, she gasped slightly, deep in her throat, as if she too wished to deny the storm of sensation that swept between them. But Jacob did not let her pull away—not that she tried. He hauled her close to his body, feeling her softness, and kissed her again and again.

Her fingers wrapped around his neck, digging into his skin. Her hips arched to his in a tormenting fashion. Slanting his head even further, he urged her to allow his tongue to sweep inside her mouth, to search, to savor, to enjoy.

When he drew away, they were both breathing hard. She was the first to wrench free.

"Fiona, I—"

When he would have apologized for his actions, she held up a forestalling hand. "No. I don't want to hear it."

He stiffened at her words. "At least give me the chance to—"

"No."

He wanted to break through her cool facade. He wanted—needed—to know she'd been as shaken as he by their embrace. "You felt it, I know you did."

"I felt nothing."

"Nothing?"

"Nothing." Her protest sounded weak to both of them.

"Why are you denying it? Why are you so afraid?"

At his demand, she jerked slightly, as if she had suffered some sort of physical blow. But she didn't speak. She merely wrenched free and leaned against the wall, splaying her hands wide as if to brace herself.

"Is that it, Fiona? Are you afraid? Has your father taught you nothing about what occurs between a man and a woman?"

"Go away, Jacob." He reached out to touch her cheek, but she shrank back. "Go away!"

Jacob opened his mouth to demand an explanation but was suddenly struck by the oddest scent. A very distinct and powerful odor, one that had tormented him time and time again throughout the afternoon.

"What is that *smell?*"

Her shoulders straightened, pushing her breasts against the flimsy barrier of the sheet, a fact that affected him with the suddenness of a fist to his groin.

"It's me, lawman. *Me!*" She jabbed her thumb in the direction of her collarbone. "Ye were so offended by the scent of lye that I took measures t' rectify the problem."

"Good Lord, you smell like a bordello."

"Insultin' me again, are ye now? Yer not content t' maul me, y' have to attack me character as well?"

"Hell's bells, Fiona, I—"

"At least I don't stink of sweat and manure and man!" With that parting shot she *harrumphed* and turned, barricading herself in the bathing room.

Jacob stared after her in astonishment. "I do not stink, Fiona! And we are not finished with this discussion, no matter how long you might try to hide."

She didn't answer.

He opened his mouth and strode to the door, stopped, hesitated.

But he couldn't bring himself to knock.

She was afraid of him, afraid of what had happened, but she wouldn't admit it. Instead, she had tried to sway him from the subject with a personal attack on his character.

His brow creased in a scowl. He didn't stink.

Did he?

Damn.

Damn, damn, damn! How was it that with one simple comment, that woman could make him feel completely beneath her standards? Dirty, unkempt . . . and randy as a goat?

The idea caused something akin to panic to settle in

71

the pit of his stomach. Jacob Grey had seen danger, had faced death, had experienced life's terrors. But those emotions paled when compared to what he felt now: a deep, overriding horror that he might—just might—be attracted to that woman, that virago, that hellion, that *criminal.*

Miss Fiona McFee.

Turning on his heels, Jacob wrenched open the door to the suite, nearly tackling one of the hotel servants, who was wheeling a trolley filled with china, tea cakes, sandwiches, and a thick broiled steak.

"Your tea, sir—"

Jacob paused, growled, then ordered, "Take it away."

"But—"

"Just take it away. I don't think either of us is hungry anymore."

He'd gone.

Fiona rested her shoulders on the panels and slid noiselessly to the floor, her eyes squeezing shut, her hands balling into fists. An ache, more powerful than anything she had ever experienced, blossomed in her chest and grew to excruciating proportions.

No. Sweet Mary and all the Saints above, no.

Her eyes opened, blinked, focusing with a tortured intensity upon the mirror opposite. Fiona barely recognized the woman who stared at her, one ravaged by guilt and dismay and an impending doom. A woman who wanted . . .

That man.

No. She couldn't possibly be so stupid. She couldn't possibly long for his attentions, his kinder words, his gentleness. He was a lawman. The worst sort of fellow, as far as she was concerned. He had no place in her life—and certainly no place in her heart.

But something about the way he'd stared at her mere moments before had eased into her aching soul like a soothing balm. She found herself forgetting everything but the feel of his hand on her cheek, the strength of his stare. The power of his kiss.

She had thought that she would hate this man forever. That he would irritate her, frustrate her, and annoy her. She had thought that would be enough to keep her emotions unencumbered.

She'd been wrong. She might try to shield her heart, but such an action would prove less than worthwhile. Whatever preventative measures she took, the truth remained. Jacob Grey had uncovered her loneliness. Her need for companionship. Affection. He'd uncovered her hunger.

But he would never care for her.

He could never respect her.

"It doesn't matter what he thinks of me," she whispered aloud, surprising herself when her voice emerged choked and tormented. "It doesn't matter at all." Rising, she turned away from the woman in the mirror. The reflected image reminded her that Jacob's opinion did matter.

Far more than it should.

Wilmington, Illinois

An eerie gloom hung over the oak-shrouded hills, as if even nature itself knew that this was not a place for joy or frivolity. The evening shadows that gathered were thick and bleak, so much so that the dozen shapes that waited behind him were indistinguishable to Gerald Stone as he moved toward where his men stood by their horses. Not until he'd nearly stumbled upon them did their faces and forms become recognizable.

Buttoning the last few fasteners of his "borrowed" jacket, he said, "I should only be gone a few minutes. Watch the perimeter guards. If their patterns vary even slightly, give the signal."

Stone heard the men murmur their agreement as he tugged at the sleeves of the prison guard's uniform. He and his cohorts had been in Wilmington for less than an hour, but they'd already rendezvoused with Billings and Watkins, the two men who had been watching Exeter Prison and charting the routines of the three dozen employees.

"I don't suppose you could have found someone with longer arms," Stone groused, eyeing his uniform with concern. The gray wool was filthy and reeked of sweat, but that wasn't what bothered him. Stone didn't mind being dirty—the nature of his activities had demanded it more than once in the last twenty years. But he did mind an improper fit. One look at the way the cuffs ended a good four inches above his wrists could cause the wrong sort of attention.

Billings grinned. "Nope." He spat a stream of tobacco into the dust at their feet. "I killed me the first guard t' get careless. He came out t' the ditch t' take a piss, an I slit his throat fer his troubles. Didn't know I was supposed t' wait fer someone yer own size."

"Never mind. Just keep your eyes open and your weapons ready."

Watkins stopped him with a hand on his arm. "I've been drinking with a couple of the guards each night at the Red Palace. Be careful. There are rumors that a U.S. deputy has been working undercover in the inner cellblock for about a month now."

The news caused Stone's first real twinge of concern. "Do they suspect us? Do they know we plan to break The Judge out?"

He shook his head. "From what I could tell, he's investigating the warden on prison conditions. Squat-looking fellow, bald, round spectacles. Watch out for him."

After checking the chambers of his own revolver and grabbing the dead guard's rifle, Stone sauntered toward the west portal. According to Watkins, the day shift had ended five minutes before. He was hoping that if he moved slowly and easily, the rest of the prison employees wouldn't pay him much attention as the night staff took their posts and the others made their way home.

His heart pounded in a heavy, measured beat as he moved from the shadows, retracing the path the now-deceased guard had made only a few minutes before. He kept his head low, his hat tugged over his brow, his shoulders hunched while his fingers stroked the hammer of his revolver with careful precision.

He managed to make it inside unchallenged. Dodging the other officers intent upon the guards' quarters, he stepped into an alcove, pausing only briefly. Mentally, he identified his location from the diagram of halls that Billings had sketched in the dust and forced him to memorize.

The heels of his boots rapped out a slow, steady rhythm as he wound through the corridors. Left. Two rights. At the first iron-barred checkpoint, he kept his head down and rubbed at his nose with a huge red handkerchief, thus covering most of his face. The chubby guard barely glanced his way, letting him into the next set of corridors.

Deeper and deeper he moved into the stone penitentiary. The air about him was rank with misery and sickness, open chamber pots, smoke, and delousing fluid. The familiar odors caused Stone's skin to crawl, reminding him all too effectively that he'd escaped his own unfortunate incarceration mere months before.

Turning left, he made his way to the far set of cell-blocks: those reserved for the most dangerous criminals. He touched a finger to the brim of his hat, nodding to the man on duty, keeping his head turned away. When the man stumbled over the task of finding the appropriate key, Stone studied him carefully, wondering if this was the deputy Watkins had warned him about.

"Warden wants t' see you," Stone muttered once he'd been let through the iron bars.

The squat man's brows rose in surprise. "Me?"

"I'm t' spell you 'til you return."

The deputy squinted at him, then shrugged and surrendered his keys. "I'll be back as soon as I can."

"Take your time."

The iron gate clanged shut and the rotund man hustled down the corridor. After selecting the proper key, Stone took a lump of soft wax from his pocket and made an impression of the instrument, then carefully put the wax away again. Moments later, he walked to the far cell.

The tall man who had been penned up for nearly half a decade glanced up from the book he'd been perusing. The cool gloom only intensified the angular planes of his face, the lean length of his body.

"How are things progressing, Stone?" he asked.

He grinned. "Right on schedule."

"Good. What about Kensington?"

"He . . . agreed to fall in with our plans."

"He put up a bit of a fuss, hmm?"

"Nothing that couldn't be handled."

"What does he know of his responsibilities?"

"Nothing more than you told me to tell him. He thinks he's preparing for another gambling junket."

"Good." Judge Krupp's pale eyes grew steely, determined. Cold. "Well? What else have you to report?"

"Our contact in the governor's office has put Grey in charge of the counterfeiting investigation. He arrived in Chicago two days ago. According to what my men there have been able to determine, he's on extended leave and intends to take a holiday—of course, we know differently, thanks to our informant. Grey has booked a suite at the Grand Estate. A private car has been pulled into the railway yard and was put at his disposal. As soon as Kensington books passage, Grey will be on the same train, under the guise of taking a 'vacation.'"

The Judge nodded. "Good. Tell your men to watch him in the mean time. I want to know where he goes and whom he talks to. If you get any more information, report immediately to me."

Stone clutched the bars, leaning closer as he murmured urgently, "Are you sure this is the way you want to handle things? The boys and I could have you out of this place in an hour. We could be on our way out of the country by dawn."

The Judge made a *tsk*-ing sound. "Patience, Stone. Patience." His gaze strayed to the line drawing he had tacked to the wall of his cell. Of the man who had put him in Exeter, who was responsible for his plight. Jacob Grey.

"I'll stay here at Exeter until the time is right. Otherwise we might tip our hand."

Stone could hear distant footfalls. Probably those of the returning deputy.

"I think you should reconsider. Let's get you out tonight, get you to Canada, Mexico. Then you can come after Grey. The man's been made a United States marshal, for hell's sake!"

"No matter." Krupp's lips grew hard. "Jacob Grey made a mistake all those years ago. A mistake for which he will pay. The time has long since come for him to fulfill that debt. If it takes another day or two in this place—or even a year—I'm more than happy to comply." His lips twitched. "Besides . . . we've gone to a great deal of effort to bait the hook. We must act now while our quarry is determined to bite."

Stone's hands clenched in frustration, but he signaled his agreement.

"Now get out of here before that fool guard catches you. I'll expect to see you again soon, Stone. Very soon."

6

"How is Lettie feeling, Alma?" Amelia looked up from her needlepoint as her sister entered the sitting room. They'd been at the McGuire home for nearly two days now, and a scowl continually creased Alma's features.

"We shouldn't have come, Amelia."

Amelia's heart sank in her breast. "I was afraid of that."

"I finally convinced Lettie to stay in her bed and sleep in a bit longer, but it took all my coaxing to get her there."

"She's not feeling any better?"

"Not a bit—but she won't admit it, won't admit that the last month of her 'waiting in' is uncomfortable at best. Backaches, warning pains, nausea, swollen ankles . . ." Alma clicked her tongue. "And we're not helping a bit. As long as we're here, she thinks she has to take care of us, entertain us, for fear we'll be disappointed with our trip."

"Oh, dear."

Alma eyed her sister, considering. "There's one more thing," she stated hesitantly.

"What?" Amelia could barely breathe the word.

78

Alma rushed to sit in the chair beside her, bending low. "I found this on her nightstand," she whispered, pulling a crumpled note from her pocket.

"What is it?"

"A letter from Jacob."

"Lettie must have been pleased to get it."

"She hasn't seen it yet." Alma glanced over her shoulder as if fearing she would be overheard. "The maid brought it in with her tea, but Lettie had already fallen asleep." She hesitated before saying, "I thought it might be important . . . so . . . I . . ."

"What does it say?"

Alma straightened in affronted dignity. "I am *not* prone to reading mail intended for other people."

"Of course not."

"But . . ." she drawled conspiratorially, "with the tea kettle so close to the edge of the flap . . ."

"The steam must have . . ."

"Pried it open a bit."

"And you . . ."

"Peeked. Just a peek." She fumbled with the letter in her hand. "I'm only too glad I did."

"Why?" Amelia breathed in trepidation.

"Jacob is in trouble."

"Oh, no!"

"Seems he's working undercover with some sort of immigrant girl. He needs Lettie's help."

"What kind of help?"

"He didn't say, but it sounds awfully hush-hush to me."

"But Lettie is in no condition to come to his aid!"

"Exactly. And this note will bring her nothing but worry if she sees it." Alma stood up and paced to the window, her ponderously corseted bosom preceding her like the bowsprit of a ship. Stopping, she tapped her lips with her index finger. "Amelia?"

"Yes, Sister."

"Are you game for an outing?"

"Whatever for?"

Alma turned. "I think we should take a little trip into town."

"Shopping?"

"Perhaps. But first, I think we should call on our beloved Jacob Grey."

"Get up."

The brusque masculine command was followed by the rude stripping away of Fiona's blankets. Fiona jumped, sleep scattering as she automatically grasped the sheet in order to prevent herself from being completely uncovered.

She cracked one eye open at the man responsible for her awakening. Her comment on his own grooming habits had evidently caused at least some sort of discomfort on his part. Jacob Grey appeared to have just stepped from a bandbox. His dark hair had been neatly combed, his jaw freshly shaven. He wore a clean chambray shirt, black suspenders, and brown woolen trousers. His well-oiled gunbelt completed the outfit. She hadn't heard him enter, making her wonder how long he'd stood there, how much he'd seen.

"Go . . . away." The words were uttered with quiet precision as she dragged a bolster over her head.

Firm fingers burrowed beneath the pillow, yanking it free. "We've got no time for your grumpiness, Fiona."

"And I've no mind fer yer dad-blasted cheerfulness!" She scowled at the way he towered above her in an unconsciously arrogant stance, feet braced apart, hands on hips. "Are ye always so chipper at the crack of dawn?"

"I've been up for hours."

Noting his smug expression, Fiona felt an immediate foreboding. Invariably, such an obvious show of pleasure from Jacob came at her own expense. "What exactly have ye been doing all that time?"

"Gathering the necessary equipment." His dark eyes sparkled noticeably as he studied her from head to toe. In an instant, she became aware of her disheveled hair and sleep-flushed skin. Far from being discouraged by the sight, he added most silkily, "Today, Fiona, we are going to see to it that you become a lady."

A *lady*. How he harped on that concept—as if she were of some unknown gender and origin, without a clue as to what she should do.

"I'm gettin' tired o' yer insinuatin' that there's something so wrong with m'education that it's going t' take a team of instructors t' fix it. I think I showed ye adequately enough that I can play the role ye've given me. Mr. Peebles didn't suspect."

"Mr. Peebles is a sweet, old, nearsighted man. He took one peek at you, draped in a sheet as you were, and lost all proper reason." Jacob leaned his hands upon the bed, causing her to roll ever so slightly toward him. "Had you worn any clothes at all, he might have taken proper notice of the way an Irish brogue kept filtering into your speech. But since he couldn't tear his eyes away from the velvety flesh of your shoulders, I doubt he would have noticed if his hair had been on fire."

Her lips tightened in pique and she scraped the covers more tightly to her body, hoping to hide the very shoulders of which he'd spoken. Jacob might not admit it, but Mr. Peebles was not the only man who found it hard to focus on much else than a measure of bare skin.

"So what are ye plannin' t' do? Hire a host o' ladies' maids to train me t' yer standards?"

"I've sent for my sister to help. In the mean time my deputy, Rusty, and I should be able to handle the first stage of the polishing process." He squinted at her as if she were to be cataloged piece by piece for further instruction. "After all, there's not too much wrong with your appearance that Mr. Peebles's creations can't fix."

"Ye make it sound as if I'm a piece o' mutton needin' some finery t' make me decent."

He paid no heed to her outburst but continued without pause: "As for the rest, a little coaching should do the trick."

Grasping her wrist, he tugged her—sheet and all—from the bed and towed her into the bathing room. "Fix your hair and put on that dress. I managed to borrow it from one of the chambermaids."

He gestured to an awful, sun-bleached calico gown draped over the side of the tub. She could only imagine how he'd managed to fanagle the garment from the unknown woman. The thought of him sweet-talking some pretty little maid caused an inexplicable pang of jealousy.

"I'll not be wearin' a stranger's clothes."

"You will—even if I have to stuff you in it myself."

He was resolute. She knew that. The stubborn line of his jaw gave ample evidence of the fact.

"Get . . . *dressed,* Fiona. When you've finished, join Rusty and me in the sitting room. We've ordered breakfast, so you'll want to hurry." Slamming the door, he left her to digest his autocratic orders.

Damn the man. Her fingers curled into the linens and she hiked them a little more securely about her chest. Sniffling, she weighed her options.

"Remember the pardons, Fiona."

The words wafted to her from the other room as if Jacob had read her very thoughts.

"Go to bloody hell, lawman," she whispered under her breath. But she didn't say it loud enough for him to hear. At least she had the sense for that.

It took only a minute to tug a brush through her hair, then don the cotton dress. Staring at her reflection in the mirror, she grimaced. Jacob might think himself an expert on women, but he obviously had a thing or two to learn about sizes. The dress exposed a far too healthy expanse of her leg, ending at a point midcalf. The waist was too loose, the bust too tight, and the sleeves far too short. In this getup, she would be mistaken as a boxcar orphan, not a wealthy British widow.

Pursing her lips in disgust, she threw open the door and marched into the other room. "Ye expect me to wear this? *This?*"

Jacob didn't even bother to glance up from his meal, but his red-headed companion choked on a piece of ham, then sat for some time coughing, trying ever so hard not to stare at the buttons straining at her bosom.

"Sit down, Fiona."

The imperious order came from Jacob.

"I—"

"Sit down or you won't be fed at all."

Deciding that in this case a good meal was worth far more than offering a piece of her mind, Fiona crossed the room to settle into the only remaining chair. She'd had nothing to eat for days but the apples, oranges, figs, and nuts she'd taken from the basket left by the hotel.

Wiping his mouth with a napkin, Jacob poked a thumb in the direction of his companion. "This is Rusty Janson, my deputy. If he gives you an order from me, take it as gospel."

Fiona considered the man with his curly red hair and freckled complexion, but she didn't respond. Rusty stared at her as if he'd just sat on a tack and considered her partially responsible. The odd mix of surprise, dread, and unease was disturbing.

Jacob shifted, regarding her consideringly. "Sit up straight."

She complied, but only because all of the food had been placed on his end of the table.

"You don't look much like a woman of quality."

"Well, *ye* don't act much like a man of refinement."

He grinned but did not offer a rebuttal.

"Go ahead and eat, then we'll get started."

She waited for him to offer her a plate, but he did nothing of the sort, returning to his perusal of the paper folded on the table and his own generous helping of fried eggs and bacon.

"Eat. Eat!" he ordered when she remained still.

"But ye've given me nothin' fer breakfast!"

"There's tea and toast in front of you."

She stared down at the meager fare, then at the men's plates, which were heaped with food. "That's all I get?"

"A true lady eats like a bird."

"Who told ye that nonsense?"

A dark light of warning entered his eyes. "My mother —God rest her soul—was a lady through and through, Fiona. I don't think I saw her eat a hot meal in all her days."

"Probably because ye forced her to fetch and tote yer meals so much she never had a chance," she grumbled under her breath.

He must have heard the comment, because his eyes narrowed in warning. "Eat what you've been given, Fiona, or do without. I don't care. Simply remember that for the next few weeks, you are to do everything— *everything*—I tell you to. Otherwise your father will be cracking rocks in the prison quarry."

Her chin tilted to a mulish angle, but she knew she'd strained the bounds of his good graces. Taking some toast in both hands, she purposefully shoved the piece midway into her mouth, chewing noisily, and creating as much of a spectacle as she could.

"Like a bird, Fiona. Eat like a bird. Otherwise Darby Kensington won't even glance at you, and I'll have no need to report favorably to the governor for your reward."

Drat and bother. He was right. By rebelling, she only defeated her own purposes. She had to focus her mind on what was important: liberating her father. Until then, she would have to bite her tongue and hold her temper.

Taking a few calming breaths, she washed the bread down with a good dose of weak tea—no milk, no lemon, no sugar had been provided—the tepid fare having obviously been prepared by an American cook. Glancing down at the crumbs littering her plate and the nearly finished piece of toast, she sighed. She really shouldn't have consumed things so quickly. Her stomach rumbled at that bare offering of nourishment. Blast it all, it wasn't fair! Those two men sat across from her, dining on enough food to feed a battalion, and all she was allowed was a bit of bread and a cup of black tea.

"I want more, Jacob."

"No."

"But I'm hungry."

"You could stand to lose a pound or two."

At that statement she huffed in fury, rising from her place and planting her hands on the table. "Ye ill-mannered, arrogant . . . *bastard!* I'll have ye know I'm fit as a fiddle."

"Not by the looks of that dress." His eyes flicked to the straining buttons. His red-headed deputy choked on his coffee.

She self-consciously tugged at the offending garment. "If ye'd bothered to get something that fit properly it wouldn't hang this way."

"Clothing is clothing. You'll have a new set soon enough." Tugging at the napkin that had been tucked into his collar, he rose. "As for now, it's time to get to work."

He pushed her into the center of the room.

"Sit."

"Beg pardon?"

"Sit."

"I'm not a dog to be—"

"Just sit down in the damned chair, Fiona!"

Grumbling invectives under her breath to keep from coming completely unglued, she complied.

"Rusty, get over here."

The deputy grabbed a handful of bacon and did as he was told.

"What do you think?"

Fiona didn't know what they searched for, but she was getting tired of having these men ogle her like she was a piece of meat.

"I think she needs to slide forward a little," Rusty suggested hesitantly.

"Perch on the edge of the chair, Fiona." Jacob waited until she'd obeyed, then asked, "Now what?"

"She 'ppears too . . . relaxed. In my experience women are usually stiff as a board."

"Straighten up."

They paused to study the effect.

"Better. Better. Now take shallower breaths."

"Glance down."

"Hands on your lap."

"Curl the fingers."

"Tilt your chin."

"Eyes up."

"Shoulders straight."

"Put your—"

"Enough!" She sprang from the chair. "Are ye tryin' t' turn m' body into a solitary cramp?"

Jacob and Rusty exchanged glances.

"Maybe we'll start with walking." Jacob took a book from the side table. "Put this on your head."

She complied, but only because she'd happened to see that there were still two strips of bacon left on the platter at the far end of the table. If she could walk that way without alerting suspicion, she was sure that she could snag the pieces and shove them in her mouth without these men being able to stop her. Such measures rankled, but the hollow pit of her stomach demanded them.

She balanced on her head the book—a very heavy, thick, awkward tome of poetry.

"Hands down."

"Relax your fists."

"Chest out—no, you'd better keep it in."

"Shoulders back."

"Walk."

She didn't wait for a second invitation but lunged forward. The book fell to the floor with a thud, but she paid it no mind and rushed to the table, where she managed to grasp the bacon, two rolls, and a butter knife. Retreating to the corner of the room, she held her makeshift weapon out in front of her.

"Don't come any closer. I agreed t' be yer puppet, but I didn't agree t' starve in the process. Nor did I agree t' be ordered about by a couple of men who don't know what they're doin'."

Jacob's lips thinned in impatience. "We're simply

trying to rub a few of the rougher edges off your personality, Fiona."

"There's nothin' wrong with me edges."

"There's plenty wrong if we're going to fool Kensington." He prowled closer. "If you're not willing to cooperate, I can do without you. It's not too late for me to find someone else. To lock you and your father up for good and give the pardons to someone else."

Her heart sank. He'd bested her. Once again he had the upper hand in the argument.

"Put the food down, Fiona."

"But—"

"Put it down."

She reluctantly did as she was told, but not until she'd hidden a piece of bacon in the pocket of her dress.

Jacob nodded in approval and drew her into the center of the room. "Pick up that book and let's start again."

By lunchtime, Jacob knew that they were all in trouble. Instead of helping Fiona to tap into her natural sources of feminine wiles—those same silken machinations she'd used with Mr. Peebles—he and his deputy had managed to underscore her self-consciousness and nervousness. So much so that by midday she was stumbling about the room like a gawky adolescent. So far there had been no messages from Lettie. He could only hope she wasn't off on some recital tour, thus leaving him completely without proper help.

"Hell, Fiona. *Try*," he muttered in frustration.

The moment he said the words, he knew he'd made a mistake. If there was one thing he couldn't fault her for, it was her effort to follow orders. After he'd issued his threat, she'd been as meek and biddable as a lamb and as tireless as a draft horse.

Her head dipped and he thought he saw a slight sheen of moisture in her eyes. A thick remorse settled in his belly. After all he'd done to undermine her confidence, he'd hurt her feelings as well.

"Fiona, I didn't mean to snap at you."

She whirled at him then, her chin proudly lifting. "Ye don't say. Ye've been doin' a mighty fine job of it all day."

"Maybe we should take a break. Have some lunch."

Her eyes brightened somewhat. "Could we go downstairs?"

"No."

"But I've been cooped up in this blasted room fer hours and hours and hours!"

"You'll stay here 'til you've been properly trained. I told you that."

"Trained. Trained?" She marched forward to poke him in the chest. "Ye and yer deputy don't know spit about what yer doin'. Are ye aware of that fact? Neither one of ye would know a proper British aristocrat if she bit ye in the arse. An' I'm tired a playin' these games that get us nowhere."

She jabbed him again, but he grasped her wrist and pulled her tightly to his chest. "If you're so knowledgeable about the gentry, then why don't you act like one instead of sashaying through this sitting room with all the grace of a swayback mule?"

Her mouth opened, but no sound emerged. This time Jacob couldn't deny that the glitter he saw in her lashes was due to her tears.

"Fiona, I'm sorry. I know you've been trying."

She didn't hear him, or if she did, she chose to ignore his apology, whirling and rushing into the bedroom. Seconds later, he heard the slam of the bathing-room door and the audible click of the lock.

"Now you've done it," Rusty drawled. "Once a woman barricades herself behind a locked door, there's no gettin' her out without some sweet-talkin' or some mighty expensive presents."

"Fiona?" Jacob marched into the neighboring chamber and pounded on the closed door. "Come out of there."

"No."

"I'm sorry about what I said."

"No ye're not."

"Fiona—"

A knock at the outer door caused him to frown, wondering if his altercation with this woman had caused such a fracas that the manager had been sent to complain about the noise.

Swearing under his breath, Jacob strode into the sitting room just in time to see Rusty admit two elderly women, one tall and stout, the other small and spry.

He stopped dead in his tracks, his mouth dropping open. Good hell almighty. The Beasleys.

He barely had time to assimilate the fact before another of his deputies dodged through the threshold. "Jacob! We've got trouble."

Jacob agreed wholeheartedly. He'd grown up with the Beasleys while living in his mother's boardinghouse. They were delightful women, fun-loving and a little bawdy, but heaven help them, wherever they went, trouble followed.

"Jacob!"

At the second call, he turned his attention to the middle-aged deputy. "What!"

"Darby Kensington just rolled into town."

"Shit." He scooped up his hat and strode to the door. Pointing to the two women, he ordered brusquely, "Wait here." Then he was gone, thundering down the servants' staircase with his deputies trailing behind him.

The wake of silence that ensued was nearly deafening. At long last, Alma and Amelia Beasley locked gazes.

"So . . ." Alma drawled.

"Mmm," her sister echoed.

"It appears that our dear Jacob is in distress."

"Yes indeed."

Alma took a deep breath, holding it thoughtfully, then releasing it in a rush. "Come along, Amelia." She swept into the hall.

"But Jacob told us to stay here."

"We'll be back soon enough."

"Where are we going?"

"To gather our things. We have a mission, Amelia. One that needs our immediate attention."

An hour later, Jacob was waiting by the base of the stairs as Rusty Janson strode toward him.

Rusty received a few odd glances as he made his way through the main lobby of the Grand Estate. With his red hair, freckled skin, and dusty shirt and chaps, he appeared decidedly out of place in the elaborate marble and gilt lobby. But the bowlegged fellow didn't notice the attention he garnered as he charged in Jacob's direction.

"We've got trouble, all right." He glanced about him, then lowered his voice to a confidential tone.

Jacob became immediately alert. "What's happened?"

"The information we've received was right: According to the men who've been following Kensington since we stumbled onto him at the railway station, Darby came in on the morning train. He made two stops—one at a tailor's and another at a rather upscale bordello. Both times he took a heavy satchel with him—as if he was afraid to leave it in the carriage with his driver. After his time at Rosie's, he went *back* to the railway station, of all places." He snorted in disgust. "Blast it all to gol-durn hell, he booked tickets for the next excursion!"

"Damn."

"He's leaving in little more than a fortnight."

Jacob felt a slow horror seep into his veins. A fortnight. *A fortnight!* He'd counted on at least a month to turn Fiona McFee into a lady. Now he had half of that to see her groomed, instructed, and clothed.

He growled, looking skyward as if searching for divine inspiration, but there was nothing upon the frescoed ceiling to provide his answers. Nothing at all.

"Oh, hell. Guess who's just arrived, Jacob."

Both men saw a tall, striking gentleman with sandy hair and a well-trimmed goatee walk through the door, followed by a host of servants struggling to carry an assortment of small trunks and satchels. One carpetbag, however, remained firmly in Kensington's own grip.

"Do you think he followed you?" Jacob asked, as he and Rusty casually turned their backs to the registration desk.

"Doubt it. He's been carryin' on like a drone in a hive for most of the afternoon. Never seen such drinkin' and high-fallutin' shenanigans, I tell you."

"You and your boys keep an eye on him, Rusty. If he leaves the hotel, I want to know about it."

"Yes, sir."

The retinue turned from the desk and made its way to the stairs. Jacob's gaze sliced after his suspect, watching his distinctive gait, the elegant swing of his walking stick.

"When Wally spells you, Rusty, I want you to make arrangements for the railway car we're using to be prepared for the same excursion train Darby plans to take."

Rusty stared at him in dismay. "You can't possibly mean you're goin' anyway. Not so soon."

Jacob's jaw firmed.

"We're going. If I have to dress that woman in ready-made and tie her to my hip . . . we're going."

Infused with a sense of urgency and mindful of the ever-ticking clock, Jacob took the hotel stairs two at a time.

The task ahead of him seemed insurmountable. Some-how, in a few paltry days, he had to turn Fiona McFee into a lady. She had to talk like one, walk like one, and smell like one. In addition, she would have to be briefed on the situation with Darby Kensington and supplied with the information concerning her alias.

Jacob had learned long before not to underestimate his foes, and he had a bad feeling about Darby Kensington. There was much more to the gambler than what met the eye. Since Jacob had begun to trail him, he'd felt a wriggling unease settle deep in the pit of his stomach whenever he was near the man. Such instincts in the past had only led to trouble.

Automatically resting his palm on the butt of his revolver, he paused at the second landing when he realized that his haste had caused him to nearly overtake the man. Standing behind one of the polished stairwell supports, Jacob studied him again.

As the gambler waited for the hotel servants to open his room, Jacob noted that he was fastidious in his dress, carefully groomed, and artlessly handsome. Nevertheless, Jacob didn't like him. Even though there had been no hard proof that Kensington was the culprit responsible for the counterfeit bills, Jacob knew—knew deep in his bones—that the elegant gambler was responsible. There was something about his smarmy attitude and easy way with women that set Jacob's teeth on edge. If ever there was a fellow destined to live his life behind bars, this one was. But he was also smart. Jacob had to give him that much credit. So far the only hope Jacob had for trapping and apprehending Kensington was a half-educated Irish street urchin with a talent for cards.

The unease Jacob had felt earlier returned. Heaven help them all if her masquerade didn't work. With Darby Kensington staying so near, they would have to be doubly careful. She mustn't be seen until she'd become an elegant widow through and through.

And for that, he feared he was going to have to enlist the help of the Misses Alma and Amelia Beasley.

Gerald Stone followed the now familiar pathway through the corridors of Exeter Prison until he reached the inner cellblocks. Approaching the bars that separated him from his long-time friend and employer, he waited for the judge to acknowledge him.

"Everything's in position?" the judge asked, marking the page of the book he'd been reading and placing it on the floor.

"I received the wire. Kensington is in Chicago. He's booked passage for the next excursion."

"Good." The judge's eyes glittered in the gloom of his chambers. "Then the next time we see each other . . ."

"I'll be taking you with me."

7

"COME ALONG, AMELIA."

Alma Beasley stepped from the carriage and sailed toward the door leading into the Grand Estate. Little more than an hour had passed since they'd come to confront Jacob Grey, only to be abruptly abandoned. After discussing the situation between themselves, they'd decided that Jacob needed help much more severely than his note had let on. Therefore, she and Amelia had arrived with reinforcements.

Stepping into the lobby, Alma didn't bother to glance behind her to see if her sister was in tow. There was no need to check. She and Amelia were more than sisters, they were kindred spirits. Wherever one went, the other invariably followed.

The door whisked in its circle with a *whack, whack* of its leather-edged panes. Hearing a squeal behind her, Alma paused, watching as the diminutive Amelia barely had the opportunity to dodge free. The contraption was left spinning in unmitigated glee.

"So sorry, Amelia."

Breathless, Amelia waved away her concern. "Lead on, Alma dear."

Smacking the tip of her parasol against the marble floors with each step, Alma marched across the lobby floor, surveying the vestibule like a practiced general, taking in the other guests, the bellboys, the maids, and the clerical staff.

"Who do you think could let us back into the suite upstairs, Sister?" Amelia asked, her voice breathy from their haste.

"That man over there." Alma used her parasol to point to the manager, who stood behind the front desk. He had his back to the women and was methodically stuffing receipts into the pigeonholes that corresponded with the numbers of each room.

Not hesitating another moment, Alma sailed toward him, her parasol clacking. Amelia followed as quickly as she could, but since she lacked at least a foot of height when compared to her older sister, she was forced to adopt a pace that approximated a sprint.

"Young man!" Alma extended her hand, ringing the brass bell on the counter with such force that the clerk started, the papers bursting from his hands and sifting to the floor like snow.

Whirling, he attempted to adopt a mask of calm.

"Yes, madam."

Upon their first real look at the middle-aged man and his raw-boned good looks, Alma's militant attitude immediately softened. She cast a glance at her sister, who smiled and returned the silent message. Then they both beamed at him as if he were a prince royal.

Leaning closer, Alma adopted a confidential tone. "I wondered if you could help us."

He eyed them curiously. "Of course, madam."

"We've a carriage outside. Our luggage has been strapped to the rear."

"You'll be needing a room then."

She smiled. "No. Thank you."

"No room?"

Amelia shook her head, echoing breathlessly, "Oh, no. But thank you all the same."

"Then where—"

"Just follow us, young man," Alma said. "Just follow us."

Jacob had just let himself into the Ambassador Suite, finding it empty of the Beasleys and Fiona still locked in the bathing room, when he heard the rattle of the doorknob. Whipping his revolver from his holster, he flung open the portal, leveling the weapon at the unknown assailant on the other side.

The porter, loaded with baggage and satchels and all manner of feminine frippery, uttered a breathy prayer and sank to his knees, the paraphernalia he'd been carrying scattering to the floor.

"Now really, Jacob. That wasn't in the least bit polite."

Before Jacob could summon any sort of an answer, Alma Beasley used the tip of her parasol to push the point of his gun away, then strode into the room, Amelia close behind.

He scowled in their direction. "I thought I told you to stay here until I got back."

Alma patted his arm in a patronizing manner. "We just ran out to pack a few things. Now we're here to stay. Where is she, boy?"

Jacob stared. "Who?"

"The girl we're to help!"

"I—"

She didn't wait for a response but turned to the porter. "Bring those inside. You can stack them against the wall for now. Jacob, make sure you give him a handsome tip."

"Miss Alma, I—"

"We would have stayed here like you said," she continued without pausing, tugging her gloves from her fingers, "but we felt that time was of the essence. Therefore we went back for our things." She whirled to confront him. "Well? What are we to do?"

Jacob stared at them in growing dismay. "I don't understand."

"Of course you don't. Men seldom do."

He had no idea what she meant by that comment.

"How did you know I was . . . that I . . ."

"Your letter to Lettie," she interrupted. "You really should have called on her yourself, you know."

Amelia's head bobbed in agreement. "She misses you desperately."

"And she's ill, you know."

"Ill?" Jacob repeated.

"Well, not ill, exactly, but not right as rain, either." Alma paused importantly. "She's about to have a baby."

"But she already has two," Jacob stammered, still not quite sure when he'd lost control of this situation.

"They're not babies any longer, you fool." Alma smacked her parasol on the floor. "You'd know that if you ever bothered to visit."

"Or write," Amelia added.

"But—"

"Nevertheless, we received your summons for help, and we are here in Lettie's place. Where is she?"

"Who?"

"The girl, the girl! My word, Jacob. If you can't get your wits about you any more than this, how can you ever perform your job properly?" Jacob had no opportunity to respond before she gestured with an imperious finger. "The *tip.*"

The porter who'd nearly been shot between the eyes was finished with his work. A fair pile of trunks and satchels had been stacked neatly against the wall. Not wanting the man to tell any more tales than necessary, Jacob gave him a handful of greenbacks, pushed him into the hall, and slammed the door. No sooner had it closed than there was a timid knock.

"Blast it all to hell, I already paid you enough money to—"

The words died in Jacob's throat when he wrenched open the door to expose Mr. Peebles. The man stood uncertainly, a box clutched to his middle, astonishment crossing his features.

Immediately, Jacob stiffened. Mr. Peebles believed

Fiona to be an extremely wealthy woman of class and decorum—and Jacob to be her lowly bodyguard. How could he possibly explain to this owl-eyed man that the commotion he'd heard was completely innocent?

"Mr. Peebles," he shouted a little too loudly, hoping that Fiona would hear and come out of the bathing room. "Hello." The little man started at Jacob's abrupt greeting. Jacob attempted to put him at ease with a smile, but if anything, it merely made the man more nervous.

"I've got the first change of clothing as requested," Peebles offered hesitantly. "I told Fiona that I'd bring it by this afternoon." He flicked a glance at the two elderly women. "Oh. Good afternoon, ladies."

Jacob had to give them credit for their abilities at play-acting. Alma didn't miss a beat as she extended her arms in welcome.

"Come in, Mr. Peebles. Come in."

"If I'm not intruding."

"Not at all," Amelia gushed. "We're the young lady's new chaperones. Pardon the mess, but we've just come ourselves."

"Is Mrs. McFee in? As I said, I spent the night finishing one of her gowns and thought she might appreciate having suitable garments to wear about town today."

"How nice." Alma drew him inside, jabbing Jacob none too subtly in the ribs in the process. "Jacob, why don't you go get our dear girl."

Jacob couldn't move. With each instant, the scene grew more horrible. "I—uh . . . she's in the other room."

After nearly two full, painful minutes of waiting in uncomfortable silence, Mr. Peebles eventually asked, "Could *I* see her?"

"Hmm?" Jacob asked vaguely, as if he had no idea what Mr. Peebles was asking.

"Mrs. McFee—could I see her?"

"Why?"

"As I said, I have her things."

"Leave them."

"But . . . but . . ." The tailor became a little nonplussed. "I can't! There are final fittings to be made. A tuck here. A tuck there." He held the box more tightly. "Can I see her?"

Jacob sighed. "I . . . don't think so."

Mr. Peebles's eyes grew wide and horrified. "Is there something wrong?" he whispered, stepping closer.

"Wrong?"

"Are we in danger?" Mr. Peebles inquired, peering around him as if Fiona's supposed murderer lurked in some unseen corner.

Swearing silently to himself and damning the situation altogether, Jacob took matters into his own hands. "No, Mr. Peebles. Mrs. McFee is merely unavailable for a fitting at this time. If you'll just give me the box."

Mr. Peebles clung to the container as if it were a foundling child. "I think . . . I should wait until I can give these garments to Mrs. McFee herself."

"Nonsense. She's . . . finishing her bath. I'll simply take this to her."

The tailor's eyes rounded in shock at such a proposition. The Beasleys gasped at the suggestion.

"I mean, I'll take it into the other room. Leave it outside her door."

A brief wrestling match ensued, as Jacob tried to take the box and Mr. Peebles held it tight, but Jacob managed to jerk the container out of his hands.

Barely able to conceal his frustration, Jacob marched into the other room, slamming the bedroom door behind him and thumbing his nose at what Mr. Peebles might think of that. The Beasleys would manufacture a story to tell him, he was sure.

Tapping on the panels of the bathing room, he waited for some reply. Nothing.

"Fiona?"

Nothing.

"Fiona, come out this instant."

There was still no answer.

"I have something for you. Mr. Peebles brought a gown for you to wear."

He thought he heard a stirring.

"I think you should try it on."

"Why? Ye'll never let me go anywhere."

The words were mumbled, but he heard them nonetheless. Setting the box on the ground, he untied the twine that held it shut and lifted the lid.

"You should see what's here. There's a dress, some socks, a pair of drawers—"

"Don't ye be rifling through me things!"

"I'm paying for them."

"Some high-falutin' banker is payin' fer them, according t'our original agreement."

She had him there.

"So don't ye' be puttin' yer grubby hands on me delicates."

He nearly snorted aloud in amusement at that. As if Fiona McFee had ever owned anything "delicate"—as if she even knew the meaning of the word.

"You'd better come out then and see them for yourself."

"No."

He sighed. "Fiona—"

"Not unless ye agree to take me somewhere once I'm in 'em."

"You know I can't do that."

"Ye can, but ye won't. Drat it all, I've been cooped up in this hotel fer days. I need t' get out!"

"It wouldn't be prudent." Not with Darby so near and Fiona still looking like a waif.

She remained quiet for half a minute. "I don't know what that . . . 'pru-dent' word means, but I don't care; I'm not a hen to be kept in a coop. I need fresh air an' the feel o' the wind on m' face. I need a good dose of spring—"

"It's the middle of August."

"—summer, then! What does it matter? M' heart is achin' t' be out in the open."

"This is Chicago, not the wide open spaces of Kansas —and don't you be trying any of that poetic rhetoric on me, Fiona. It won't work. My sister gave me enough of that when we were younger, and it has no effect on me."

He heard no retort, no sound of any kind for some time.

"Fiona?"

"What!" The word was sharp. Bitter.

"Come out."

"Not until ye agree t' take me somewhere—anywhere. Just fer an hour."

"No."

"Then ye can wear that dress yerself and say yer the blasted Queen of Sheba fer all I care!"

"I'll have your father—"

"I'm beginnin' t' believe that m' father an' I would have a better time of it in jail. At least there they'd feed me three times a day—an' not with no blasted weak Yankee tea!"

She'd called his bluff—and apparently she knew it. There was no time to ask another woman to help him. Even if there were, where would he find another female cardshark that he could hold under his thumb?

"I'll take you out for thirty minutes. We'll go for a drive."

"An hour."

"Forty-five minutes, and you can wear your new clothes."

He could almost hear the flywheels turning in her brain.

"Ye've got yerself a deal, lawman."

Less than an hour later, Fiona's heart was beating with an unaccustomed excitement as she was led from her suite into the hall. Finally—*finally*—she was to be allowed outside—and not just dressed as a simple working woman, either. She wore the suit that Mr. Peebles had made for her.

Jacob didn't like the costume. She'd known that from

the moment she'd appeared fully dressed. A nearly palpable wave of disapproval flowed her way with each step she took.

He had the sense to hide his reaction, introducing her to the two old women who claimed to be her chaperones. She was confused by their arrival. Jacob had made no mention of supplying companions, but she supposed she should have expected something of the sort. Jacob was concerned about propriety—and in truth, she was a little glad that she had the elderly women to buffer some of the tension between her and Jacob.

The minute the Beasleys and Mr. Peebles rounded the bend of the staircase, Jacob stopped her with a hand on her arm.

"Great holy hell, Fiona. *What* are you *wearing?* You look awful."

"Thank *ye* very much," she offered pithily.

"I told you to order something nice."

Fiona glanced down at her severe ebony suit and frowned. As far as she was concerned, there was nothing about her appearance to inspire such language. She had dressed with great care for her role as a British widow. She'd carefully donned each item: coarse linen drawers and a knee-length chemise, a stiff black corset and corset cover, three lawn petticoats and two of black chintz, a bustle, bustlepad, black underskirt, bodice, and swag. The entire ensemble had been finished with thick black cotton hose, leather boots and gloves, and a broad-brimmed bonnet.

Fiona knew she had made no mistakes. Society dictated that a woman in mourning should wear no colors that could be seen by the outward eye. Black wool covered her body from neck to toe—although she had forgone the use of a veil, since she already felt as if she would expire from the weight of her costume.

"Ye ordered me t' dress appropriately. This is the proper outfit for a British widow in full mourning."

"You're dressed like a crow."

She didn't glance in his direction, but she felt the way

he studied her body from the tip of her severe black bonnet to the high-necked suit with its dead-on row of jet buttons, the unadorned draped skirt, and practical black hightop boots.

"I'm attired like a woman o' grief."

"I hate it."

"Yer opinion isn't really an issue, now is it?"

"Part of the plan we've developed is for Darby Kensington to notice you. He'll never take a second glance in that getup."

She sniffed in disdain and tugged at her sleeves. "On that, ye are wrong. Men are intrigued by women in mourning."

"Who gave you that idiotic idea?" he whispered. Placing a hand at her waist, he ushered her down the stairs. "Hell. We'll simply have to make some adjustments to your wardrobe before Mr. Peebles can get any farther."

She glared at him suspiciously. "What exactly do ye plan to dress me in? Feathers?"

"If necessary."

They had reached the last few steps when Jacob suddenly took her wrist, forcing her to stop.

"Wh—"

"Kensington." The name was but a puff of breath.

She immediately knew who Jacob referred to. She'd seen enough gamblers in her lifetime to know the type. Darby Kensington was tall, broad-shouldered, with waving gold hair and a carefully trimmed mustache taught to curve at the tips and a neatly groomed goatee. He fairly reeked of money and swaggering assurance.

She sensed the way Jacob's attention diverted from their prey to focus on her.

"He's very handsome, don't you think?" Jacob asked. By his very tone it was evident that he expected her to deny such a thing, to show she could remain unaffected by his charm, but Fiona couldn't prevent needling him.

"I suppose."

"He's also very good at cards."

She tilted her chin to a regal angle. "Not good enough."

Darby Kensington turned from the desk, his ebony walking stick tapping out the closing distance.

Jacob's grip tightened. "Come along. It's too soon for him to see you."

She glared at him. "Ye mean I'm not enough of a lady?"

"Exactly."

His response irritated her beyond belief. What under the holy stars did he *want* of her? She hadn't said hell or damn in at least an hour, she'd washed the lye from her skin and combed the tangles from her hair. For the past few minutes, she'd taken great pains to walk as if a poker had been shoved up her arse—just as Jacob had insisted before they'd left the room—and he *still* wasn't satisfied.

Jacob must have sensed a portion of her thoughts, because when she took a step forward, he scowled at her. "Fi-o-na," he warned. "Don't."

She flashed him an innocent smile. One worthy of the cherubs she'd once seen painted on the walls of Saint Michael's Cathedral. "Don't what?"

Any warnings he might make were far too late. Darby Kensington had climbed the first tread. Fiona, seeing the opportunity, pretended to stumble, gasped, and threw her arms around the gambler's waist to catch herself.

Behind her, Jacob swore, grasping her shoulder and snatching her free.

"Are you all right, madam?" Kensington inquired, but he didn't quite look at her face. Indeed, after a cursory examination of the woman who'd all but collapsed at his feet, he returned his attention to his mail.

All of Fiona's old instincts bubbled to the fore at his rudeness. Was she of so little consequence that this man wouldn't even meet her gaze? Was she so lowly, he couldn't take the time to see for himself if she was bleeding or sick or in need?

"Of course I'm all right, ye big—"

Jacob wrapped his arm around her elbow and pulled her after him.

"So sorry, sir. She's not quite used to these new shoes."

Not allowing Fiona to respond, he dragged her out of the lobby, past the Beasleys, Mr. Peebles, and their carriage, not stopping until they'd reached the side alley and its vestige of privacy. "I told you not to call attention to yourself!"

"The bloody bastard didn't even have the courtesy t' see fer himself if I was all right."

Jacob sighed in irritation and planted his hands on his hips. "What did you expect, dressed up like a bat?"

Her eyes widened in disbelief. "This is a *very* pretty dress."

"For a maiden aunt."

"Mr. Peebles copied the latest styles."

"Making them as severe as possible in the process."

"But ye told me to dress like a widow!"

He opened his mouth, closed it, then opened it again. "Maybe in the future you could refrain from delving so *deeply* into *deep* mourning."

She blinked, a bit of her hurt dissipating beneath the hidden meaning of his words. "Do ye mean t' say I can wear some o' the colors then?"

"I think your dearly departed husband has been gone long enough for that."

"A little blue?"

"And purple and rust."

"Hmmm." She liked that idea, liked it very much. Black had never really been her favorite choice in clothing. It was far too . . . far too . . .

Practical.

"Very well. I'll talk to Mr. Peebles."

She took a step, but he stopped her, linking her arm through his own so that she wouldn't charge ahead full steam.

"No, Fiona." He sighed. "It's become patently clear to

me that neither of us is properly suited to prepare you for this endeavor."

She eyed him curiously.

His mouth pursed as if he'd been forced to take a bitter medicine, but then he schooled his features into a mask of determination.

"I suppose that since my sister is unavailable . . ." He glared at the two elderly women who had followed them out of the hotel and were waiting eagerly next to the curb. "We'll have to make do with the Beasleys."

Their ride through town was a brief one—just enough to satisfy Fiona's craving for a bit of fresh air. Then Jacob hustled her back to the hotel, taking the rear staircase this time.

He waited until Fiona had retired for the night before confronting the Beasleys. Standing at the threshold to the sitting room of the Ambassador Suite, he demanded, "Well, how much do you already know?"

The two women exchanged glances.

"Only what you said in your letter," Alma responded carefully. "All we know is that you're working undercover with an immigrant woman."

"Her name is Fiona, Alma. We discovered that this afternoon."

"Yes, *Fiona.*"

"We also know that you need our help in . . . refining her a little," Amelia stated.

"As well as serving as her chaperones."

Jacob sighed. That about summed things up in a nutshell. "You seem to know most of it." He took three steps into the room. "Now it's time you were told the rest. Then, once you are completely aware of what's involved in . . . *helping* me, you can make up your mind whether or not to stay."

8

"SUPPER!"

Dub Merritt hooked the ring of iron keys to his belt, then took a battered tin tray of food from a dented iron trolley and strode toward the last cell at the end of the rear corridor. His shift at Exeter Prison had been a long one, causing his back to ache and his feet to throb, but he had only these last few meals to deliver, then he could exchange his uniform for a cool nightshirt and sleep the brunt of the afternoon away.

Thank heavens he only had one more week of working undercover in the prison. Once his report on Warden Carmichael's extreme disciplinary practices had been made to the governor, Dub could return to other assignments and—with luck—the fresh country air he loved.

Sighing, he rapped his cudgel on the bars. A dirty stream of sunlight studded with dust motes shot across the narrow cubical, illuminating a cot, a pitcher, basin, chamber pot, and a single chair. Times being what they were, room in Exeter was sparse, forcing the inmates to share two, sometimes three convicts to a room. But this little space was residence for a single fellow. A tall angular prisoner with a shock of gray hair who, by virtue of his nature and his reputation, had the iron and stone area to himself.

Dub knew all about this man—every lawman in the state knew about him. He'd once been a circuit judge. But he'd forsaken his noble calling to form a vigilante group known as the Star Council of Justice and had terrorized most of Illinois under the guise of apprehending those who had somehow escaped the law's influence. Dub knew only a portion of the details regarding his crimes, but it was said that The Judge had killed for money. Dub tended to believe such claims. There was an aura about The Judge, a sense of lingering power that caused the other convicts to call him "The Judge" behind his back—and "sir" to his face.

"Rise and shine, Judge!" Once again Dub rattled the iron bars with his cudgel and slipped the tray with its bowl of broth and a sliver of rye bread beneath the door. "Eat it now, or I'll be feeding it to the dogs, y' hear?"

For a few seconds there was no movement, causing Dub to squint at the shape half shrouded in shadow, half streaked with sunlight. "Judge?"

Just when his heart began to quicken ever so slightly in alarm, the man rolled over and stared at his captor, his eyes a piercing steel gray that echoed the glint of the iron chains of his suspended bunk. For a flickering moment, his gaze was filled with a stark hate, a bitter determination. Although Dub sensed the emotions were centered inward, he took an involuntary step away, then frowned at his own display of nervousness.

"Be up and about, mind you," he warned briskly.

The Judge got up, unfolding himself bit by bit, until he stood tall and slim and lean. The buttery glow from the window streamed over the side of his face, illuminating the craggy features that were always impeccably clean and groomed no matter what the hour.

He retrieved his meal, his movements revealing an innate grace. One that was bred into a man by old money and a thorough education.

"Thank you, Dub."

Ever polite, ever solicitous. It was enough to give a man the shivers, Dub thought as he nodded awkwardly in acknowledgment and returned to the trolley of similarly laden trays. Once there, he shot a quick glance over his shoulder, wondering how, while the other prisoners foundered and sickened on the weak fare, this man—exjudge, murderer, and thief—had managed to stay so hale and hearty on the meager diet.

"Was there something you needed?"

The Judge had caught him in his scrutiny. Even though it was Dub who stood on the proper side of the bars, he found himself strangely defensive.

"No, no. Enjoy your meal."

Enjoy your meal. He scowled in disgust at his own remark. This man was a prisoner—the worst sort of criminal. He had turned on his own kind. He'd betrayed his fellow lawmen.

But even as something within Dub warned him to go, he found himself watching in fascination as The Judge withdrew a linen napkin from the box of personal belongings beneath his bunk. He sat down, spread the square of fabric over his lap, then proceeded to eat his meal with the care and deliberation of a guest at the finest of hotels. The whole time he tasted, chewed, and enjoyed, his eyes were trained upon a clipping he'd glued to the opposite wall. The tiny scrap of paper displayed a line drawing of the man who had uncovered The Judge's perfidy and brought him to heel: Marshal Jacob Grey.

Turning away, Dub resisted the urge to cross himself. He was not a superstitious man; he prided himself on that fact. Yet he could not deny that as he stared at The Judge, he felt as if a goose walked over his grave. There was something about the man, something deep in his eyes. A glint of purpose that did not bode well for the object of his concern.

Wrapping his fingers around the handle of the trolley, he pushed it, the wheels squeaking and complaining the entire way, toward the outer door. Just as he was about to leave, the portal opened from the opposite side, admitting Dub's replacement for the next shift. He didn't know the man's name, but after spending only three weeks at Exeter, that was not unusual. His face was familiar, at least.

"Merritt." The angular man nodded, the visor of his cap casting his face in an odd sort of shadow. The cuffs of his jacket seemed to have been hemmed far too high. "Any trouble today?"

Dub straightened and hooked his thumbs around his suspenders. "Not a bit. Quiet as lambs. The heat's got them dead on their feet."

"Mmm." The unfamiliar guard propped the heavy door open with his toe. "What an apt choice of words."

Unable to assimilate what the man meant to do, Dub watched in astonishment as the stranger drew his revolver from his holster and aimed it at Dub's chest. Dub's arms lifted in reflex, his legs buckled. An explosion of sound reverberated, the noise bouncing on stone and seeming to echo again and again. Dub felt a searing pressure strike his ribs, felt his limbs give way, then the smack of his body striking the rough rock floor.

Oh, God. Oh, God. The prayer slipped silently from his lips. A warmth began to spread over his chest, down his side. His eyes squeezed closed, then flickered open again when he heard the sharp rap of bootheels next to his head.

The man who had shot him stepped over his prone body without bothering to glance down. He moved with the casual, cocky assurance of a person who knew that Fate intended to work to his advantage.

The sound of the gunshot had roused the other members of the cellblock, and the prisoners rushed to extend their arms through the bars and gawk.

The guard lifted his revolver, sighted. Dub's eyes closed tightly again, blocking out the horrible vision he saw, one clouded by a haze of pain and denial. But he couldn't dam the sounds, the shots, the thud of a prisoner dropping to the ground, another, another, another.

Dub choked on a sob. *Oh, God. Oh, God.* But God didn't hear him—or perhaps He did. For as The Judge carefully removed the line drawing from the wall and walked from the room with a casual disregard for all that had occurred . . .

Dub knew he was the only man alive.

"She's very beautiful, Alma."

"Lovely."

"We should have no troubles as her chaperones."

"No troubles at all."

"However, I shouldn't think a little matchmaking would be amiss."

"No indeed."

"I've always longed to attend a fall wedding."

At the word "wedding," Fiona's eyes popped open, immediately taking in the darkened room, the closed draperies, and the two shadowy figures hovering near the foot of her bed.

She automatically grasped the sheets, pulling them tightly to her throat. Was she forever to be caught unawares first thing in the morning? But this time there was no need for protecting her modesty from a gentleman's eyes. The Beasleys beamed, pleased that she had woken up.

"Good morning, my dear," Alma offered.

"Good morning!" the tiny one echoed, wagging her fingers in an added greeting.

Feeling disoriented, Fiona sat up in bed and propped her shoulders on the headboard. Still clutching the blankets, she stared at the pair as if they had been conjured from some sort of dream.

"I do believe we've frightened her, Alma," the little one whispered in a voice that, despite its tone, could have been heard quite well in the opposite room.

"Nonsense, Amelia." The larger woman marched to the far side of the room, where a pink-papered box had been left near a pile of assorted trunks—those belonging to the Beasleys, she supposed. Fiona rubbed her eyes and pushed the hair from her forehead, wondering who had brought the baggage into her room, and when. Had she slept so soundly that all manner of visitors had crept into her bedroom? Or had the things been brought by only one person? Jacob?

The thought caused a strange tingling sensation to plunder her veins. She still had no nightclothes to wear, so she had been forced to slip beneath the clean sheets completely unclothed. If Jacob had come into the room, how much had he seen? What had he thought? Had he gazed at her, studied her?

"You're a little pale, my dear. Aren't you feeling well?" The question came from Amelia, who had noiselessly approached and now patted the top of her head. At a glance, she knew that the question had been uttered with real concern.

"I'm a bit confused," she answered, her gaze bouncing from one woman to the other.

"Don't you remember, dear?" Amelia's apple-withered face bunched into a web of tiny wrinkles as she grinned. "We're to be your chaperones."

The events of the last few days rushed to the fore, and with them the complex tangle of emotions. The Beasleys. Alma and Amelia. Jacob had left her to their care.

"Jacob has since found rooms for us across the hall."

"But the manager let us in here this morning so that we could store our things."

Manager? Fiona clutched the covers even more securely.

"He was very congenial."

"Very handsome."

"And so young—only midfifties, wouldn't you say, Sister?"

"That would be my guess."

The two turned their attention to Fiona.

"Tell me, dear: Was your father a pastor? Or did you just return from some sort of religious mission?"

"Mission?"

"Your dresses." Amelia grimaced. "I don't mean to be

rude, but they must have come from charity barrels or something of that sort. Only Mr. Peebles's creation seems fit for wearing—although I'd say it's a trifle severe." When Fiona didn't answer, she made a dismissing gesture. "No matter. We're here to help you. You'll be needing to shop."

"Shop?" Fiona glanced from one elderly woman to the other. "But Mr. Peebles—"

"Has enough on his hands with finishing your suits and gowns. We'll need to spend some time gathering your accessories," Amelia inserted.

"You're just confusing her with your prattle, Amelia."

"I don't mean to."

Alma sniffed and lifted the lid of the pink box, pushing aside a layer of tissue paper. "Nevertheless, perhaps we should wait until later before offering any more comments." She crossed to the bed. "Come along, dear. We'll see to it that you have a bite to eat, then we'll help you dress."

Fiona opened her mouth to explain to these women that she had no clothes other than the garments they thought were part of a charity donation and the black suit they'd complained was too "severe," but Alma shook her hands and the creation she held fell to the floor in a slither of silk and lace.

"Oh."

It was the only sound Fiona could manage to push from her throat. Never in her life had she seen such an exquisite garment. The wrapper had been formed of raw ivory silk interspersed with hand-stitched lace and cutwork. Beneath, another lining of pale pink silk enhanced the gossamer quality of the robe.

"Come along, dear. We haven't much time."

Somewhat shy of her nakedness, Fiona edged toward the side of the bed.

"She's quite bashful, Alma," Amelia murmured *sotto voce.*

"A proper young lady to the bone," Alma commented in satisfaction. "Close your eyes, Amelia."

To Fiona's infinite amusement, the two elderly women squeezed their lashes tightly shut and waited. Needing no further encouragement, Fiona slipped from the bed and slid her arms into the waiting garment, wrapped the edges around her body, and tied the shiny pink sash.

Daring a peek, Amelia sighed. "Lovely."

Alma's head bobbed in satisfaction. "Definitely a color you should wear to attract the men."

One of Fiona's brows rose. "Men? What men?"

"Why, any men, of course," Amelia answered as if the question was a moot point.

Fiona was unable to completely assimilate the woman's remark. Alma had taken her arm and steered her in the direction of the small table and chair in front of the window. Motioning for Fiona to take her seat, she proceeded to fling the curtains aside.

"Jacob told me not to open—"

"Nonsense. You're much too pretty to be hidden in the dark." Planting her hands on her hips, Alma surveyed the room, then turned her attention to Fiona. "Eat, girl," she ordered, motioning to the tray. "You'll need your strength for the day ahead. After all, there are things to do, places to go, and gentlemen to snare."

How could Fiona confess that at that moment, wearing this delicious silk wrapper, she found herself inexplicably wishing she could snare one single man's attention: Jacob Grey's.

By the time Fiona had dressed and she and her chaperones had finished breakfast, Jacob still hadn't made an appearance. The Beasleys were far from concerned, however, telling her that Rusty had dropped by to report that Jacob had business to tend to that day and Fiona was to dedicate her time to studying with the Beasleys.

Amelia patted her hand when the mere mention of Jacob's name caused Fiona's heart to sink, a fact that must have been mirrored in her face.

"Is there a problem, dear?"

"Problem?"

"You appear troubled."

She hesitated, then said, "I don't know how much he's told you about . . . my situation."

Alma *harrumphed.* "We've been told all we need to know—and I must say, Amelia and I are shocked."

Fiona's eyes widened, wondering what Jacob had said to them. "Shocked?"

"He should have come to us sooner—as if he and Rusty know anything about the genteel training required of a lady in this day and age."

Amelia nodded decisively. "Indeed."

A spark of hope was kindled in Fiona's breast. "Exactly! I tried to tell him that very thing. But Jacob . . ." She sighed. "He doesn't like the way I walk or the way I talk. He says that I need *lessons* in how to be a lady."

The two women pursed their lips in dismay.

"Oh, my." Amelia sighed.

Alma sniffed. "I had no idea the man was so dense."

When Fiona's brow creased, they rose from their seats, circling her and studying her up and down. She became overtly conscious of the tight coronet of braids she'd fashioned of her hair and the somber mourning gown she wore. The same one that Jacob had hated the day before.

"Obviously, we have a thing or two to prove to Mr. Grey."

"Quite."

"And that tailor . . . If this is an example of his work, we'd best keep close tabs on him."

"I dare say, we'd best take over altogether."

"Indeed."

"The effect of the hair will need to be softened."

"As well as that suit."

"She'll need proper underthings."

"Shoes."

"Hats."

"Fans."

"Gloves."

Alma squinted, then said, "It shouldn't be difficult."

"Not at all," her sister echoed.

Fiona stifled the urge to retreat from them as they examined her so intently. "I don't understand."

"It's quite simple," Alma stated, puffing her bosom out in great importance. "Men are glorious to look at, delightful to hold, and oftentimes dumber than an ox. They have no concept of what makes a woman . . . a woman."

"No indeed."

"But Jacob told me that you could help me to become proper."

Hmph. The sound came from both women at once.

"He's a fine man," Alma began.

"Quite adorable."

"Tall."

"Handsome."

"Devoted."

"But he's spent so much time hiding behind a badge and a gun, I'm surprised he knows what to do with a woman."

Fiona felt the heat of a blush begin to stain her cheeks and damned the telltale reaction. Especially when Alma pointed a finger in her direction and waggled it teasingly.

"Just as I suspected, Amelia."

Amelia clapped her hands together in glee. "They've kissed."

"No!" The word burst from Fiona's lips.

"No sense in lying, girl. It's as plain as day that the two of you—"

"Share certain intimate emotions."

"I was going to say that."

"So sorry, Alma."

Alma took a deep breath. "I'm pleased."

Fiona could not fathom why—unless it was because they had known Jacob for some time.

"Your behavior will make our job easier."

The fire settling into Fiona's cheeks intensified. Did that mean the women thought she was loose? That she and Jacob . . . that they'd . . . that she would . . .

"The secret to being a lady of quality," Alma broke into her thoughts, "is *feeling* like a lady of quality." Leaning closer, she lowered her voice to a confidential murmur. "It's not something that is taught, mind you." She waved her hand dismissingly. "I'm not saying that it doesn't help to know how to speak, to keep your knees together when you sit, or the simple common courtesies. But that's simply the polish."

Amelia nodded. "The polish."

"I said that."

"Yes, Sister."

Alma patted Fiona's hand. "Being a lady is indulging in the feel of silk on your skin—even if no one ever knows you're wearing it. Being a lady is smelling good, appearing pretty, and putting people at ease because you are at ease. But most of all . . ."

Both women smiled at each other, then at her.

"Being a woman is enjoying making a man stare at you when you walk into a room—"

"Finding a way to make his eyes kindle—"

"Moving and talking in such a way that he can't tear his glance away—"

"Making him want to spend more time with you than with his horse—"

"Amelia!"

"Well, it's true!"

"Nevertheless, such a thing didn't need to be said."

Fiona had been watching the two open-mouthed, as if following the trail of a bouncing ball. She wouldn't have guessed that these two elderly maiden sisters with their bluish-colored hair and wrinkled features would even know of such things, let alone speak of them so freely.

"No need to appear so shocked," Alma stated.

"We may be getting on in years—"

"But we're not dead." Alma nodded emphatically to herself. "Get your bonnet and your shoes. We've got work to do."

"Work?"

"You can't possibly feel like a goddess in that getup. We'll need to do some shopping."

"Immediately."

Fiona reluctantly pinned her bonnet to her hair. "But I'm not supposed to leave the room."

"Horsefeathers. You've got a mourning veil to wear with that awful costume, haven't you?"

"Yes."

"Put it on. Nothing gives a woman more privacy—"

"—and allure—"

"—than a veil. It drives a man to distraction."

Fiona draped the veiling over her face, feeling a twinge of excitement, but one pang of unease still remained. "Jacob won't like it if we leave."

"A man should never be indulged too much with things he likes. Especially if it interferes with a woman's buying habits. That's why we intend to charge the expenses of the afternoon to Mr. High-and-Mighty Grey himself."

Fiona was quite sure that she would carry the memory of the shopping expedition with her for years. After explaining Mr. Peebles's role in her transformation, she found herself being sandwiched between the two women on the seat of Lettie McGuire's carriage. They hustled to Oak Street, Alma erupting into full steam as she charged down the brick steps to the grim little room where Mr. Peebles worked.

"Stop!"

Alma threw open the door, swinging out an imperious arm. Mr. Peebles was nearly struck with a fit of apoplexy. A pair of scissors flew from his hand to clatter against the brick wall.

"Madam?"

"You must stop this work at once."

Amelia drew Fiona in behind her, the two of them entering much more timidly.

"Stop your work." Alma pointed to the yards and

yards of black cloth flooding the floor and the cutting tables.

"But—"

She flipped the veil from Fiona's face. After being apprised of the situation with Mr. Peebles and the stories he'd been told, Alma was more than willing to play along—indeed, she appreciated the drama involved. But she had refused to hear of any more widow's weeds being worn.

"This woman has been put in my charge." She took a self-important breath.

"Mine too," Amelia reminded her.

"Yes, yes. We have come to correct a grave error."

Mr. Peebles clearly had no idea what the Beasleys had in mind.

"Look at this child. Just *look.*" She pulled Fiona forward. "Isn't she beautiful?" When Mr. Peebles didn't answer, she prompted, "Well?"

"Why, yes."

"Would you doom her to a life alone?"

He clutched a bodice piece to his chest. "Why, no."

Alma beamed at him. "Marvelous." She whirled, spying Mr. Peebles's hat and cane. Grabbing them, she slapped them on his chest. "Come with us."

Within minutes, the four of them were barreling down Michigan Avenue. For most of the day, they darted in and out of boutiques, millinery shops, glove-makers, cobblers, fabric warehouses, and department stores. The Beasleys selected parasols and hosiery and underwear— stating the last was a necessity, since true ladies wore nothing harsher than lawn on their delicate skin. The elderly women also purchased bolts of satin and silk and batiste, instructing Mr. Peebles on how they should be constructed. Whenever possible, they bought a few pieces of ready-wear that would require only minor alterations.

At midday, the Beasleys drew a halt to the frenetic pace, taking Fiona and Mr. Peebles to a small tea room for a light repast. Then they returned to work.

By the time the sun was beginning to set, the carriage was heaped with feminine frippery.

"Mr. Peebles, I fear that we will bury you alive if we store all these materials in your shop."

Mr. Peebles, whose face was barely visible beneath a heap of hatboxes and frilly mantles, blew a flounce away from his lips, saying, "Yes, madam."

"Call me 'Alma,' please."

"Very well . . . *Alma.*"

"I think we should see that you're boarded at the hotel as well."

Mr. Peebles's eyes widened.

"Don't you agree, Amelia?"

"Yes, I do, Alma."

"Do you have any objections, Fiona?"

Fiona couldn't even summon the energy to speak. Her feet throbbed, her head ached, and the black suit made her itch all over.

"Very well. It's settled. You will be returning with us."

A veritable army of hotel bellboys and cleaning staff helped carry Fiona's bags from the curb into the hotel. She was just emerging from the revolving doors when she glanced up to see Darby Kensington stepping from the elevator. His attention was immediately drawn to the parade of boxes and bags with their exclusive labels. He immediately began searching for the source of such luxuries. Upon seeing Fiona and her chaperones, he tipped his head, smiling.

Fiona's posture straightened bit by bit. Beneath the veil, her chin adopted a regal angle.

So that was what impressed this man. Yesterday, dressed in these same widow's weeds, he hadn't bothered to offer her a glance when she'd nearly tumbled into his arms. But this evening, at the blatant display of her supposed wealth, he couldn't make contact fast enough.

"Let's get you upstairs, dear. You're tired and in need of a nice long soak." Amelia took her hand while Alma frowned intimidatingly at the gentleman who'd had the audacity to stare at her charge.

Fiona complied. But as she walked past Kensington, she momentarily paused. He reacted immediately, his interest quite obvious. But before he could speak she averted her head and began to climb the stairs.

Alma and Amelia were right: The secret to being a true lady lay in one's power over men. Yet, with this man, rather than feeling like a goddess, she'd felt more like a spider. A black widow, she thought with great irony. Glancing over her shoulder at the man who overtly watched the twitching of her bustle, she thought:

I will trap you. I'll trap you like a fly in my web. Then Jacob will have to admit that I'm a woman to be reckoned with.

9

After retiring, Fiona didn't sleep much at all. At first her dreams were restless and overanxious, filled with cards and gamblers and midnight trains. She didn't know why, but suddenly, after a day of shopping and fussing, this entire situation was becoming far more real. For the first time, the depth of her situation stared her square in the face. She was about to confront an alleged criminal, a reportedly dangerous man. And it was her job to snare him so completely in his own worst nightmare that he couldn't escape.

That thought led her to another, and another, and another, until she invariably began thinking of Jacob. She hadn't seen him at all that day, and she found that the thought disturbed her no end—far more than it should. Drat it all, why did the mere thought of him consume her so? He'd done nothing but annoy and frustrate her for days—years, if the truth be told. But somehow those emotions had altered, intensified, become something else. Something far more dangerous. More sensual.

The hall door snicked shut and Fiona was instantly awake, knowing that Jacob had finally returned. Her heart began a slow, deliberate beat. Her breathing became mysteriously shallow. Closing her eyes, she willed herself to fall asleep, to ignore him, to forget he even existed. But she could no more deny his existence than fly. She needed to see him. Just once. She told herself it was simply to make sure that he was safe and well, but even she didn't quite believe such an excuse.

Grabbing the wrapper Amelia Beasley had brought early that morning, she padded into the doorway of the sitting room, watching Jacob as he wearily made his way to the settee and began to remove his boots. He looked so tired. Weariness etched his face and hung heavily on his shoulders. She felt the irresistible urge to approach him and smooth away all signs of exhaustion with a sweep of her hand. To cradle him against her, to . . .

Dear sweet heaven, what was she thinking of? Jacob wanted nothing of that sort of response from her, and she shouldn't even entertain such nonsense.

The thought of just how far her emotions were beginning to stray from their usual track filled her with a twinge of fear, then a wave of pique. Marching into the sitting room, she lifted her chin to a proud angle. "Where have you been?" she demanded.

He barely looked at her. "I do have a job to do, Fiona. Some of the success you will hopefully have will be due to the arrangements for railway cars, meals, and payroll for my men."

"What about my father?"

"He's fine."

"I want to see him. Now," she said without preamble.

"No." He looked up at her, his eyes dark. "It wouldn't be safe."

Their gazes locked. Held. An uncomfortable tension began to soak into the room around them. Fiona felt it creeping into her bones and lodging there like the cool lick of slow, white lightning. Once again, her breath came shallow and quick. She became conscious of the slight gleam of sweat on his skin, the dark curls she could see at the neck of his shirt.

"Please, Jacob. Please let me see him."

He grew still, and the evening shadows stroked his form like a mantle of dusky feathers. The effect served to soften his features, add a vulnerability. A sadness.

"If someone were to follow—"

She rushed forward, kneeling on the floor and gripping his arm. As her fingers dug into the muscles of his forearm, she sensed his weakening resolve. "No one will notice. No one will care. Please. The Liberty Hotel is only a few miles from here. Take me this evening, while it's still dark. This will probably be the only chance I'll have to see him for some time. *Please.*"

Jacob turned her to face him. She appeared so very young in the moonlight. So very fragile. The thought brought him up short. Fragile? Fiona? The same woman who would have wrestled him to the ground at any given moment and beat the living tar out of him?

But seeing her shrouded in a silken wrapper that was so very appealing, her soulful eyes, her breathy anticipation, she appeared entirely irresistible. He felt the unaccountable urge to touch her, just once, to confirm that her skin was really as soft as velvet.

When had she grown so sweet? So appealing? Had the Beasleys done something to her? Had they cast some mystical spell that made her look so soft, so womanly in the shadows?

The tip of his thumb stroked down the line of her cheek, causing her to blink in astonishment. Emboldened by her reaction, wanting to see how far she would let him go, he cupped her jaw, absorbing the shape, the angles, the heat. The nudging of her chin against his palm was the only reaction she offered. After a day of worrying about her safety, about her activities, he found that even the simple caress was not enough.

Slowly, he bent, giving her every opportunity to back away. When she remained still, quiet, he touched her lips with his own.

The kiss was little more than one friends might exchange, but the sensations that rippled through him were far less simple and he broke free, shuddering slightly. But her wide-eyed stare only seemed to invite him to reaffirm what he'd experienced, so he bent again, his lips brushing, then growing more bold, more intimate.

As their kiss deepened, intensified, Jacob couldn't account for his behavior. He only knew he couldn't deny this instant, this embrace. All day he'd been tormented by the thought of what it would be like to hold her, touch her. He'd tried to drive such ideas from his head, but they'd only returned, much stronger than before.

Lifting his head, he struggled to breathe. She stared at him with eyes that were dark and molten.

Cursing himself for his behavior, Jacob drew back, summoning a stern frown. "I won't offer you an apology for that." His voice was far too rough, far too strained to offer much credence to his words.

She touched her fingers to her lips and he saw the way they trembled slightly, even though her retort was tart. "I didn't plan to ask for one."

Jumping to her feet, she took two steps away as if returning to her room, paused, then faced him again. "What's come over us?" she asked, somewhat feebly.

He shook his head, unable to offer her a comforting answer.

"I never expected that you . . . we . . . would ever . . . kiss or . . ." She shook her head and said firmly, "It isn't real. It's a trick of the night. Such . . . yearnings will vanish with the sunrise."

"Perhaps they will."

His answer failed to comfort her. In fact, she looked slightly wounded. She retreated into the darker puddle of shadow to be found by the wall. "I think ye should know that I'm not the sort to . . . I mean, I've never . . . I haven't . . ."

He stood, crossing to touch her arm. For some reason, he couldn't bear for her to think that he'd found her to be a woman of easy virtue. "I know, Fiona."

Her chin tilted proudly. "It isn't that I haven't been

attracted to men—or they to me. There just hasn't been . . . too much . . . time . . . in one place."

He touched her wrist. Her skin was cool, soft, smelling slightly of lilacs. "I know."

"What about you? Have there been many women you've . . . kissed? . . . loved?"

He released her and moved away, scuffing his toe on the carpet, uncomfortable that he'd opened the way for such admissions. "Some. A few." But when he thought about it, he couldn't remember the last time he'd spent an evening with a woman for the sheer pleasure of her company and conversation. There had been a few brushes with passion, little more.

"I would have thought that ladies all over the country would've been beating down your door."

"The nature of my work tends to discourage them."

"Then they're fools, Jacob Grey." The statement was but a whisper, obviously expressed with some reluctance, but spoken all the same.

When he would have tugged her into his arms again, she stepped away. Slightly ashamed by his boldness, he slid his hands into his pockets, watching her as she stood in the glow of the gas lamp.

"I'll just be getting dressed. Then you can take me to my father."

He waited until she was nearly in the bedroom. "It won't happen again. The kisses, I mean."

She looked at him over her shoulder, her eyes dark with meaning. "I wouldn't be making any promises you don't intend to keep."

Her words crouched in the darkness like a living thing. Pulsing. Gnawing at his limited control.

Jacob's mouth went dry. This woman, this child, this irresponsible creature, knew him much better than he had ever known himself.

Lettie McGuire shifted from within her nest of pillows, yawning and stretching her arms over her head. For the first time in weeks she'd slept, actually slept. True, it had simply been a series of catnaps strung together, but her pregnancy had been so uncomfortable of late that any real rest at all was welcome.

Smothering another yawn, she tugged the bell pull and waited for the arrival of her maid. Mildred Wimps entered mere moments later, her broad face wreathed in a smile, her chubby hands clapping together in pleasure. "My, what a fine sleep you've had!" She rushed forward as fast as her stout body could go, reaching to plump the pillows so that Lettie could sit.

"I can't think what came over me to stay in bed for so long," Lettie replied.

Mildred made a clucking noise with her tongue. "It's all that writing you've been doing. You know how you pace and fret and fuss 'til a poem's been written down. I'd dare say that the baby was plumb worn out and wasn't above letting you know it needed some rest of its own."

"Even so, I'm afraid I've neglected the children over the past day or two—and the Beasleys!" Her hands flew to her mouth. "I forgot all about the Beasleys! They must think I'm an awful hostess."

Mildred's brow furrowed. "But they're gone."

"Gone?"

"They packed their things and went to help your brother—or so they said." She tugged a crumpled note from her pocket. "We found this in their room."

Lettie perused the hastily scribbled note, then read it again, stifling a very unladylike snort of laughter.

"I could send the driver to retrieve them if you think it best."

Lettie held up a hand to stop her, smiling broadly. "Not on your life. It's apparent that the Beasleys have it in their head that they're engaged in a mission of grave importance." She settled back into the pillows. "Let them carry on with their plans and drive Jacob to distraction with their meddling." A smug grin teased her lips. "It will serve my brother right for not coming to visit me as he should have done."

* * *

Fiona knew long before they reached her father's room that Mickaleen was in fine form. She could hear his warbling serenade from the top of the stairs. She paused, spearing Jacob with an incredulous gaze. "Ye haven't given him whiskey, now have ye?"

Jacob's mouth opened, then shut, and he shrugged.

"Hell's bells, man," she muttered, striding in the direction of the noise. "Haven't ye got even a wee bit o' sense?"

She would have thrown open the door, but it was locked. Fiona was forced to wait until Jacob approached, took a key from his pocket, and allowed her to enter.

The sight she saw caused her to frown in dismay. Mickaleen McFee, a spry man with the legs of a bandy rooster, was perched atop the bureau, clinging to the mirror and bellowing Irish love songs at the top of his voice, a pint of whiskey held firmly in his grip.

"Papa!"

Her call alerted the two guards, who were trying to get him down but seemed to have little effect at all on the little Irishman himself.

"Papa, ye'll be climbin' down from there now or I'll be takin' a switch t' ye meself, d'ye hear?"

Mickaleen offered a silly grin and stared blearily in her direction. "Fiona! Me wee lass, me dearlin'."

"Get down, Papa."

He rolled his eyes at her tone and whispered conspiratorially to one of the guards, "She's a spry one, she is. Full of vim and vinegar. T'ain't a man alive that could tame that one," he added, jerking a thumb in her direction.

Fiona felt the betraying sting of a blush begin to infuse her cheeks.

"Come along, Mickaleen." Jacob took control of the situation, signaling to his men. Between the three of them, they were able to lift Mickaleen bodily and dump him on the bed.

The whole process must have caused Mickaleen's head

to swirl, because he cracked one eye open, attempting to focus. "Marshal Grey, as I live . . . an' breathe."

Fiona sank onto the bed beside him. "Papa, are ye ill?"

He waved aside her concern. "Nah, not a bit, I tell ye. I'm fit as a beetle in a bottle o' beer!" He took a swig of the whiskey before she could stop him and emptied the bottle, then held it up in Jacob's direction. "Thank'ee kindly fer the . . . kindnesses." He waggled a finger in the lawman's direction. "Jest see t'it that ye guard me daughter well, fer if ye don't . . . I'll . . ." His words trailed free, his hands dropped to the pillow, and his eyes flickered shut. A drunken snore began to ebb and fall from his lips.

Sighing, Fiona stood, took a rumpled quilt from the foot of the bed, and drew it up to her father's whiskered chin. When would she learn that things would never really change? She'd had such hopes for this visit. She'd thought that her father would be worried about her, that he would rush to hug her, to hear all her news. Instead, she'd found him as she usually did: drunk and sleepy.

Fiona sighed. He'd never been a cruel man. He loved her, she knew. But sometimes she wished with all her heart that she didn't have to be the strong one.

She patted his shoulder and bent to kiss his cheek. Then, without a word, she turned and left the room, leaving Jacob to follow her.

Back at the Grand Estate, Fiona preceded Jacob into the Ambassador Suite and quickly stripped off the heavy black bonnet and leather gloves. She'd worn her widow's weeds to visit her father, but what had been the point? No one had seen them leave, no one had seen them come, and the time with her father had been completely disappointing.

"Tired?"

She jumped a little when Jacob spoke. He'd moved so quietly behind her that she wasn't prepared for his nearness.

"A little."

"You should go to bed. You have a big day tomorrow."

"I suppose."

She crossed to the window, then remembered she wasn't supposed to show herself. Her sigh eased into the silence.

"He *does* love you, Fiona."

She didn't bother to ask how Jacob had so easily read her thoughts.

"When I was a little girl, I was quite sure that my father was the most wonderful man in the world. He brought me to a new and exciting country and filled my life with adventures. In all the years that followed, those adventures never dimmed."

"They merely skirted the edge of the law."

"Maybe so." She plunged her fingers beneath the heavy coils of hair that had been pinned to the top of her head, hoping to ease some of the tension. But the tension she felt hadn't been caused entirely by the weight of the braids.

"He loves you," Jacob stated again.

"Yes. But sometimes I wonder if I'm not just a bother t' him."

"You keep him out of jail."

"Is that t' be my lot in life?"

He walked toward her, slowly, deliberately, stopping mere inches away. "What *do* you want, Fiona?"

"More." The word slipped reluctantly from her lips, but she refused to make an attempt to retrieve it. "I want *more*, Jacob Grey."

Although she began to tremble, deep in her shoes, she couldn't prevent herself from saying, "I still remember that afternoon so long ago—the first time I saw you." She licked her lips to ease their dryness. "I'd never seen a man without his shirt, let alone his pants." Her words became breathless, slightly rough. "I've always thought that it was wrong for me to stare at you so keenly. But I can never seem to regret looking my fill."

"Any girl would feel the same way."

"Would they? My father wasn't much of a teacher as far as manners were concerned. I never really knew if I'd committed some unpardonable sin."

"No."

"Even so . . . I sometimes think of you . . . that way." The admission was hesitant, nearly painful, but it had to be said to clear her mind. She glanced up at him, but he made no effort to stop her hasty disclosure. "I've often wondered what ye look like now. That way."

She felt the heat of a blush tinge her cheeks from her boldness, but as much as she might wish to do so, the words could not be retreated. Fiona saw the way Jacob's Adam's apple moved convulsively as he swallowed, and she wondered if his throat had grown as tight as hers.

"Am I wicked t' think such thoughts?"

"No." The word seemed to tear from his throat.

"Am I damned?"

He took her by the shoulders. "No."

Drawing her close, he kissed her eyes, her cheek, her lips. She sighed and melted into him, splaying her hands wide over his chest. He'd brought such turmoil to her life, such anguishing questions. But she couldn't stop him. She didn't want to.

His mouth brushed her ear, causing her to tremble. Clutching at his shirt, she wondered how such an innocent gesture could cause so much feeling, so much pleasure.

"I'm not a beautiful woman, Jacob."

"According to whom?"

"My hair is quite ordinary, my features too plain."

He drew back, his brow furrowing as he studied her. For the first time Fiona felt him *really* looking at her—not as a nuisance, but as a woman. She didn't know what he saw, but a certain wonder seemed to spread over his features, causing a strange warmth to puddle in her stomach.

"Never believe such lies." His fingers stroked her jaw, her temple. "Even in black and dressed like a crow, you manage to set my heart tripping."

"Truly?"

"Truly."

He kissed her softly, sweetly, then gathered her close for one soul-wrenching embrace. "Now, go wash your face, relax, take off a few of those damned layers, and I'll go order us some supper. I don't know about you, but I've developed a bit of an appetite over the last few hours."

The word *appetite* hung over their heads, shivering, reminding them that there were other hungers going unfulfilled. But before Fiona could say anything, he strode from the room.

Jacob returned nearly an hour later with several members of the hotel staff toting chafing dishes and china. To Fiona's ultimate delight, he had dispensed with his rule about ladies eating like birds. There were plates of roast beef and potatoes, three kinds of bread, preserves, steamed vegetables, and sliced fruit. Then, for dessert, ice cream.

Much later, Fiona sighed in delight, licking the last of the creamy treat from her spoon. "I've died and been reborn in a better place."

Jacob eyed her in fond indulgence, enjoying the act of watching her far more than he had eating his own dessert. Over dinner, he and Fiona had talked about inconsequential things—the weather, horses, the Beasleys—and with each minute that passed, he'd noted an odd occurrence. She was beginning to relax in his company, her speech growing smoother—not the affected British accent she used with Mr. Peebles, but a Midwestern American inflection with just a faint lilt of the Irish. For some reason, it delighted him no end.

"There's a bit left in my bowl," he teased when she sighed in infinite regret.

Fiona pulled a face, then cast a longing glance at his bowl. Seeing her gaze, Jacob laughed and pushed it toward her. He couldn't help it. When she looked at him that way, he wanted to grant her every wish.

"Eat it."

"Thank you ever so much. For that I shall be especially cooperative tomorrow."

"I only wish I'd known that ice cream proves to be a far more powerful bribe for you than two pardons."

There was the scrape of a key in the lock. The outer door opened and Rusty stepped inside, but Jacob barely noticed the man as Fiona scooped the ice cream into her mouth.

"This is my favorite food in all the world," she proclaimed between spoonfuls.

"Obviously."

He chuckled in delight when she poked the tip of a milk-covered tongue at him.

"Jacob?" Rusty approached the table, his hat in his hands.

Jacob was still smiling, an echo of his laughter shimmying through his body. But when his deputy stood looking at him, his eyes so bleak, so hollow, the humor immediately bled free.

Rusty looked at Fiona, then at his friend and superior. "There's a problem. I think you'd better come with me. I've already fetched our mounts from the livery."

At the mention of horses, Jacob rose. The instincts he'd come to trust so much in the past nearly pummeled him with their intensity. Something was wrong. Terribly wrong. The mention of mounts only served to underscore such a point. That meant that either speed or privacy was of the essence.

Immediately, his fingers curled around the hilt of his revolver. His eyes cast a searching glance about the room. When his gaze returned to the woman beside him, he realized that he must have transmitted a bit of his caution to her. Or maybe, being a woman who had also learned to live on instinct, she'd caught Rusty's unspoken messages as easily as he.

Jacob choked on a searing epithet. "Go get the Beasleys. As soon as they've arrived to stay with Fiona, we'll go."

Rusty nodded and hurried to follow orders.

The door closed quietly behind him and Jacob immediately began dousing the gaslights, leaving only one lamp to cast a meager glow. For once Fiona didn't balk at his cautious attitude, didn't question. She jumped from her seat to check each of the windows, shutting out the slightest slivers of moonlight that managed to escape the closed draperies. Then she turned.

There was an obvious fear in her eyes. A stark foreboding. "My father?"

Jacob shook his head. "Rusty would have said something if Mickaleen was at the root of his concern."

They were the only words either of them spoke for some time. When Rusty tapped on the door, they started, having sunk so deeply into their own ruminations.

Jacob slid his revolver free. Only a precaution, he silently reassured her with his eyes, but he knew that Fiona was not quite so naïve.

"Rusty?" he murmured next to the door.

"Yeah."

Holding his weapon at the ready, Jacob slid the bolt free and opened the door.

"The Beasleys are dressing. They'll be here in a minute or two."

Jacob nodded, then turned to Fiona. "I can stay here with you until they come."

Fiona shook her head. "Go. It's obvious that ye have business t'attend to."

The Irish brogue had returned, this time brought on through fear. Jacob regretted the loss.

She studied Rusty's sober face. "Just as it is obvious that Rusty needs you, *now,* but he won't tell ye anything for fear I might worry."

Rusty's bristly brows rose in surprise, but Jacob felt only an odd sense of pride. She understood. This woman understood the demands of his job. She didn't seek information or reassurance, she merely understood.

"Go gather our horses, Rusty. I'll be right down."

The deputy nodded and disappeared to do as he'd

been told. The parlor became hushed, still. The light from the single lamp offered an intimacy that neither one of them could ignore or forget.

Closing the distance between them, Jacob slid his revolver back into its holster.

"You'll be fine until the Beasleys come."

"I know. I'll just head back into the bedroom and wait . . . unpack a few of the things we bought today . . . or something."

"You've been shopping?"

"With the Beasleys."

The words they exchanged meant nothing on the surface. They merely offered a noise to fill the awful silence. A silence that reminded them that, despite the truce that had been declared between them, despite the kisses and the laughter, there were dangers lurking in the darkness outside this room. By combining forces, Fiona and Jacob had invited those dangers into their lives.

"Don't open the door for anyone but the Beasleys."

"I won't."

He saw the strength that radiated from her. The pride. This woman was a survivor; she had learned long ago to defend herself. But he couldn't still that tiny part of him that wanted to be the protector, to show her there was still some honor in the world.

"I want you to take this." He bent to remove the tiny derringer he kept hidden in the top of his boot.

Her eyes widened when she saw it. "But ye said—"

"Never mind what I said." He placed the gun in her hand.

"I can't shoot it," she admitted shame-facedly, remembering her earlier lie.

"Here." He put her fingers in position. Not allowing her to demur, he drew her shoulders to his chest and wrapped his arms around her, showing her how to hold it braced away from her body. "If you should need to use it, just pull back the hammer, aim, and squeeze the trigger. *Squeeze* it. If you jerk it, your shot will go wild."

She nodded.

His instructions finished, there was nothing more to say, but he found that he couldn't move. His eyes closed and he breathed her scent, felt the softness of her hair on his cheek. She felt so good pressed next to him this way. When he shifted, the bustle she wore collapsed, offering him the sweet shape of her thighs, the tickle of her skirts.

His hands moved of their own accord, sliding slowly, ever so slowly up her arms, over that scratchy black wool, until he encountered the delicate shape of her shoulders. Resolutely, he turned her to face him, peered down into those incredible topaz- and cinnamon-colored eyes. This woman was beginning to twine right into his every thought. How and when and why didn't matter anymore.

"You were right." The phrase emerged as a husky warning of his intent.

One of her brows lifted in silent query.

"I made at least one promise this evening that I am definitely unable to keep."

With that, he bent to kiss her, needing her softness, her sweetness, a portion of her youth and optimism.

Her hands wound around him, and not even the potent reminder of the revolver pressing into his shoulder blade could dampen the rush of pleasure he felt when she gave freely of herself, offering her passion and her strength.

He had only a minute to enjoy the embrace. But as he retreated, he knew that the memory of it would last much longer. So much longer.

She watched him go, the hand that held the revolver dropping to her side, the other lifting to touch her throat. When he hesitated one last time to stare at her in that ugly dress . . .

Jacob realized he had never encountered a more lovely woman in all his days.

"What's the problem, Rusty?"

As soon as they'd left the hotel, Jacob drew Rusty into the alley, where they could talk with some privacy.

"There's been some trouble at Exeter Prison in Wilmington."

Jacob didn't need much more of an explanation than that. He knew that Judge Krupp had been moved to Exeter after an attempted prison escape at his previous location—an attempt that had succeeded in freeing his friend and long-time ally, Gerald Stone.

"Let's go."

It took nearly an hour to reach Exeter on horseback. Rusty used the time to brief Jacob on Krupp's escape. As well as the casualties.

Stepping into the cellblock where it had all occurred, Jacob fought the roiling of his own stomach. He'd seen death. He'd seen violence. But never in his career had he seen such senseless slaughter.

"What leads do we have on the men who did this?"

The deputy in charge frowned and spat on the floor. "None. We're quite sure Gerald Stone had a hand in this. We knew he'd try to get to Krupp sooner or later."

"Sir!" A young guard burst into the room. "The midnight watch just discovered Bob Wilkens, one of the day guards, strangled and lying in a ditch just outside the prison. "By the looks of him, he's been there more than a day or two."

Jacob sighed. "Well, at least we know how Stone got into the prison." He surveyed the dingy walls spattered with blood, the limp bodies being wrapped in sheets and carried out of the room, where they would be taken to a long line of hearses waiting in the inner courtyard. "Who was on duty?"

Rusty touched his arm, warning him with a glance. "Jacob, I think we need to talk," he murmured so softly that no one else could have possibly heard him.

Jacob had learned well enough over the years to trust his deputy. He'd learned to read his thoughts, his expressions, and his gestures. Knowing that he was about to tread on dangerous ground with his questions, he nodded, following the bowlegged lawman from the room. Dodging the prison staff and convicts who went quietly about their grisly business, they weaved through the tangled corridors, making their way steadily downward until they stopped in front of a door that read "Infirmary."

"Only one guard was on duty in Krupp's cellblock last night," Dusty said. "One of our own men. Dub Merritt."

A sick lump of dread wedged in Jacob's stomach.

"The governor hadn't released him from his special assignment to investigate the prison. Dub got caught in the middle of a business that wasn't his own."

With that, Rusty opened the door, revealing the hushed, somber interior of the room. There were five bodies lying on the cots. Five bodies covered in bloody sheets. All still, so still.

"Take him away as well, poor bastard." The stolidly shaped medical officer sighed, stepping away from the corpse he'd examined. "Cause of death: shot to the head."

Jacob's hand clenched over his revolver. *No. Not Dub. Not Dub.*

"He's over here."

Jacob nearly wilted visibly when Rusty led him to another bed. One where the stained sheet rose and fell in a shallow pattern of breaths.

Seeing their intention, the surgeon took a rag to wipe his bloody hands. "What will you be wantin' me to do with the man?" He shook his head. "I've stopped the bleeding—for a time. But he needs a hospital. Real doctors."

When Jacob's brow rose, he shrugged. "I'm not so blind to my own skills that I think I can help that one. I'm a simple doctor. Trained over twenty years ago on the battlefield. He deserves someone with a little more finesse."

"Who knows he's here?"

It was Rusty who answered Jacob's question. "We've kept things as quiet as we can. If Stone discovers he's left a witness . . ."

Rusty didn't need to finish his sentence. All involved knew the seriousness of their situation.

"Send a messenger to inform Dub's wife of what's

happened, but don't let her return with you. Not yet." His eyes swept the dirty room. "Not here." He moved a few steps closer, taking Dub's hand as if the action could infuse a little of his own strength into the arms of his colleague. "Publish a list of the dead. Put Dub's name on it. Then arrange for one of the hearses to meet us outside the rear door. We'll draw it into line with the others but detour once we're out of the prison walls. We can take Dub to Holy Mercy Hospital."

Rusty nodded to show he'd understood. Needing no further bidding, he went on his way, leaving Jacob alone with the doctor and the wounded man.

"Is there anything else you'll be needing?"

"No." Jacob hooked his foot around the leg of a rickety chair, pulling it close to the side of the bed. "No. I'm just going to sit here for a while." Dub appeared so pale, so fragile, so weak.

And no man should be left alone to die.

The omnipresent midday heat followed Gerald Stone like a sluggish wake as he stepped into the rear room of the printer's shop, taking great pleasure in the exuberant way Krupp finished his meal. It was good to see that his appetite had returned.

"Well?"

"I've been able to discover that the man being guarded at the Liberty Hotel is one Mickaleen McFee."

Krupp's brows rose. "Who, pray tell, is that?"

Stone shrugged. "I've no idea. No one really appears to know him. He's a petty thief of some sort."

"Yet Jacob has him living in a hotel at taxpayer expense? Then he brought the woman to see him, the same woman our man in the governor's office says has been employed to help Grey?"

"Yes."

"Mmm." Krupp wiped his lips and took a sip of wine. "What an interesting twist in events. They must be using the man at the Liberty Hotel to hold something over the woman. To *make* her cooperate. Keep your eyes on him."

Stone nodded but didn't leave. "We have another problem, I'm afraid."

Krupp's fingers tightened around his glass, but he didn't speak, knowing from the tone of Stone's voice that what he had to say would be serious enough to warrant his caution.

"Dub Merritt is alive."

"Who?"

"The guard delivering meals in your cellblock during the time of the escape."

Krupp's eyes narrowed. "I thought that you assured me he'd been listed as one of the dead."

Stone shifted uneasily. "He was. I had one of our men obtain a copy of the report. But I saw Merritt this afternoon."

"Where?"

"A few of our men noted a great deal of activity in and around the back streets surrounding Exeter. The bodies were being removed, but one of the hearses made a stop at the infirmary instead. Two of our boys followed the hearse, the other came to get me. We caught up with the conveyance at Holy Mercy Hospital. I saw Dub unloaded myself. He had a companion on his journey."

"Who?"

"Jacob Grey."

Krupp's lips twitched ever so slightly in irritation. "How very coincidental."

"Grey must know we're responsible."

"Of that I'm sure."

"What should we do?"

Krupp's fingers closed so tightly over the glass that it threatened to shatter. A thousand ideas tumbled through his brain and, with them, an overwhelming rage. Summoning the last dregs of control he possessed, he said, "Nothing."

"But—"

"It's too soon to do anything yet." He took a healthy swallow of wine. "But the prison guard is another matter." His head bobbed in a curt nod. "Another matter indeed."

"What do you want me to do?"

"I'll take care of him. That way Jacob will have no doubts that I have returned to haunt him like the devil he claimed I was."

10

"I WANT *OUT* OF THIS ASSIGNMENT!"

Jacob pounded the desk of Walter Carruthers, one of the governor's aides and the man responsible for recommending that Jacob be put in charge of investigating the counterfeiting ring. The governor had since turned the direction of the operation over to Carruthers, and in Jacob's opinion, the man was far too zealous. He had stipulated that every detail of the mission must have his approval first—a needless waste of time and manpower.

"I understand your position, but—"

"No, dammit, you don't!" Jacob pointed in the general direction of the city that waited just beyond the office windows. "The men responsible for the prison break won't stop here, do you understand? They'll be out for revenge."

"They'll be on the first train heading toward Mexico."

Jacob leaned upon the shiny surface of the desk. "I know Krupp; I know Stone. Neither one of them fears the law. They were lawmen themselves. Now they've got some twisted vision of their own power. They think they're above any kind of retribution, that they've been

141

given the right to punish whoever and whatever they please."

"Now Jacob—"

"Don't patronize me!" He took a deep, calming breath. "I agreed to help you with this counterfeiting ring. I agreed to enlist Fiona McFee as an accomplice in the venture. But this thing with Krupp has to take precedence. I am needed elsewhere." Each word was punctuated with the frustration he felt.

"Why?"

Jacob growled in frustration. "Because Krupp has killed over a dozen men in his escape. He nearly killed one of our own."

"What makes you think you're the man to stop him? We do have other officers at our disposal, you know. The city has jurisdiction over this matter as well."

"Dammit all to hell, I *know* these men. I know what they'll do next."

What Jacob didn't say was that they would be coming for him. He knew that fact to his bones. He wouldn't be so lucky as to escape their wrath now that they were free. It was his testimony that had landed them both in jail. His and Lettie's and Ethan's.

He could feel his face blanch. Ethan wasn't due back from his investigations for another day or so. As soon as he arrived, Jacob would warn him. But Lettie and the children . . . Lettie had played an integral part in bringing the Star Council to justice once before. She wouldn't be safe from their forms of retribution. He had to warn her. He had to see to it that she hid somewhere safe until Krupp could be caught.

"You will *not* be dismissed." Carruthers's voice cut through the ensuing stillness.

Jacob's hands clenched. "I want to speak to—"

"I've spoken with the governor and apprised him of the situation. He agrees that you are needed in your current capacity."

Slapping the desk, Jacob whirled and paced the room.

"Don't you *see?* Unless you take me off this assignment, you're only jeopardizing it. The counterfeiting is a completely separate issue. But if Stone and Krupp come searching for me while I'm on that train, all the preparation, all the hard work, will be for nothing."

Carruthers's brows lifted. "Do you actually think Krupp and his men value any revenge against you above their freedom?"

"Yes!"

Carruthers steepled his fingers and peered at Jacob over their tips. Several minutes ticked by. Long, tension-fraught minutes. Then he sighed and shook his head. "I'm sorry. We need you where you are." Lifting his pen in obvious dismissal, he murmured, "Goodbye, Jacob. Have a good journey. And see to it that you bring Kensington back in irons with absolute proof of his guilt."

Jacob's hands curled into fists. "You've made a mistake."

"*Goodbye,* Jacob." He scrawled something on the paper he'd perused. "You're a resourceful man. If, as you say, you think Krupp and Stone will come gunning for you, then prepare yourself. Take a few extra precautions, a few extra weapons."

Jacob stared, wondering how the man could be so naïve. Grabbing his hat from the chair beside him, he stormed from the room, knowing that if Krupp and Stone came hunting for him . . .

He'd need more than a few extra weapons.

"Good morning, dear."

Fiona turned from the window, where she'd been sleepily examining the new day through a slit in the curtains.

"We're glad you're up."

Smiling, she grunted her acquiescence. Two days had passed since Jacob had been summoned away in the middle of the night. Since then the Beasleys had proved to be excellent tutors, showing Fiona by example and by pointing to women who passed in the street what was expected of a lady of manners.

Fiona was surprised by how little effort it took to adapt to her new role. Her success was due in large part to the fact that she'd always been good at copying people—their behavior, speech, manner of dress. But what proved even more helpful to her was the fact that she didn't see much of Jacob during that time. There was no pressure, no nervousness on her behalf, because the man she hoped to impress was not to be found. So what did it matter that just the thought of his absence caused a hollow ache to settle into her chest?

"We've a special surprise for you today," Amelia whispered as she stepped closer.

"Jacob is here to check your progress."

Jacob. The sound of his name had the power to make her heart beat a little faster, and she damned the fact. Over the past few days she'd convinced herself that the feelings she'd experienced in his arms were an aberration, a moment of whimsy. But as if to dispute such logic, a flurry of anticipation plundered her veins.

"Shall we show him what you've learned? Hmm?"

Fiona nodded, knowing that the elderly women needed a response, but she was unable to form any sort of coherent reply. Jacob was here. Here. He would see the clothes she'd bought, the manners she'd adopted.

Would he be pleased? Her fingers twisted together, betraying the intense longing for his approval. Please, please, let him be happy with how much she'd changed.

"Come along, dear. We need to hurry."

Alma nodded. "Sister and I are about to demonstrate a point."

"A point?"

"Never you mind." Alma patted her hand. "It's simply time Jacob took off the blinders and saw things as they really are."

After that cryptic statement, the women helped her brush her hair and tie it with a pink ribbon. All the while, they bandied comments to each other—comments Fiona only partly understood.

"When you talk to him, Amelia, remember the element of mystery we wish to employ. It is very important."

"Just a glimpse of her."

"Then we'll send him packing."

"A man should have to wait, after all."

"Downstairs, I think."

"I'll talk to the *maître d'*. A spot by the window."

"Perfect."

"Remember, Fiona—"

She jerked to attention when they addressed her.

"Posture, attitude, and gentility." Alma parroted the phrase that had become their motto.

"Posture, attitude, and gentility," Fiona repeated.

"Very good."

The two women beamed. "Come along."

They led her into the sitting room, just a step or two past the threshold, then stood in front of her like a human barricade, allowing her little more than a glimpse of the face she craved to see.

"Jacob, you'll have to leave."

Peeking over Alma's shoulder, Fiona noted the way he glanced up from his plate of eggs and bacon. He appeared tired. Worried. Was it because of her or whatever business he'd had with Rusty?

His eyes met hers, briefly, spontaneously, and she thought she saw a spark in their depths. One that warmed her blood. The determination she'd felt earlier surged in her breast. She would make him proud of her. She would make him happy with his decision to trust her in this task.

"Beg pardon?" Jacob asked blankly, tearing his attention back to the sisters.

"You'll have to leave," Alma announced. "It isn't proper for a bodyguard to eat in the same room as his employer. Especially when that employer is a woman."

He returned to his food. "We all know the true situation here. I don't think that such precautions would prove necessary."

"Jacob," Alma said sternly. "You have entrusted us with this woman's reputation and honor. You will leave."

"But—"

"Go. If you're so hungry, you can eat in the dining room downstairs."

"But—"

"Go!"

He sighed in frustration. Then he untucked his napkin and threw it on the table. "Come on, Rusty. Maybe downstairs we can finish our meal without being nagged."

The two men stomped from the room, leaving Fiona with her chaperones. When she would have wriggled past them to make her way to the breakfast table, they shook their heads.

"You'll want something hot, dear," Amelia offered quickly.

"And much more filling than the bird food those men ordered for you." Alma's bosom expanded with a breath. "Therefore, I think we should see to your *toilette* and—"

"—take you downstairs."

"Exactly."

The elderly women pushed her into the bathing room, repeating a ritual that had become familiar to Fiona over the past few days.

Until accepting Jacob's challenge, Fiona had never been aware of how much effort was involved in becoming a *grande dame* of society. She was instructed to soak for thirty minutes. "Long enough to open the pores and soften the skin," Alma proclaimed importantly. After stepping from the scented waters, she was wrapped in a huge towel and set on a stool. Alma and Amelia went to work, coiffing her hair, rubbing oil into her skin, trimming her nails, and dabbing perfume behind her ears.

"Which dress, Alma?"

"The rose-striped, I believe."

Amelia bustled from the room, returning with her

arms laden. "Here are her unmentionables. While you're helping her into her foundations, I'll send a chambermaid to fetch Mr. Peebles from the parlor."

Alma helped her get up. "Slip into your drawers and camisole, then meet me in the other room," she ordered, closing the door.

Fiona dropped the towel and did as she was told, sighing at the cool caress of China silk on her skin. Never had she imagined that undergarments could be so delightful. These were delicate as a cobweb, as sleek as rainwater.

After stepping into the first petticoat, she joined Alma. Minutes later, she was dressed in the rest of the underpinnings needed to support her gown. Yet when Alma held out a pale pink underskirt for her to don, her eyebrows rose. This was the first day she had been given something other than the ugly black suit she'd ordered from Mr. Peebles. After confronting him in his shop, the Beasleys had completely changed Fiona's wardrobe orders, never letting her see what they planned for her to wear. While shopping, Fiona had helped pick out shoes and gloves and hats in all sorts of styles and shades without a clue as to what she would wear with them. Through it all she'd seen women wearing sherbet-colored gowns and she'd yearned to wear something that feminine.

She eyed the pink skirt with obvious hunger. "I'm supposed to be in mourning. Isn't that a trifle . . . cheery?"

"Trust me, dear."

Sure that Jacob would be angry at the dash of color, but not willing to argue with Alma Beasley, she allowed the taffeta creation to be slipped over her head.

"Amelia?"

"Yes, Sister?" The call came from the sitting room.

"Have you called for Mr. Peebles?"

"He's just arrived."

"Have you retrieved the gown from our room?" Wishing to keep tabs on which deliveries had been made from

147

which stores, the Beasleys had arranged for all the boxes and bags to be delivered to their room.

"Yes indeed."

"Well, bring it in here."

Amelia's apple-withered face appeared around the edge of the door. "She's ready?"

"Of course she's ready!"

Amelia grinned and bounded inside, her frail arms fairly heaping with skirts and flounces and ruffles.

"Here you are. Mr. Peebles is waiting in the other room in case any alterations need to be made."

"Good. Hand me the items as I call for them, Amelia. Blouse."

A sheer delicate shirtwaist of ivory silk with lace insets was pulled over Fiona's arms, then fastened with tiny pearl buttons down the front.

"Overskirt."

Next came the first layer of the gown, a heavy skirt made of ebony satin with a deep flounce that fell from her knees to the floor and yards of fabric that mounded over her bustle and cascaded into a train. As Alma reached beneath the garment to adjust the tapes and buckles that would control the degree of puffed fabric, Fiona indulged a small sigh of regret—the only breath she could manage beneath the tight lacing of her corset. Her underslip might be pink, but the gown would be black.

"The swag, please."

Fiona gasped in delight, seeing that her fears were not to be realized. The gathered apronlike garment of black and pink stripes was draped around her hips, then tied in the back with a huge bow.

"Jacket." Alma paused to apologize. "I know the heat is dreadful, dear, but your position as a widow *does* demand you wear a coat. But I have instructed that it be of the 'open' variety, meaning that it is not necessary to button anything more than the vest."

She handed Fiona the outer covering, one that would have been somber in its ebony color if not for the *faux* vest of a smaller pink and black stripe that fastened at her waist and the pink silk piping, which lined the high collar and military-style cuffs.

"Now the shoes."

Amelia ran into the other room, returning with a box that she opened to reveal a pair of black and pink satin hightop boots with jet buttons.

"Sit, please."

Fiona took her position on a small chair, and the two women slipped the shoes onto her feet and fastened them with a pair of buttonhooks. Then Alma turned her attention to dressing Fiona's coiffure with sparkling, jet-tipped hairpins, while Amelia hurried to collect the rest of her accessories.

Prior to stepping from the room for Mr. Peebles's final vote of approval, a tiny bonnet was pinned to the loose curls piled on top of Fiona's head. A small swathe of illusion veiled her eyes. She'd been given bob earrings with jet and garnet stones, pink gloves, and a black and pink parasol.

"Well, Mr. Peebles, what do you think?"

He whirled from his perusal out the window, then paused, barely breathing, his lips slowly tilting in delight.

"Stars and garters, Mrs. McFee! You look like an empress!"

She laughed—she couldn't help herself. She felt like royalty. She felt invincible.

Mr. Peebles fussed over her for a few minutes, restitching the hem of her flounce when it proved too long, adjusting the drape of her skirt. Then he nodded his approval. "It's time," he pronounced.

The Beasleys grinned in pleasure.

"Let's go see what we can find for breakfast."

Amelia patted her hand. "Just remember: You are a beautiful woman. Be proud of that fact. Not everyone is blessed with such a state." Then the two women glanced at each other and giggled.

As they walked from the room, Alma muttered for all to hear, "Can't wait to get a glimpse of Jacob's face when he sees you. It's been a long time since I've seen the man so pole-axed."

Pole-axed? Jacob?

Never.

Jacob scowled in the direction of the Grecian pillars that led from the dining room into the main lobby. There was no mistaking the two elderly ladies who peeked around the *maître d'*, then grinned and waggled their fingers in acknowledgment.

"Come along, Amelia."

He heard Alma's command from yards away. Why she was always bellowing that same instruction to her sister he didn't know, for Amelia never strayed from her side.

"Good morning, Jacob."

"Ladies."

The women met each other's gaze, evidently very pleased with themselves.

"She's here."

"Who?"

Alma rolled her eyes. "Who else?"

Jacob grew still. "You didn't bring—"

"Fiona? Yes!" Amelia inserted, taking the chair beside him and whispering, "We decided she should make an entrance."

"I thought I told her to stay in the—"

The words died in his throat as a tall, elegant creature stepped under the arch. If not for the fact that both elderly women bent close and punched him in the ribs, he might not have recognized her. Fiona appeared wealthy, refined, and sophisticated in her stylish suit and feather-topped bonnet.

He found himself unable to breathe. Never in all his born days had he thought that Fiona McFee could ever look like . . . like *that*. Automatically, he rose to his feet, ignoring the napkin that dropped to the ground. She found his gaze, smiled ever so slightly, then looked away—just as a proper woman should.

After that slight pause, she walked forward. His awe at

her appearance dimmed somewhat as Jacob stood frozen, praying that she could carry off her role. He grew more tense with each step she took, wondering what Fiona would do to reveal her true identity: Trip on the rug? Swear? But to his infinite surprise, she surveyed the room with a cool gaze as she made her way into the dining hall, bustle swaying, parasol tapping.

The *maître d'* snapped to attention, leaning close for her murmured instructions. Then he led her to a table in the solar, seating her in the sun between two potted ferns.

"Bravo," Alma whispered, casting an I-told-you-so glance in Jacob's direction. "There's no need to keep her locked in her room, Jacob. The girl can play her part. However, she shouldn't sit alone."

"It would invite the wrong company."

As if Amelia's words had been uttered by an oracle, Jacob saw Darby Kensington wending his way through the tables.

"Damn," he whispered under his breath.

"Oh, dear. He was watching her several days ago when we returned from one of our shopping expeditions. She was wearing her veil, so I doubt he'll recognize her." Her lips pursed in disapproval. "It was obvious that it was the size of her retinue that attracted his attention."

Jacob scowled at the news. "Stay here, ladies."

He crossed the distance in slow, measured steps, not wanting to startle Fiona into revealing herself or call Kensington's attention to his own presence. But his fingers automatically rested on the hilt of his revolver.

Hell, he was too far away to prevent the ultimate confrontation. He saw the way Darby paused a few feet from her table. Fiona glanced at him—a brief, proper glance—then studied the menu.

Darby moved closer, speaking, the words low so that Jacob couldn't hear.

Abandoning her study of the menu, Fiona caught Jacob's eye. He was close enough to hear her say, "I am afraid, sir, that you are taking frightful liberties."

Darby was far from dissuaded. "With one so beautiful,

I pray I can be forgiven." He paused, then said, "I hope I might also be allowed to join you for a moment."

"What do you think, Mr. Grey?"

Jacob nearly stumbled when she caused Kensington to turn and measure the worth of his adversary.

"What say does . . . Mr. Grey have in your choices?"

One of her brows rose. It was obvious that Fiona found him far too assured of himself.

"He is," she stated slowly while beckoning to a waiter, "my bodyguard."

At the word "bodyguard" it was Kensington who demonstrated his surprise.

"You find yourself in need of protection?"

"Don't all women?" She handed the menu to Jacob. "Would you be so kind as to order for me, Mr. Grey?"

He silently applauded her tactic—one that relegated him to the role of a mere servant while managing to pique Kensington's interest all in one move.

As Jacob gave an order for fresh fruit and a tray of sweetbreads, part of his mind centered on the pair at the table.

"I haven't seen you at the hotel before today."

Jacob thought he saw her eyes twinkling. "Haven't you?"

"Surely I would remember someone like you."

"Why is that, Mr. Kensington?"

The waiter retreated, allowing Jacob to eavesdrop openly.

Kensington's brows rose and he leaned on his walking stick. "You know me?"

"I know *of* you."

Jacob didn't understand where Fiona was leading the conversation, but he hoped she wouldn't go too far.

"Your reputation precedes you."

"Oh?" Kensington drawled, bending even closer.

"Your reputation with *cards*." A very subtle chiding note feathered her tone, causing him to grin.

"Only with cards, Miss . . ."

"Mrs."

152

His good humor dimmed ever so slightly.

"As my late husband used to say—"

"Late husband?"

"Yes, Mr. Kensington. I am a widow."

"You have my condolences."

"Which are appreciated, but unnecessary. You see, my beloved groom was very old, very rich, and very talented. Prior to his death he passed on to me his wisdom, his money, and his craft."

"What craft would that be?"

She paused, then drawled, "Gambling, Mr. Kensington." After her announcement, she stood up. "Mr. Grey, I am no longer very hungry. Will you please cancel my repast?"

"Yes, ma'am."

"Then I should like to go for a drive if you deem it prudent."

Jacob's lips twitched in amusement over the use of a word that days ago she hadn't even known.

"I'm starving."

Fiona waited until the carriage had pulled well away from the hotel before speaking, but she wasn't about to hold her tongue completely.

"You were wonderful in there." Jacob's comment caught her by surprise. "I never dreamed you would find a way to capture Kensington's attention in a manner that would appear so natural, yet so intriguing."

"I didn't ruin anything?" She waited on tenterhooks, aware of the fact that she'd failed him too many times in the past few days when she'd been unable to grasp the finer graces he'd thought she should employ.

He squeezed her hand beneath the fullness of her skirts. "The man's interest was clearly engaged. Not just because of your mention of gambling, but also because you are so lovely."

She tipped her head, studying him through the veiling of her hat.

"Do you really think so?" She couldn't prevent the question. She needed to hear him say the words.

"I do." He touched her chin, then, after ascertaining that her parasol hid them from the sightlines of the hotel, he leaned forward to place a gentle kiss on her lips.

She smiled, a spark igniting the same slow heat that invariably eased through her veins when she found herself in his company, his arms.

"The Beasleys met with Mr. Peebles and made sketches of this dress for him to copy."

"I like it."

"I suppose this was what you had in mind when you hired Mr. Peebles?"

"No." The answer was low, rich, husky.

"No?"

"It's better, far better. You look . . . you look . . ."

"What?"

"Like a lady."

It was the highest compliment he could have given her, but there was more. Brushing his thumb across her knuckles, he said, "But you've always been that, haven't you, Fiona? You've always been a lady—inside, where it counted."

She shook her head, but he touched her cheek, halting the refusal. "I was wrong. Being a lady isn't how you speak or walk or act. It's how you . . ."

"Feel inside."

He smiled. "Yes. I think that's it."

"So what happens now?"

He grew serious. "I haven't wanted to tell you before now—I didn't want you to feel pressured—but Darby has booked himself on a tourist train that leaves the day after tomorrow."

Fiona felt a pang of anxiety. So that was why he'd been gone so much of late. He must have been taking care of details for days.

"Yer sure?" she asked, her nerves injecting a note of the Irish, one that seemed to occur less and less under the Beasleys' tutelage.

"We've determined that Kensington has purchased a ticket. I've made arrangements for a private car for you and me."

"What about the Beasleys?"

"Well . . ."

"And Mr. Peebles?"

"I can see the Beasleys have been instructing you quite thoroughly as to the servants required of a woman of station."

"You were the one who worried about what people would think."

"So you need to drag two old ladies along?"

"Chaperones."

"As well as a tailor?"

"We've ordered an entirely new wardrobe. The Beasleys and I have spent all our time taking care of the accessories and such."

"I gathered that from the stack of bills. As of today, I've seen nothing to warrant them but your wrapper and that dress."

She cast a worried glance in his direction, wondering if she and the Beasleys would be scolded for their excesses. "The Beasleys are keeping everything in their room for now."

"There's no need to appear so concerned, Fiona. After seeing the results, I'm more than happy to deal with the consequences." He released her hand to cup her cheek. "More than happy." Bending forward, he pressed his lips to her own.

Dear heaven, would she ever get enough of this man? Ever—

Without warning he jerked away, pushing her to the floor.

"What in—" Gunfire erupted, and the dull smack of a bullet striking the carriage filled her ears.

11

"WHAT IN HEAVEN'S NAME?"

Jacob wasn't listening to her. Infused with a sense of purpose, he covered her body with his, shouting instructions to the driver. They rode pell-mell through the streets, not slowing their pace until it became clear that they'd lost the gunman. Finally the carriage clattered to a stop in the alley between a pair of brownstones.

Jacob waited, his hand on her shoulder, keeping her flattened in an ignominious heap at the bottom of the carriage until he was sure that they were safe. When he finally offered his hand, Fiona was trembling so badly she could barely stand.

Seeing her predicament, he swept his arms around her and lifted her onto the seat. "Are you hurt?"

She shook her head, still dazed by all that had occurred in such a short period of time. "No." Her eyes fell on the seat. A jagged hole had appeared in the leather, and stuffing and horsehair popped out at the edges where the bullet had exited.

"Someone shot at us," she said, stating the obvious. Even the words sounded unreal. "Who?" She grasped Jacob's hands. "Who shot at us?"

Seeing her distress, Jacob spoke quietly to the driver, instructing him to check the streets and ensure that no one was still looking for them. It was an obvious ploy for privacy, but the man didn't seem inclined to object.

As soon as he'd gone, Jacob hauled Fiona into his arms. She clung to him, not caring that her actions could be interpreted as weak. At this moment she needed him. Needed his strength.

"Why was someone shooting at us?"

Her head was tucked beneath his chin so she was unable to see him, but she could feel the way he stiffened. "I think they were shooting at me."

When she would have straightened, he held her still. "Shh. It has nothing to do with you."

"How can you be so sure? You warned me that my involvement with Darby Kensington could prove dangerous."

"That's true. But you met with Kensington just a few minutes ago. Did he strike you as threatening?"

"No."

"I doubt he's responsible."

"Then who did this?"

He stroked her back with his hands, remaining silent for some time before saying, "Years ago, my sister, her husband, and I were responsible for putting a vigilante group behind bars. The leaders of that group recently escaped from prison. I have reason to believe that they would like to exact revenge on those they think responsible for their plight."

She drew back in concern. "What are you going to do?"

He stared into the distance, deep in thought. "It's too late to back out of the affair with Kensington. My brother-in-law, Ethan, will be joining us on the train— he's made some contacts with Kensington, so he'll be the one to arrange a poker match between the two of you. Once he and I are on the train, I doubt we'll be followed. But my sister will need to be warned. She'll need to leave town."

"Where will she go?"

He thought a moment, then nodded decisively. "My mother died a few years ago, leaving the family boarding house to my sister and me. Neither of us has been back there in years. She'll be safe there. The townspeople know her. They will protect her there."

Jacob framed her cheeks with his hands. "I know you're shaken, frightened—and you have a right to be. But I've got to warn my sister, then we'll go back to the hotel."

"Of course."

"Wilt!" he called to the deputy waiting a few yards away. "Let's go. The McGuire home."

It wasn't until they stopped in front of the imposing facade of a huge brownstone mansion that Fiona remembered that Jacob's sister was *the* Letitia McGuire, the celebrated poet. The thought managed to distract her from her fear ever so slightly. Three years before, when Fiona had read Letitia McGuire's biography in one of the literary papers, she'd been stunned to discover the woman was from the same family as this man. Now she was about to meet her.

"This is your sister's home?" she asked as they stopped.

"Yep. She's the only sister I have, thank heaven. One of her was enough." The words rang with a quiet indulgence, an obvious affection.

The carriage rolled to a stop, and Jacob took his revolver in hand. He scanned the quiet neighborhood, the trees, the corner park, before jumping to the ground and helping Fiona to alight.

"Hurry inside. Don't bother to knock."

He kept his back to the door, he and Wilt standing with their weapons ready should it prove necessary. The very fact that they thought someone might have found them so quickly caused Fiona's skin to crawl, and she hurried up the stairs and into the strange house.

From the other side of the door, she could hear Jacob

instructing his deputy to search the grounds and warn the servants. Then he joined her inside, shutting the door.

Seeing her still shaking, her arms wrapped around a coat rack, he smiled in reassurance. "No one followed us," he murmured.

"Yer sure?" The fear brought out the brogue, as usual.

"Quite sure."

She looked carefully around her, seeing the dark elaborate wood, the roseate window above the door, the polished floors. "I don't like comin' into a person's house without even knocking."

"Lettie's family. She won't mind."

Lettie's family. The phrase echoed in her head, reminding her again that Letitia McGuire was this man's sister.

How long had Fiona revered that woman and her work? Since the age of three, Fiona's father had apologized for her lack of formal education and had insisted that she at least have a knowledge of the arts. Whenever they'd gone to a city large enough for such entertainments, he'd seen to it that she found her way into the great stages and auditoriums of America—whether he had to sneak her in through a rear door and hide her in the shadows of the balcony, or volunteer to help with the striking of the sets if Fiona could sit on a stool and listen.

From those experiences, Fiona had gathered a wide artistic background. She'd seen plays and operas and revivals. She'd listened to the most celebrated tenors and orators. But her favorites had been the poets—men and women alike—who had recited their work in the hushed caverns of theaters across the country, somehow finding a way to paint Fiona's world with rainbows. She couldn't bear to think that one of her idols, one of her heroes, was in danger.

"Come with me." Jacob took her hand and made his way to a huge staircase that circled the wall of the vestibule. "Lettie!" he bellowed.

There was no response at first. Then a young girl wearing a black dress and white apron poked her head over the upper railing.

"Where's Lettie?" Jacob asked, not bothering to explain to the maid who he was.

"With the children," she replied, obviously mystified.

"Gather the rest of the servants and take them into the kitchen. There will be a man there to talk to you," Jacob ordered cryptically.

Not waiting to see if he'd been obeyed, Jacob hurried up the remaining stairs. The faint sound of talking and laughter led him up another flight to the floor above. Once there, he took her through the hallway of what appeared to be an entire story devoted to children. The walls had been papered in colors more lively and delicate than those dictated by fashion. The doors they passed had been flung open to reveal a bedroom with one small bed and a doll house whose contents lay scattered on the floor and another room with a tester laden with iron soldiers poised for battle.

Without pause, Jacob strode into a sitting room and playroom. The noises came from the quarters beyond, and the splash of water testified that it must hold the bathing room.

"Jake, come here at once!"

Fiona eyed Jacob curiously, but he hadn't altered his step, didn't even appear to notice the imperious summons. When a little boy streaked naked into the room, he laughed and knelt to hold out his arms.

"Uncle Jacob!" The bright-eyed imp changed his direction in midstride to rush into the older man's arms.

"Hey, Jake." The two hugged, and it was obvious that the love they shared was heartfelt.

The little boy drew away, his hair and dark eyes gleaming wetly. "Didjya bring me a present?"

"Jake, please. Mind at least some of the manners you've been taught."

Hearing a softer, feminine voice, Fiona glanced up,

then grew still as she was flooded with an almost overwhelming shyness.

Lettie McGuire. *The* Lettie McGuire. Not only had she been brought into this woman's home, but she'd also had a glimpse of her personal life. Her children.

The toddler in Lettie's arms smiled, then hid her face in her mother's shoulder.

"He takes after you, Jacob," Lettie said to her brother, gesturing to Jake. "He has no sense of the social graces." She paused meaningfully, and when Jacob didn't respond, added, "Such as the proper introductions."

Until that moment Jacob appeared to have forgotten completely that he'd brought a visitor with him. Fiona could feel herself flushing to the roots. How silly to imagine he would think someone like her was worthy of the social niceties.

For a moment, she felt like a fraud. Her hair seemed too elaborate, her dress too new. But when Jacob stood and smiled at her, his eyes lingering upon her in a familiar, almost heated way, the inadequacies eased somewhat.

Ruffling his nephew's hair, he gestured to Fiona.

"This is Fiona," he stated simply.

"How gracious you've become, Jacob," his sister teased, rolling her eyes. Setting the child on the floor, she walked forward, her hand extended. It was at that moment Fiona realized that the huge Mother Hubbard apron she wore had not been bunched around her waist as she had first supposed. This woman was pregnant. Very pregnant.

"I'm so pleased to meet you," Lettie exclaimed, taking Fiona's hand. Then she patted her bulging stomach and winced, the color of her cheeks ebbing. "As you can probably guess, I don't receive many visitors lately. I've received several short notes from the Beasleys. They informed me of your project and asked my advice on a few pieces of your wardrobe. I'm pleased my brother allowed you to visit me."

Fiona wanted to say something—something profound and memorable—but she didn't dare open her mouth for fear that in her excitement her brogue would thicken to a point of becoming unintelligible. Instead, she bobbed a curtsy, then could have kicked herself for the action. It was something that a backstairs maid would do for her mistress. Damn, damn, damn.

"Lettie, have you heard anything from your husband?"

Fiona could have hugged him for drawing the attention away long enough for her to gather her equilibrium.

"He returned home a little earlier than expected. He's gone to the bank."

"I'll get him later." He strode to the window, peering out through the curtains.

Lettie's brow creased. "What's wrong?"

He hesitated before saying, "Krupp escaped. A few minutes ago, someone shot at Fiona and me."

Fiona saw the way the color bled from Lettie's skin. She began to weave, and without thinking, Fiona caught her elbow and helped lead the woman to a chair. When she would have drawn away, Lettie caught her hand, squeezing it in silent gratitude.

Jacob abandoned the window to kneel beside her chair, taking her other hand. "I think you should go away for a few weeks until they can be apprehended. Take the children and some of your servants. Leave tonight while it's dark and tell no one where you're going until you're on the train."

"Where . . . where shall we go?"

"Take the children to Madison—to Mama's old boarding house. You'll be safe there. Warn the townspeople that Krupp is loose. They'll keep such a close eye on the roads and trains that he won't be able to get within twenty miles of you."

She nodded to show she understood. "Fiona, will you tug the bell pull for me, please?"

Fiona did as she was told. Within seconds a thin, gaunt woman appeared. "Fern, pack a few things for the children and myself—enough for a few weeks. We'll be going away for a little while."

The servant appeared startled by the abrupt order, but she left to comply.

"Mama?" Jake looked up at Lettie with worried eyes, and Jacob bent down to speak to him.

"You and your mama have to take Celie away for a while. Can you help me? Watch over them? See that they're safe?"

The little boy nodded, but tears glistened uncertainly in his lashes.

Jacob hesitated before telling his sister, "I need Ethan with me. He has been helping me with a counterfeiting suspect for weeks. I need him a little longer."

Lettie pressed a hand to her stomach but didn't protest. "As long as you take care of all this. Soon."

"We'll finish up with the business on the train as soon as we can. I'll send Ethan to you in Madison within a couple of days."

Jake tugged on his pantsleg. "Will you come see us again soon, Uncle Jacob? Will you bring my present when you come?"

Despite the serious note that had invaded the room, Jacob chuckled. "How do you know I have one?"

"You always have one."

"Why?"

"Because I'm your favoritest little boy an' you're my Uncle Jacob."

When Jacob grinned in pleasure, it became obvious to Fiona who had taught the boy such a response. She wondered how often Jacob came to see his nephew and what they did when they were together. They were quite natural together—and uninhibited. Jacob showered his nephew with obvious adoration and didn't seem to care who saw it. A curious reaction for a man who was usually so guarded.

"I'll come see you in Madison—but you might be asleep when I come."

"You can wake me. I'll letcha."

Laughing, he drew the boy close for a hug. "All right. If you help your mama and go straight to bed when she tells you to go, then I'll wake you first thing."

Jake had to consider the rewards of a present over going to bed, but he conceded.

Jacob turned his attention to the little girl who had moved to hide behind her mother's skirts. "What about you, princess? Would you like your present too, Celie? Hmm?"

She slid her index finger into her mouth and did not respond. If anything, she held a little more tightly to Lettie's knee. Fiona was intrigued by the way her reticence bothered Jacob.

Lettie caressed the top of the girl's dark head in reassurance. "It's okay, sweeting. That's your Uncle Jacob."

The relationship didn't impress the young girl.

Lettie sighed. "She was a baby when you last visited." One brow rose pointedly. "If you came more often, she wouldn't be so shy."

"I know, I know. But I have to—"

"Work will always be there, Jacob. Children grow."

Fiona shrank back into the shadows as Jacob and his sister began an obviously familiar argument. She was feeling more distinctly out of place with each word that was said, but she couldn't deny, deep in her heart, that she wished she belonged. She wished she could stroke the dark curl from Jake's brow, tease Celie from her shyness, and offer Lettie her aid.

"Now Lettie . . ."

"Don't you 'Now Lettie' me, Jacob Grey. Don't you think it's high time you had some children of your own?"

"Leave the subject alone, Lettie."

Fiona thought she detected a slight stain of red infusing his cheeks. The idea that Jacob might be embarrassed by the twist in the conversation caused a curious feeling to settle in her stomach. A tingling. A warming. A hint of dread.

Glancing down at the boy who had wrapped his arms around Jacob's knees, she suddenly felt as if someone had punched her in the stomach. Lettie was right: Jacob should be married. He should be having children of his own. Dark-haired, dark-eyed boys and timid little girls. He had a natural way with youngsters; he would make a marvelous father.

Staring at him openly, she wondered why he had never married. As far as she had ever known, no woman's name had ever been linked to his in even a casual way, let alone intimately.

The question must have been displayed quite baldly across her face because when he looked at her—really looked at her—his arms tightened ever so slightly around his nephew.

Fiona became still, seeing in his gaze a stark craving. He *wanted* a life such as his sister enjoyed. He *wanted* a home, children, the intimacy of marriage. For one brief second his need, his vulnerability, his rage—at what Fate had given and he had denied himself—was as plain to her as the corresponding feelings she harbored herself.

"We'd better go."

Reluctantly, he set the boy on his feet. The mood, that moment of sharing, was shattered.

Lettie followed them into the hall. "Tell Ethan I'll take the ten o'clock train."

"I'll send some men around to help. Be careful, Lettie." He took Fiona's hand and led her from the room.

"Jacob?"

Lettie stood silhouetted in the doorway, appearing at the same time fragile and strong.

"Take care of yourself, of Ethan."

"I will."

"Then promise you'll take some time off to visit us, really visit. We could stay in Madison for a few weeks—just like old times."

He nodded.

"Promise?"

"Yes."

"The children need you—and so do I." The words were filled with an evident devotion. "There was a time when I couldn't lift my little finger without having you squawk. Now I'm lucky to see you once or twice a decade."

There was no mistaking the gentle rebuke. Jacob's eyes became warm, filling with a light that Fiona had never seen the man adopt. Releasing her, he joined Lettie, taking his sister's face in his palms. Smiling, he stated, "I'll return before that baby can be born, and I'll stay until the christening."

Her answering smile was tremulous. "I'll hold you to your word."

As he placed a kiss on Lettie's forehead, Fiona took an involuntary step backward. She could have been invisible for all the attention these two people gave her—and it was just as well. A tightness gripped her throat, her heart. No one had ever looked at her like that, not even her own father. No one had ever loved her so unconditionally, so completely.

She wanted that love. From someone, just once before she died. The hunger gnawed at her with a strength she could scarcely credit. But as Jacob joined her again, she also knew that such emotions did not come to people—common folk—like her.

"Come along, Fiona. We've work to do."

"Goodbye, Fiona," Lettie called, but Fiona couldn't acknowledge the woman. Walking outside to where the carriage waited, she fought an unaccustomed threat of tears, and the very action filled her with an untold rage, an untold regret.

Damn Jacob Grey to hell and beyond. No man had ever made her want so much. No man had ever made her rue so much.

No man had ever made her feel so lonely.

The carriage rattled to a stop at the rear entrance of the Grand Estate. Grasping Fiona's hand, Jacob led her into the kitchen and through the startled clusters of kitchen staff members who were preparing for the afternoon-rush.

"Go on up to the room and stay there. I've got to find Ethan and—"

"No."

She stopped in the middle of the stairwell, fighting to catch her breath beneath the tightness of her stays. Pressing a hand to her ribs, she gasped, "Not until you tell me the rest of what's happening."

Jacob grew quiet, causing Fiona to wonder if she'd stumbled upon a tidbit of information that he'd surmised.

"You aren't telling me everything, Jacob Grey."

He pulled her forcibly up the servants' stairs. "Get in the room and stay there until I tell you differently."

"Why?"

He refused to answer, drawing her into the suite and locking the door. Hurrying to the windows, he drew the drapes, plunging the two of them into darkness. Parting one a sliver, he peered into the street below.

"What are you searching for?" she asked some time later, when the quiet had become almost unbearable. "You told me that the leaders of a vigilante group were looking for you. How many? Are they alone in wanting revenge, or are they bringing a whole army with them? What are you so afraid of?"

He didn't answer immediately, and she wondered if he meant to ignore her, until he answered softly, "Ghosts."

The word was so starkly painful for him to utter, she found she couldn't press him for more answers. To her surprise, he continued: "Do you have ghosts, Fiona? Past events that return to haunt you?"

"Don't we all?" she echoed, thinking of how hard she'd worked these last few days, how hard she'd tried to bury her immigrant status, only to have the past rise like a specter.

He remained still, so still.

"Well, I've made quite a few enemies in my time."

"I suppose your job demands it."

They faced each other, neither moving. Jacob was the first to shift, resheathing his weapon and prowling toward her. "Do you consider yourself one of those enemies, Fiona?"

His words took her by surprise. As did the expression he wore. One that was intent. Serious. Hungry.

"I used to think so."

"And now?"

He stopped mere inches in front of her, cupping her cheeks.

"The Beasleys," she breathed in warning. "What if they're—"

"There's no one here."

"How can ye be so sure?"

"There's no one here."

Then there were no more words. His head bent, his mouth taking hers in a searing kiss, one that searched for the answers she had been so reluctant to give. Answers to the true depth of her feelings, her uncontrollable needs.

He drew her close, and their brush with death caused her to cling to his shoulders, his arms, needing his strength and heat much more than she could ever admit. When his hands fumbled with the buttons of her suit, she moaned deep in her throat, pulling away to whisper, "Yes, yes."

Finally he managed to free the fasteners enough to reveal the next layer of clothing. His sigh of frustration brushed across her lips. "What in the hell do you have on?"

"Only the true trappings of a lady."

"Right now I would wish you into your washerwoman costume."

"You just can't seem to make up your mind."

The teasing light faded from his eyes, replaced by a seriousness she could not ignore. "I think my mind is set."

She could barely breathe at what she saw deep in his gaze.

"I want you, Fiona. I don't know when all this happened, I don't know how. I only know that I spend too much time thinking of you, wondering what you're doing when I'm not here."

The words hung in the air, bold, powerful.

When she didn't speak, he asked, "Does that surprise you?"

"No."

"It does me."

When her eyes averted in hurt, he forced her to look at him. "It surprises the hell out of me that I could feel this way about *any* woman. In the past, my overriding concern has been my job. Only my job. I never allowed anyone close enough to care."

She touched his chin, his lips, her fingers trembling noticeably. As much as she wished she didn't have to be the voice of caution, she knew she had to think of where all this would leave them. "Don't indulge your feelings, Jacob."

His eyes narrowed in confusion. Obviously, it wasn't the answer he was expecting.

"I can never be enough for you."

"You're more than I've ever wanted."

"I'm not good enough for you."

"Like hell."

"I've lied, I've stolen, I've cheated." Those were the ghosts *she* had to contend with. She knew that Jacob didn't want to be influenced by such things, but she saw the way his eyes dimmed. "You've spent your whole life putting people like that in jail."

"The governor is willing to pardon you."

"But are *you*, Jacob?" There it was, her greatest fear: Could Jacob Grey, lawman, forgive the fact that she had a past? One that he had spent a lifetime pursuing? "Can you forget what has occurred, can you drive it from your mind, can you give me a fresh start, living each day with no regrets?"

"Of course."

"Such a simple answer, but said without a moment's thought."

He tried to brush her concerns aside, but now that she'd started, she refused to quit. "What will you do when someone recognizes me? When someone realizes that you, a U.S. marshal, are openly consorting with a known criminal? What will you do when you have to introduce me to your colleagues, your governor, knowing that all along they are quite aware of what I've done?"

"You'll be pardoned."

"But can a pardon erase what has passed?"

He didn't answer; but he didn't have to. The confusion written on his face was enough for her.

Bit by bit, she slipped from his grasp. "I suppose I have my answer, then."

"Fiona—"

"No." She held up a hand. "Don't apologize, don't try to explain. Right now, I don't want to hear the words. I don't want to hear that I'm right in my assumptions. You might not say so out loud, but I'd hear the pity in your voice. The silent recriminations."

Reaching behind her to sweep her train out of the way, she retreated several steps. "I suppose we were only fooling ourselves into thinking that a mule in horse's clothing could be anything but a mule."

Dub Merritt moaned and roused himself from sleep. In the time he'd been at Holy Mercy Hospital, he'd learned to recognize the staccato footsteps of the woman who served as his nurse, the grumblings of the medics, the slow, weary gait of the doctor. But something had awakened him. Something not quite right.

His lashes opened. Dawn had not yet come; night had not yet passed. Of all the hours he had grown to dread in his life, this was it. During his stint at Exeter, the gloom of midnight lingered far too long, reminding him that it would be hours until his shift ended. In the hospital, his dislike of this portion of the day had not dimmed. In fact, it had increased. He often woke to such overwhelming darkness, that pressed upon him like a woolen shroud, reminding him too eloquently that he was mortal. Weak. Alone.

"Hello, Dub."

The words melted out of the shadows beside his bed, startling him. He jumped, his heart beginning to pound unaccountably.

"Who's there?"

"A friend. An associate."

But the tone of the words was far from congenial. A chill lingered behind them. A threat.

Dub's fingers clenched at the blankets, drawing them beneath his chin. Blinking, he tried to see a face, a shape, anything to help him pinpoint the identity of his visitor. But the curtains had been drawn around his bed, blocking out what little light might have seeped into the ward from the hall. His chest ached, his body throbbed, but the presence would not leave him alone.

"Who?"

"I told you . . . a friend."

When he received no name, no reassurance, Dub released one hand, slowly inching it across the bed and curling it beneath the mattress.

"Searching for something?"

The query was low, nearly feral. Quiet. Long before he reached the spot where the knife should have been hidden, Dub knew what he would find.

Nothing.

In an instant, he recognized the man who stood beside his bed. He'd heard that silky tone in prison.

"Judge . . . Krupp."

"Very good."

Dub's strident breathing filled the silence. "What . . . do you . . . want of me?"

"How much did you tell him?"

"Who?"

"I don't play games, Dub."

Dub licked his lips. He felt weak, so weak. His body was on fire; the beating of his heart settled in the pit of his stomach. But he didn't dare surrender consciousness. Not with the threat of this man so near.

"I didn't . . . tell him . . . a . . . thing."

"Neither am I a fool."

The keen bite of a blade pricked his neck, and Dub gasped.

"What did you tell him about the prison break?"

"Your . . . name."

"And?"

"I . . . described the man . . . who shot me."

"I see. Tell me: What information do you intend to offer me in return?"

"I . . . don't know . . . anything."

The knife bit deeper. Dub could feel a trickle of blood seep down his throat.

"What's on the lawman's mind?"

"I—I . . . don't—" He bit off the excuse when the blade slid a fraction of an inch to one side. "I don't know!"

"There's a woman with Marshal Grey. What is her name?"

"I don't . . . know about . . . woman."

"Give me her name."

"I don't . . . *know!*" Krupp cruelly grasped his hair, jerking his head back and causing his neck to grow taut beneath the blade. Dub sobbed. "I . . . don't know! I . . . swear!"

"Surely you've heard something of Grey's current case."

"No!" The knife sliced, burned. "I've told . . . every . . . thing!"

Krupp stepped away, the blade lifted. Sobbing, Dub pressed a shaking hand to his throat, feeling the warmth of his own blood. His consciousness wavered, a weakness closing in, but he couldn't surrender. Not yet.

"You'd better not have lied to me."

Dub shook his head, having no energy for more of a response.

"Oh, and Dub . . ." Krupp slapped something on his

chest, something that rattled suspiciously like a stiff piece of paper. "Pass this on to your lawman friend when next you meet."

Dub reached to take it, but his hand never touched the spot. There was a rush of air, a slight whistling, then a pain, an overwhelming pain, as the knifeblade plunged into his chest. Then there was nothing but the haunting threat of death. Here. Alone.

In a darkness that was not quite dawn. Not quite night.

12

THE HALLS OF THE WALLOBY BANK AND TRUST WERE QUIET, eerie. Without customers and employees, the establishment inspired a cool, unsettling feeling to wriggle into Jacob's gut. Much like tiptoeing through a crypt.

Ignoring the unsettling comparison, Jacob made his way resolutely through the tangled corridors until he saw a thin brushstroke of yellow from beneath the door to the president's office. Holding his revolver at the ready, he stepped noiselessly inside.

"It's about time you got here."

Ethan McGuire turned, holding aloft two glasses of amber liquid. "Pull up a chair."

On the surface, he spoke the usual banalities expected of a man who is about to entertain his brother-in-law, but Jacob sensed the undercurrents wrestling beneath the surface.

"You heard?"

McGuire's startling blue eyes grew even deeper in color. "Imagine my surprise: I go home for a little tea and sympathy, only to discover my house as empty as a ghost town."

"I—"

Ethan waved away anything he might have said. "You did the right thing. I appreciate the deputies you sent with my family." He stroked the side of his glass with his thumb. "I just wish all this hadn't happened so close to the baby's arrival." His tone became steely. "So we'd better get this counterfeiting mess wrapped up, hadn't we?"

Jacob's lips twitched into a reluctant smile. Although he and Ethan had developed a grudging sort of friendship and respect over the last few years, he couldn't deny Ethan's love for his sister. That same love that had convinced Jacob to believe Ethan's avowals of innocence so long before.

"Let's get to work."

Ethan set his glass down and rolled a map onto the blotter of the desk. "I've marked in blue all those areas where I was able to find strong evidence that Kensington is the man responsible for the spread of counterfeiting. Those circled are the areas where I've found bankers who would be willing to come forth with information and testimony if he's tried."

"So all we have to do is catch the man red-handed."

"Exactly." He pointed to the other markings on the map. "I traced the train's path, here, in red. Those areas shaded in yellow are the spots where stops will be made, as well as the approximate routes the horse-and-buggy excursions will take."

Jacob leaned close. "I've got men stationed in most of these areas already. I've been trying to get them all in position the last couple of days."

"How many will go on the train itself?"

"Nearly a dozen."

"Good. I've taken care of my own passage. As you'd requested, I'll board a separate car, be seen with Fiona one or two times at dinner as if we are distant acquaintances, then casually introduce her into one of Kensington's card games." He grinned. "I've already developed a bit of a . . . losing reputation with the man, so I'm sure to be given an invitation. But I warn you: Once she's been admitted into his magic circle, I plan to leave the train and return to my wife."

Jacob nodded in understanding. "I appreciate the fact that you're still willing to come at all. Kensington has met Fiona and expressed some interest, but whether or not he'll allow her to play cards with him is another thing. We need someone like you, someone who's already been a part of his games, to help ease her into his serious bouts of poker."

"Do you think she's ready for the job?"

A reluctant smile touched the corners of Jacob's lips. "You know, I think she is—if we can just remind her to stay calm enough so that she'll refrain from speaking with that Irish brogue of hers."

"What about your expenses?"

"The government has picked up most of the tab. I've used a bit of your own money for the rest." His brows lifted. "The Beasleys have a rather expensive taste in clothing."

"Goaded on by my wife, no doubt. I've seen her cutting pictures out of her ladies' magazines to copy."

"They've kept most of the purchases hidden away in the Beasleys' room, but what I've seen of the results is well worth the expenditure."

"Are you sure you have enough money to cover any extra expenses?"

"Plenty. Thanks. I also appreciate the use of the private railway car you've put at our disposal. I think it will give her ruse an air of authenticity."

"What about your own men? How will they travel?"

"I've arranged for a boxcar to hold mounts and ammunition. The rest will be scattered throughout the train itself."

Ethan's eyes narrowed. "A boxcar . . ." he murmured more to himself than to Jacob. "Did you know that Kensington also arranged for a boxcar?"

Jacob felt a shiver of unease trickle down his spine. "Whatever for?"

"Well?" Stone asked as Krupp stepped inside the abandoned tenement complex.

"Dub Merritt won't be telling tales." Krupp moved to the grimy window and peered out to ensure he hadn't been followed. Because of its position below ground level, he could see little more than the boots of passersby, but he didn't care. There were no bars to obstruct his vision. Night had closed in, casting a beautiful sooty depth onto the rough stones. The blackness eased into his soul, soothing him after so many months in prisons where at least one gas lamp was kept eternally lit.

"Were you able to find out anything about the woman Jacob has holed up in the Grand Estate?" While he'd tended to business, Krupp had sent Stone on a ferreting mission of his own.

"According to the chambermaid I bribed at the hotel, her name is Fiona McFee. She's a wealthy British widow, and the gossip being whispered through the staff at the Grand Estate has it that she's a gambler as well."

"A gambler? Consorting with Jacob Grey?" Krupp's finger rubbed the side of his nose. "Doubtful. The man wouldn't openly associate with anyone of that nature."

"That's all I've been able to ascertain so far."

"McFee . . . McFee. You followed one of Jacob's deputies to a hotel in the middle of town. Wasn't that the name of the prisoner being held there?"

Stone grinned, nodding. "I'd say our Mr. Grey is using the man as a hostage of sorts."

Krupp's features lightened ever so slightly. "Of course! Use a gambler to trap a gambler! He must be holding the old man over the woman's head, so to speak, hoping that she can entice Kensington into her confidences. Unless she does what he wants, he'll probably punish the old man somehow."

"What do you intend to do?"

Krupp pursed his lips, but he couldn't contain the smile that curved at the edges of his mouth. Laughing softly to himself, he moved to the far cupboard. There he withdrew a knife, which he slid into his boot, and a pistol, which he tucked into his waistband beneath his coat. Grinning, he turned to his partner.

"I think it's time we raised the stakes a bit."

"In what way?"

Krupp leaned close. "Grey is using that old man as leverage. What would he do if that source of influence were suddenly removed?"

Stone's mouth twitched in an answering smile. "A man in his custody."

"A man he's sworn to protect."

Stone laughed. "He'd have a devil of a time explaining himself to the powers that be."

"Come along, Stone. We've got a little job to do."

He'd only taken a step when Stone caught his arm. "All of this is well and good for trapping Grey, but what about his sister and her husband? They helped to land us in jail."

"Patience, my good man. Patience. First we take care of Jacob. His loss will be devastating to them both. People in mourning make mistakes. Once we've taken care of him, we'll move on to less important targets."

It was morning when a scream erupted from deep inside the Liberty Hotel. Across the street, Stone was casually walking away, but Krupp lingered in the shadows of the alley, listening with great glee as the hotel staff found the two bodies that had been dragged into the corridor, lawmen who had been guarding a mysterious old man with a penchant for good whiskey and fried eggs.

Turning, Krupp finally left the scene, knowing that the old man was gone as well, his body still hidden, undiscovered. He'd passed from this world, his wide, sightless eyes and clenched fists revealing he had not been ready for his assailant. Nor had he been ready for death.

As the commotion behind him became frantic, Krupp joined the rest of his men, swinging onto the back of the mount that waited. "Come along, boys," The Judge called, signaling for them to fall into line. "We've got some ground to cover and a lawman to catch."

"Jacob!"

Rusty burst into the bank office early the next morning, startling the two men who had drunk whiskey and planned until the wee hours before falling asleep in Ethan's office.

"Come with me. Now!"

The red-headed deputy didn't wait to see if Jacob followed but ran from the room. After a moment's hesitation, Jacob did the same, Ethan close on his heels.

A pair of horses waited outside. Rusty had mounted his own gelding and was holding the reins to Jacob's animal as he ran from the building.

"Ethan? Jacob? Jacob! What in the world?"

Neither he nor Ethan answered as a carriage pulled alongside them and two elderly women peeked out the window, nearly obscuring their charge. Turning into the street, they urged the horses into as brisk a pace as possible with the congested traffic.

The hospital was a good six miles away crosstown. As soon as the stone edifice came into view, Jacob felt a cold bitterness seep into his stomach. He didn't need to be told why his deputy had brought him here. As the walls grew closer and closer, he sensed the reason behind Rusty's errand: Dub Merritt must have died.

After all that had happened to the man, Jacob should have been prepared for the possibility. Nevertheless, he found himself filled with a silent rage, an acrid frustration, knowing that they'd lost their only witness to the prison massacre—not that it really mattered. There was enough evidence against Krupp and Stone to see them hanged for murdering the men of Exeter. But Jacob hated death. Especially the senseless death of a lawman.

After leaving their animals with a boy near the front stoop, the three men took the inner stone steps two at a time. Even from a distance, Jacob could hear the hushed murmurs of the staff members who waited outside the ward door. A ward that had been cleared of all other patients to allow the bevy of lawmen who had arrived more room to perform their grim duties.

When Jacob would have stepped inside, Rusty stopped him.

"You'd better prepare yourself."

Jacob caught more than a simple worry in Rusty's gaze. A cool finger traced down his spine. His deputy evidently had much more on his mind than the death of a fellow officer.

"What's wrong, Rusty?" Ethan asked.

The deputy didn't speak but merely glanced down at the toe of his boot, then up again.

How had Jacob failed to see that the overt concern his deputy displayed had been directed at him? His reactions. His strength.

Rusty drew him to the side, away from the curious medical staff. The foreboding Jacob felt burgeoned, grew, swelling inside him with such a dank, overwhelming power, that for the first time in years, he experienced a very real twinge of fear.

"Rusty?" It was the only word he managed to squeeze from his tight throat with any sense of normalcy.

"They think Dub died late last night, judging by the blood."

The chill grew stronger. "Do you mean to tell me that the stitches pulled free and no one noticed all that time?"

Rusty shook his head. "He didn't die of the wounds he received at Exeter."

Jacob's chin lifted ever so slightly, as if bracing for a blow. Without waiting for Rusty to explain any more, he stepped into the ward.

Immediately, his gaze flew to the far side of the room where Dub had been ensconced in the last bed. Upon his first glance, the entire scene took upon itself a haze of unreality. He absorbed each minute detail as if time had suddenly ground to a halt, becoming slow, so slow.

He saw the huge puddle of blood beginning to dry on the scarred floorboards, the sheets drenched with more of the stuff, stained with huge patches of scarlet. He noted the way Dub's fingers lay waxen and lifeless, extending toward the door as if pleading for help. The sightless eyes that lay open to the shadows. The grimace of a painful death.

Jacob's boots echoed hollowly on the floor as he moved forward. In a dream. This had to be a dream. He knew Dub. Knew his wife. The son he liked to bounce on his knee. Dub liked warm whiskey on cold January evenings and delighted in conning the iceman into giving him a lump in the middle of July so that he could chip it into little pieces and chew on them for most of the afternoon.

"Dub?"

The name slid unwillingly from his lips, conveying quite eloquently the disbelief he felt. The room around him shrank, stinking of death, of fear. The blade that had been driven into Dub's chest had not been removed, and Jacob felt a surge of anger, wondering why the hospital staff had left him this way, in all the indignities of such a demeaning death.

But as he drew to the foot of the bed, a slow horror seeped into his breast, and he knew why the man had not been disturbed until he'd arrived. Blood covered everything and gleamed garishly beneath the dim gaslight. Even so, there was no disguising the note pinned to the man's chest, held in place by the blade of the knife. Nor had its crimson hue completely obliterated the symbol that had been scrawled upon the none too subtle missive. An eight-cornered star inscribed with three letters: *SCJ*.

Jacob had seen that sign often enough in the past to know immediately what it meant. At one time he had even been a member of the vigilante group known as the Star Council of Justice. He'd thought he'd been righting wrongs, helping his fellow man. Instead, he'd become embroiled in a band of mercenaries led by a corrupt judge. They'd been after Ethan then. Ethan, Lettie, and Jacob.

"Krupp." He hadn't heard Ethan approach, but his pronouncement came as no surprise. "He did this."

Jacob's eyes squeezed closed, and he fought the bubbling nausea. But even though he kept his lashes tightly shut, he could not avoid the image emblazoned on his mind. The sight of his friend. His colleague. The eight-pointed star.

Blinking, he looked again, sure that he must be mistaken. The sight was just as horrible, just as real.

Jacob's hand tightened around the hilt of his revolver and his jaw grew hard. "Find The Judge. *Find* the bastard! Then bring him to me."

A gasp tore through the macabre silence and Jacob whirled, his gut wrenching when he saw Fiona standing in the doorway.

"Damnation! What's she doing here! Catch her and take her back to the hotel!"

Rusty rushed to get Fiona, but she'd whirled and dodged from the room.

"Where'd she come from?"

"She was in the carriage with the Beasleys. No doubt they followed us here."

"She won't know the significance of what she's seen," Ethan murmured.

"Not yet."

"But if Krupp is anywhere nearby . . ."

Rusty came back, shaking his head. "I couldn't catch her, but the carriage seemed to be on its way to the hotel."

"Rusty, I want an extra man who does nothing but follow her wherever she goes. Have another man assigned to the Beasleys. Despite what I say, those women tend to disobey my orders and leave the suite when they please."

A silence settled about them. An awful gloom.

"What about Dub?" Rusty asked. "Someone's got to inform his wife."

The leaden weight of responsibility threatened to choke Jacob. "I'll tell her." He could barely force the words from the tightness of his throat. Swallowing in an attempt to ease the pressure, he reached forward, closing the eyes of the man who had suffered so much.

"I'll tell her," Jacob said, walking from the ward, the crushing yoke of his job settling even more firmly into place, reminding him that he had no time—no right—to seek out Fiona and comfort her. There were things he had to tend to first.

Fiona waited for hours. Night piled deeper, Chicago grew looser, less staid. And Jacob didn't return. She tried not to think too much. She tried to push the images she'd seen from her mind, but she couldn't deny the way her instincts screamed that something was wrong, very wrong.

Finally, she heard him enter. She waited, not wanting to intrude if he'd brought Rusty with him for a conference, but there were no noises. So much so, she wondered if she'd imagined that he'd returned.

Her feet made no sound as she tiptoed over the carpet, padding out of the bedroom and moving through the silver bars of moonlight that spilled onto the floor from the windows. Inexplicably, the draperies had been flung free and the panes thrown wide. The Beasleys had not been responsible for such a state. After Fiona had returned to the carriage appearing so pale and shaken, they had acquiesced to Jacob's orders to keep Fiona in her room and hidden from sight. Jacob alone must be responsible for the change.

Seeing the man sprawled in the chair and staring into the evening, she doubted such unaccountable actions had been done out of spite or even to catch the breeze. No, Jacob's face told her clearly enough that he wanted to escape, that the room had been closing in on him, threatening to smother him. This man loved the outdoors, the wide spaces of the prairie, the solitude, the grandeur.

But upon rounding his chair and seeing him head-on, Fiona realized that her suppositions had been correct to some extent, but there was more she could only guess about. So much more.

She had never seen Jacob this way. His hair was disheveled, his eyes bloodshot and a bit vague. His clothing hung untidily upon his body, the buttons only partially fastened, causing the edges to gape and expose the dark hair dusting his chest. In the lax fingers of his left hand, he held a squat glass of whiskey. Judging by the bottle at his feet, it wasn't the first tumbler he'd consumed.

"Jacob?"

The silence pounded between them, loud and keen. Fiona began to believe that he'd been so immersed in his own thoughts that he hadn't heard her until he spoke.

"Go away."

The order was stern and implacable. But there was something buried in its depth. A thread of need. Of utter desolation.

"What happened today? At the hospital? Who was that man?"

"No one that concerns you." The words dripped with scorn, and she prepared to march into the other room. But she stopped, knowing that was exactly the reaction he expected.

Without uttering a word, she pulled a chair next to him and sat upon the cushions, drawing her feet beneath her and resting her chin on her knees.

Several minutes passed. "Go to bed, Fiona."

"I don't want to leave."

"Well, I wish you would."

She didn't move, and he sighed in frustration.

"Is there nothing in this world that fails to bring out your stubbornness?"

"Very few things."

He took a healthy swallow of the whiskey, obviously hoping to shock her by his open indulgence. She was not shocked. Indeed, she found herself wanting to startle him a little as well. Taking the glass from his hand, she took a sip, allowing the fiery liquid to trip down her throat and warm her stomach, then handed it to him.

"Not the best I've tasted, but certainly not the worst."

His eyes narrowed. "Is there anything you haven't done?"

"So very much." Her earnest reply took him by surprise, but he didn't comment. Gesturing to the liquor, she asked, "What's driven ye to drink, lawman? Ye've seen death. Ye've seen men killed. Why should a stranger in a hospital bed be so different?" This time she consciously used the lilting brogue of her childhood. Not because she was nervous or tense, but because it was employed as a sort of endearment. An intimacy to be shared with someone who'd grown close to her.

Closing his eyes, he rested his head on the back of the chair. His pose displayed an overwhelming weariness.

"Tell me what's wrong."

"It's not something a man should discuss with a lady."

One of her brows lifted. "As I recall, you've spent most of your time telling me that I'm no lady."

"Is that new?" He gestured to a pale blue nightshift barely hidden by her wrapper.

"Of course it is. You've had me sleeping in a sheet."

"Mr. Peebles must be very quick."

"This did not come from Mr. Peebles."

He frowned at her.

"The Beasleys and I have been shopping off and on for days. We went again this morning. That's when we saw you rushing toward the hospital." She saw the way his body tensed, muscle by muscle.

"You were told to stay at the suite."

"With our departure growing so near, the Beasleys insisted we finish our errands."

His gaze blazed a trail from her head to the tips of her toes. Fiona found her muscles becoming relaxed, her movements more sinuous.

"Tell me, Jacob: Do you like my new things?" The question held the same husky fire as the scotch she'd drunk. For some unknown reason, she found herself wanting to push this man, to make him see her as a woman, not a criminal, to make him confide in *her,* Fiona.

"It's very nice."

"We found a few more things this afternoon at a little boutique near Lake Shore."

His gaze grew steely. "I thought I posted a guard outside your room and sent word that you weren't to go out?"

"So you did."

"But you went anyway."

"I had chaperones."

"The Beasleys are no match for the kind of people you need to be avoiding."

"We went in disguise and took your guard as well."

"Disguise?"

"I wore my ugly black suit and a veil."

He swore, lifting the glass to gulp another healthy portion of liquor. "A veil isn't going to keep the wrong sorts of people from recognizing you."

"You would be surprised." She lowered her feet to the ground, crossing them at the knee—an action that caused the edge of her nightwear to shift and reveal a sliver of her calf. "People feel awkward around the bereaved. They don't bother to look at you. They don't *want* to—as if by seeing your face they'll be touched by your tragedy."

Jacob started, clasping her wrist. "Have you experienced tragedy, Fiona?" There was a cutting bite to his question. In an instant, he radiated a patent fury, an overwhelming frustration. His reaction disturbed her—almost frightened her. Lunging up, he planted his palms on the arms of her chair, leaning close. "Have you, Fiona?"

She didn't know how to respond. This wasn't the Jacob she knew, the unflappable lawman, the easygoing gentleman. No, this man had a hardness to him, revealing the things that he'd seen and experienced that no one should ever know.

He grasped her cheeks. *"Have . . . you?"*

He didn't give her time to respond. His head dipped and his mouth closed over hers, fiercely, hungrily. Fiona was startled by the blatant need he revealed. It was as if he wished to drown himself in her, to forget everything that had occurred but this moment, this kiss.

Fiona wondered if she should be miffed or even frightened by the overwhelming passion he displayed. But as his tongue flicked out to graze the corners of her mouth, she found she didn't care, didn't care at all. Few men had given her a second glance. She and Papa had never really stayed in one place long enough to develop any sort of relationship. Even if they had, Fiona had discovered in the past that few men found her type of woman desirable. They wanted meek, fragile creatures in bonnets and ribbons.

But Jacob . . . Jacob wanted her. Now.

She pushed him away, framing his face in her hands, needing to see that what she'd sensed was true, that the passion he'd displayed was for *her*, Fiona, and not just for the convenience any female might provide.

The fire she saw reassured her. He scanned her hair, her cheek, her neck, and the skin beyond, which pushed above the scooped bodice of her wrapper.

"When?" The word was a bare whisper escaping from his lips.

Her brow creased in confusion.

"When did you become so beautiful?"

The words caused a blooming in her heart, filling an empty portion of her soul that she had always denied existed.

Closing her eyes, she drew him down to her. As their mouths met, softly, gently, she savored the storm of sensation such a simple embrace inspired. Her fingers tightened, pressing into the stubble on his jaw. She found the contact oddly exhilarating, tantalizing. She had never dreamed that a man's face with a shadowy growth of beard could rub so deliciously on the palms of her hands, sending a rush of gooseflesh over her skin.

The kiss deepened, became something pagan, needy. Fiona gave in wholeheartedly, abandoning the voice of caution that told her this wasn't real, couldn't be real. She didn't care anymore. She didn't care if such an embrace was transitory or if it led to nothing permanent. She didn't want to think of the consequences or the future. She wanted to drown in the here and now.

He stood, pulling her with him. Her arms automatically swept behind his neck while his wrapped around her waist, bringing her tightly to the planes of his hips. A slow ache settled in the pit of her belly, one she had never really experienced, not this desperately.

Seeking to ease it, she shifted closer, closer, rubbing herself against him in such a way that caused him to moan and break away.

They were both breathing hard. The stridency of their panting could not be ignored.

"Dammit, I don't want this to happen," Jacob whispered.

"I do." Her admission was stark, honest.

His eyes clouded, adopting a hint of worry. "We don't belong together. We mix like water and oil."

"Does it matter?"

"This is wrong."

"Why?"

"I should be protecting you, shielding you from this very thing."

"Why?" She drawled the word again. "Life is so short, Jacob."

He cringed, hauling her close to bury his face in her shoulder.

"Don't say that. Nothing will happen to you. I swear it."

There was a desperation to his words, one that echoed with hidden meaning.

"Jacob?"

"Promise me that you'll be careful."

"What—"

"Promise me. You won't go anywhere without *me*, do you understand. I don't care if the Beasleys have you swaddled in iron, I won't have you taking any more chances."

"If that's what you want."

He bent to kiss her again, passionately, boldly, then abruptly drew away. "Now go to bed."

"But—"

"Tomorrow will be a big day. We'll need to make last-minute preparations for the journey. The day after, we'll be boarding the train and your role will begin." When she hesitated, he urged her in the direction of the bedroom. "Go."

Reluctantly, she complied, but he stopped her again just as she would have disappeared into the bedroom.

"There will be no more such . . . encounters, Fiona."

She glanced at him over her shoulder, noted the rigid line of his spine, the resolute expression. Smiling, she whispered, "Liar."

He looked away. Obviously, he couldn't deny that what had occurred between them would ultimately prove stronger than any hasty resolutions he might make.

"Do you have any worries about the upcoming excursion?"

"No."

"Your role—"

"The Beasleys have been excellent tutors. I think that even you will be pleased with all I've learned." She wanted to tell him that the Beasleys hadn't been solely responsible. Jacob had also taught her and taught her well. He'd shown her the power connected with being a woman. She would probably never become meek, and she would certainly never become fragile, but she had learned the importance of having a man see her as a woman.

This man.

Jacob.

"I want this job to be finished as quickly as possible. I need to be back so that I can help take care of Krupp. Only then will I take some time off to go home to Madison. I promised Lettie I'd be here before the baby is born."

His abrupt statements caused her brows to raise.

He stood for some time, surrounded in a bar of moonlight, so serious, so inscrutable. "Things are brewing, Fiona. Things that I can't explain—that probably can't *be* explained. But know this: If anything happens to me during the journey, return immediately to Chicago. Rusty and the Beasleys will help you. Then I want you to go to my sister. She'll see to it that you receive an appointment with the governor. Hold him to his bargain."

The warning as well as his unspoken worry caused a shiver of disquiet.

"What's wrong? That man at the hospital: Was he someone you—"

He shook his head. "There's nothing you need to concern yourself about. Dub Merritt was involved in business that had nothing at all to do with your own duties." He chose his words carefully, saying, "I've merely discovered that the past can be a very difficult thing to outrun."

That was something Fiona *could* understand.

Specters from the past had a tendency to pop up at the most trying moments. Fiona had learned that such gremlins didn't soften with age but sometimes grew more powerful, more worrisome.

She felt a sudden kinship, the tumbling of final barriers. The two of them weren't really so different as Jacob might have her believe. They were haunted by mistakes they'd made as well as events over which they'd had no control. And did the past and all of its mistakes really matter when compared to a person's tomorrows? If it didn't, why not live the day for what it could give, for what it could mean? For the comfort she could offer Jacob Grey?

He needed her. Maybe just for the moment. But he needed *her*—not as an actress, not as a gambler, but as a woman.

Fiona retraced her steps, knowing that with each step, her commitment to this man increased, her emotions intensified, her need expanded. Stopping mere inches away, she took him by the hand.

"Come with me, Jacob."

He regarded her questioningly.

"You're tired. You need to rest."

When he still didn't move, she tugged until he followed her.

"While I, for that matter, need the warmth of a pair of arms wrapped around me while I sleep."

13

He didn't demur.

Their feet made no sound as Fiona and Jacob approached her bedroom.

"The Beasleys—"

She shook her head when he would have inquired as to the whereabouts of the elderly women. "They're in their own room across the hall."

"I thought I relayed a message for them to stay with you."

"They did, for a time. But with the guard you posted to follow our every move, I couldn't see the point. Once he took his position in the hall, I insisted that the women get something to eat, a periodical to read, and go to bed."

His lips twitched in wry amusement. "You and the Beasleys avail yourselves quite freely of money which isn't your own."

"We do whatever needs to be done."

She stopped in the center of the bedroom. For several minutes, neither of them spoke. Fiona felt the way the darkness shivered about them, expectantly.

"You look so tired."

He didn't answer, not that she had expected him to. It would have been against Jacob's nature to admit that he needed anything, even something as basic as sleep.

"Will you rest with me?" Her hands spread wide over his chest, feeling the strength to be found beneath his shirt. "Will you lie with me?"

His breathing hitched ever so slightly. She felt the action beneath her fingertips, and it gave her a spark of hope. She might not have a future with this man. She might fall short of the type of woman he should claim as his wife. But he was hers this night, and the next, and the next. And Fiona McFee was not above begging for Jacob Grey's attention.

A reverence stole through her body, a hunger that throbbed so deeply in her it became a near spiritual ache. There was nothing she wouldn't do for this man, nothing she wouldn't give to keep him. But since that could never be, she would offer him her most prized possession: She would offer him her heart.

Only three buttons kept his shirt closed, and she loosened them, one by one by one. His skin was warm next to her own, the faint friction of hair arrowing down into the waist of his pants tickling her hands.

He stopped her only once. "You don't have to do this."

She allowed all she felt to appear naked on her face. "Yes. I do."

After that, he didn't try to prevent her from continuing. When she slid the shirt from his shoulders, allowing it to fall to the floor, he closed his eyes. Her palms ran over his skin, testing the shape of his shoulders, his chest, the arch of his ribs, the taut muscles of his stomach. Then she began to work on the fastenings of his pants.

Fiona was not a naïve woman, but she had never seduced a man. Indeed, she had never seen one completely aroused. So when he pushed his trousers to the floor and stepped free, she gasped, staring at the part of him that stood so proud, so full, waiting, wanting.

He was watching her closely. Fiona knew that if she

refused, if she showed the slightest sign of retreat, he would walk from the room, and this night would never be spoken of again. But rather than being frightened by what she saw, she was emboldened. He desired *her*.

Her fingers tugged at the sash holding her wrapper closed. The covering plunged to the floor in a rush of fabric, leaving her clad in nothing more than a nightshift of sheer silk.

In an instant, Fiona knew that she had thrilled him even more with such a move. Moonlight spilled through the draperies, piercing the delicate weave of her gown but leaving her body in shadow—hinting at what lay beneath without allowing it to be seen.

His hands snared her hips and pulled her closer, rubbing her stomach to him, against that hard, heated ridge.

Her eyes closed and she surrendered herself to the flood of sensation spilling through her veins. Her fingers sank into his hair, that dark, silky hair. A feeling like she had never experienced bubbled inside her, building, blooming. A restlessness consumed her, an inexplicable languor. She needed to arch, twine her body about his own, even as she longed to lie down.

His head came down, his lips pressing to the spot beneath her ear. She gasped, never having known that such an innocent location could send a bolt of reaction spearing to her abdomen. One of her legs bent, rubbing his thigh, and he sighed, stringing a row of kisses across her jaw, down her throat, to the hollow between her collar bones.

Her fingers curled into his hair. Her breath came in short, uneven pants. "Don't stop. Please, don't stop," she whispered desperately.

She thought her words might have startled him because he drew away. He swept her into his arms, carrying her to the bed. Laying her atop the tangled covers, he stood back one last time, silently offering her the opportunity to reject him.

Fiona held out her arms, knowing that she could never

turn him away. As long as he would have her, she would be there for him.

An expression approaching humility crossed his face, and he sank onto the bed. But when she expected him to draw close for a kiss, he moved lower, taking her nipple between his lips and suckling.

Lightning shot through her and she arched, her fingers plunging into his hair in an effort to push him away, then to pull him closer. She gasped again and again, scarcely able to absorb the sensations he'd created. She'd never dreamed that such ecstasy could be found in a man's embrace. Why had no one told her what to expect?

His mouth strayed lower, to her ribs, her navel. He followed the ridge of her hip bones, then, when she would have pulled him up again, he rolled her onto her stomach.

Gripping the pillow, she squeezed her eyes shut as he blazed a tormenting trail of kisses from her ankles to her calves. His tongue explored the insides of her knees and slid up her thighs, skirted the swell of her buttocks, lingered in the small of her back. Then he continued up her spine to nuzzle her shoulder blades, her neck.

By the time he'd turned her to face him again, she was writhing with need. Her arms wound about his shoulders, drawing him down for her own kisses, her own explorations.

When his weight settled over her, she welcomed it gladly. She wrapped one leg around his hips. She would do anything for this man. Anything to make him happy, to give him pleasure. But when his hand slid between them, resting low on her woman's mound, she cried out, realizing that he would not be the only one who would be gratified. Biting her lips, she arched her head into the pillow as the aching of her lower body intensified, increased, building like thunder within her. His fingers slid intimately over her, providing a delicious friction, and she lifted her hips from the bed, seeking to intensify the sensation.

Then he shifted, his hand moving away. She would

have whimpered in protest, but the sound died in her throat when the strength of his palm was replaced by another sort of pressure, a more intimate and tantalizing hardness.

She bucked under him, needing . . . What?

Jacob drew away and the hardness nudged her, testing the delicate flesh. She held her breath, her hands clenching, her body tightening, as, bit by bit, that hardness moved closer and closer.

Slowly, powerfully, stretching her, gauging her readiness, Jacob moved above her, infusing her with a heat such as she would never have dreamed. There was a little pain, a little tightness, but the sensation was so new, so frightening, so wonderful, she couldn't push him away.

When he rested on her, fully, heavily, her eyes blinked open. What she saw filled her with a joy that could know no bounds. He loved her. Dear heaven above, there was no disguising what she saw in his gaze. Yes, there was passion. Yes, there was a mindless need. But he also loved her. He *loved* her.

The thought gave her strength as well as a frantic pleasure. She began to move, tentatively at first, then, when he moaned, more boldly. Soon there was no time to think. Her eyes squeezed closed and she gave herself up to the moment, to the indescribable feelings.

A taut anticipation brewed deep in her body, a delicious pain. She found herself moving, lifting, twisting, anything to intensify the feeling, to assuage it. She didn't know what her body sought, she only knew she needed more. *More.*

Just when she thought she would lose all coherent thought her body grew still, tightened. She paused in her frantic movements, her legs holding him firmly to her. She felt Jacob shake; he had braced himself on his arms and she noted the trembling of his body. Then, without warning, he thrust into her, deeply, powerfully.

Fiona cried out, her body imploding, contracting. Jacob groaned and shuddered, spilling a warmth into her womb, a sweetness. Then, bit by bit, their bodies seemed to drain of all energy and he lay upon her, pressing a weary kiss to her ear.

Later, so much later, he lifted himself to his elbows, easing the weight of his body. Fiona felt a twinge of disappointment. The heaviness of his body had felt too wonderful, too comforting, too real.

Smoothing the hair away from her face, he examined her curiously. She saw the regrets lurking on the fringes of his consciousness. She pressed a finger to his lips, stopping the apologies before they could be formed.

"I gave myself freely. Don't take that away."

Closing his eyes, he rolled to her side, then gathered her close, resting her head upon his shoulder.

"I do care for you, Fiona," he murmured into the darkness.

For now, it was enough that he had said the words. Even though they weren't the ones she wanted to hear.

"What does *S-C-J* stand for?"

Dawn was beginning to peek over the tops of the buildings across the street, and Jacob had rolled from bed long enough to shut the drapes. But Fiona's question halted him in midstride.

She sat up in bed, pulling the linens over her breasts.

"I heard the policemen whispering the letters over and over again. At the hospital. Does it have anything to do with the vigilante group that is looking for you?"

He shook himself loose. Whipping the curtains shut, he turned, but even the deepening of the shadows could not conceal the way he'd become suddenly tense. Suddenly wary.

"Don't concern yourself with these things."

"What happened to that man?"

He walked to the washstand in evident agitation and poured a healthy measure of water into the basin.

"He was a lawman. He was injured."

"Someone *killed* him."

His head reared, and he met her gaze in the mirror.

"I saw the knife. What happened?"

"I told you before: It has nothing to do with you."

The words were harshly spoken, but she refused to be cowed.

"You came to me for help, you embroiled me unwillingly in your business. I think I have a right to know about anything that might affect me in the long run."

"What makes you think it has anything to do with you at all?"

"Don't take me fer a fool, Jacob. The Beasleys an' I are in a carriage an' we see ye rushin' t' the hospital as if ye were bein' chased by the hounds of hell." When her brogue got the better of her, she took a deep breath to calm herself again. "What *happened?*"

Jacob splashed some water over his face. When he straightened and wiped the moisture away with a towel, an unaccustomed agitation had begun to nibble at her nerves.

"Dub Merritt was . . . wounded in a totally unrelated situation."

She waited until he turned around and she could read his face, his eyes.

"Do you swear that it has nothing t' do with me or my father?"

"I promise."

"Then it must have something to do with the vigilantes."

"Yes," he supplied reluctantly. "He was a witness to their escape.

"Poor man." She sighed. "Poor, poor man." She leaned on the headboard. "So what happens now?"

"We board the tourist train as scheduled."

"What happens with *us,* Jacob?"

He dropped the towel on the dresser and moved to the window. "I don't know."

Although she'd been expecting such an answer, it wasn't any easier to accept.

"At least yer honest with me."

He sighed as he opened the drapes a crack. The

rose-colored light spilled over the sharp planes of his profile and limned the tousled waves of his hair.

"I've grown to care for you, Fiona. I never thought I would."

"But?"

He shook his head. "I've been a lawman for so long, I don't know how to be anything else. I started in the business when I was just a boy, pinning up wanted posters and running errands for the town marshal. How can I stop being what I am?"

"No one is asking you to stop."

"I know that. But you were right: If you and I were to . . . make something permanent of this, there would be ramifications."

She pleated the sheets with her fingers. "If I could erase what I've been, I would."

"I understand that." There was a wealth of empathy in his tone. "And I know I'm partially to blame. It shouldn't matter to me what other people think, but . . ." His voice became low, defeated. "Dammit all to hell. It does."

Fiona's heart became tight, brittle, as if Jacob had taken it in his hand and squeezed. Somewhere, long before, she'd heard that love conquered all. But she was beginning to see that the trite phrase did not hold true in all occasions.

"Will I see you after we've caught Kensington?"

He paused, then said, "I don't know."

She stared down at the sheets again, at the bed where she'd given him her heart as well as her body. At that moment, she realized that pride had no place in her situation. "Then will you at least let me have this? . . . For as long as it can last?"

He regarded her sadly. "You deserve more."

"I'll take whatever you're willing to give me."

He shook his head. "I should walk out that door."

His words caused her to throw back the covers and rush across the room, wrapping her arms around his waist. "No. Stay with me. Give me what you can. Then, if you can't offer me any more, I'll go. Without a fuss."

His fingers curled into her hair.

"Fiona—"

"Please!" She stared up at him. "Please."

Not allowing him to reconsider, she pulled him across the room. Pushing him down upon the featherbed, she straddled his hips and placed desperate kisses across his chest, his jaw, his cheek. It didn't matter that she had allowed him to see the way he'd broken her pride. All that mattered was that he'd agreed to offer her a few crumbs before he left her.

"All right." The words were a mere puff of capitulation, but she heard them and smiled.

"You won't live to regret your decision."

"I know." His fingers wove through her hair, and he said again, "I know."

Then he drew her down for his kiss, leaving her with the consolation that at least she would have the comfort of his lovemaking.

Even if he denied her his unconditional love.

14

Sunlight streamed through the hallway of the Grand Estate as Fiona let herself out and crept to the stairs.

She'd left Jacob sleeping in her bed. It was barely seven in the morning—a late sleep for Fiona, who was growing used to rising early for her "lessons." But judging by the way Jacob lay sprawled across the bed, breathing so heavily as to approach a near snore, she didn't think he would awaken soon to find her gone.

Fiona didn't know what drove her to dress in her own skirt and blouse, to sweep her hair into a simple braid, and tiptoe down the rear stairs. She hadn't changed her mind about all she had decided the prior night. She would continue to help Jacob in his endeavors to trap Darby Kensington. She would stay with him as long as he would allow her. She would love him for whatever time he deemed.

But this morning, as the harsh light seeped beneath the hems of the draperies, she'd found herself driven to remind herself of her roots, her real reasons for all she'd done.

"Miss?"

She'd descended only a few steps when the soft call came from behind. Glancing over her shoulder, she saw that one of Jacob's men had followed her. The same guard Jacob had ordered to keep her in line.

"I don't believe you should be going anywhere," he murmured.

Her hand slipped from where it had been concealed in her skirt, and she pointed the tiny derringer squarely between the man's eyes.

"Leave me alone." The words were blatant in their sincerity.

The young man—he couldn't have been much more than eighteen—shrank away ever so slightly.

"But Miss—"

"Leave me alone." Lifting her skirts, she raced down to the servants' entrance and dodged into the morning heat.

Fiona didn't pause to reconsider her actions. Jacob would be angry, there was no doubt of that. But tomorrow she would be leaving on the tourist train. She would be adopting the role that was somehow becoming more familiar to her than her own behavior. She had to see Mickaleen one more time. Just to reassure herself that her choices had not been entirely selfish.

The traffic this early in the day was surprisingly heavy. Although the wealthy might sleep in until the sun had climbed well into the sky, the working classes had been up for hours. Fiona was forced to fight her way through the bunches of men in their business suits, farmers with their suspenders and plaids, and women with shopping on their minds.

Fiona didn't have the money to hire a carriage, so she walked the short distance to the Liberty Hotel. Her weariness pressed in upon her, making each step an ordeal, reminding her all too eloquently that she had not rested well the night before, but she continued nonetheless, refusing to be daunted.

There was some sort of commotion at the entrance,

and a crowd had gathered by the front stoop. Pausing for only an instant, Fiona slipped through the alley to the delivery door. From there it took only a moment to find the staff staircase and climb the three flights to Mickaleen's room.

As she eased into the hall, she hesitated. There was another large cluster of people who had banded together near the far end. They murmured softly to themselves, nodding gravely. Fiona thought she saw a man carrying a medical bag disappear down the opposite steps, shaking his head as he rounded the bend.

A slow dread began to drizzle through her veins. Her lungs constricted, making it difficult for her to draw breath.

Plunging her hand into her pocket, she clutched the key that she'd stolen from Jacob's vest, the one engraved with the Liberty Hotel insignia. She waited, pressing the raised number into the pad of her thumb until the gaggle of onlookers had cleared. Her father's guards must have momentarily left to help with whatever emergency had occurred, so now was her chance.

Her heart pounded as she moved toward the appropriate door. "Papa?"

There were no sounds on the other side—not that she was not completely surprised. Her father had grown used to lying abed in the mornings. After the life of hardship he'd endured, she couldn't completely begrudge him that fact.

Slipping the key into the lock, she dodged inside, her eyes blinking to become used to the gloom. Evidently, she was not the only person who had received Jacob's edict to leave the draperies closed.

"Papa?" she whispered again. There was no answer. Drat it all, her father was becoming increasingly hard of hearing, but she didn't dare speak any louder for fear that Mickaleen's guards would return and find her.

Tiptoeing to the window, she drew one of the draperies aside, hooking it to the stanchion embedded in the wall.

Let Jacob chide them both if he found them basking in the sunlight. She needed to talk to her father, and she needed to see his reactions.

She frowned as she noted the empty, rumpled bed. Her father's belongings had been flung over the only chair, and since his room was not so palatial as hers, there weren't many other places where he could be.

"Papa?"

The word was uttered in vain. Unless he'd crawled under the bed, he wasn't here.

Keen disappointment settled on her shoulders, nearly smothering her with its weight. She blinked at the tears that rose to her eyes. She'd so set her heart on a kind word, a bit of brogue that wasn't her own.

Dejected, she walked toward the door. Her hand closed around the cool metal, but then she paused, not really knowing why. A chill skittered down her spine, and a horrible feeling of loss flooded her chest. She remembered the crowds at the front door, the people in the hall.

"Papa?" The word eased from her lips so softly, it was barely audible.

Trembling, she turned, seeing again the bed, the rumpled covers that appeared to have been pulled all to one side.

Her hands tightened into unconscious fists as she took a step, another, another. Rounding the corner, she first saw one bare foot, two pale legs, a tangled nightshirt.

"Oh, Papa," she whispered, sinking to her knees. "Papa, no."

But the blood-spattered head she drew onto her lap was stiff. The hand she touched was cold, so very cold.

"How could you just let her go like that?"

Jacob scowled at the young deputy he'd left in charge of following Fiona.

"She pulled a gun on me, sir."

Jacob stabbed the youngster in the chest with his finger. "Boy, it's time you learned that if you plan to be a lawman, there's going to be a great many people who'll be doing that in the future."

With that, he signaled to Rusty. The two men rushed outside, mounted their horses, and led them as swiftly as they could through the press of traffic to the Liberty Hotel. As they reined to a halt, the manager, who'd been standing on the boardwalk, hustled to meet them.

"I was just about to send word." The man wrung his hands together. "Your men . . ."

"My men?" Jacob repeated in surprise. He'd been so intent upon retrieving Fiona that he'd forgotten there were other guards in place at this establishment.

"I'm so sorry. I know this is a terrible loss."

Jacob looked at Rusty. His deputy had grown pale beneath his freckles.

"What happened?"

The manager wilted in open distress. "We don't *know*. The maid . . . she found them early this morning. They'd been brutally murdered, then dragged into one of the linen closets."

Jacob's stomach churned.

"What about McFee?" he demanded through a throat that had suddenly grown tight.

"The gentleman in the room?" The manager became still. "I don't know. We didn't check."

The words had barely been spoken when Jacob dismounted and brushed past him, dodging into the hotel and up the stairs. Racing down the hall, he came to an abrupt stop when he saw that the door had been left slightly ajar.

No. Dear heaven, no.

But even as he swung the portal wide, he knew what he would find there.

Fiona.

Her head was bowed, her hair gleaming in the sliver of sunlight that pierced a pair of mishung draperies. Her position behind the bed blocked most of his view, but as he walked forward, her clear dejection struck him to the core.

She didn't know he was there. Not by a movement or a glance did she reveal that she had sensed his presence. He moved as quietly as he could, his eyes quickly surveying the scene, seeing with a lawman's calculation what must have been a struggle, a struggle that had ended with Mickaleen McFee being bludgeoned over the head with the iron bar that lay on the floor.

"He had a bad heart."

He started when Fiona suddenly spoke.

"He drank too much. He ate too well."

Her fingers brushed at the curls that spilled untidily over her father's forehead.

"I'd prepared myself for the fact that he would die in any one of those manners."

Jacob knelt beside her. "Come with me. You shouldn't be here."

She didn't move. "I only wanted to see him. Talk to him."

"I know." She had wanted to tell her father about *him*. Jacob knew that, knew it as surely as he knew that the sun rose and set each day.

"He was a good man. Deep inside. Where it counted. Even *you* would have to admit that."

"Yes."

Her chin suddenly trembled, her features crumpling. "Now I'm alone, Jacob. What am I going to do?"

Her naked misery wrenched at his heart. Gently, he lay Mickaleen's head on the floor and drew her to her feet, wrapping her tightly in his arms. She trembled violently, like a wounded bird, her hands clutching at his back.

"I'm completely and utterly alone."

Then she began to cry. Not soft gasps and wordless tears, but deep, heartfelt sobs that wrenched her entire body and threatened to shatter her in two.

Jacob pulled her as tightly to his body as he could, but it wasn't enough. It would never be enough. Her grief was too raw, too real to be eased by anyone else.

Rusty stepped into the room. When he would have

withdrawn, Jacob shook his head, gesturing with his eyes that his deputy should care for the body.

Signaling to another man who waited in the hall, the pair stepped quietly around the bed, wrapping Mickaleen in a blanket, then taking him outside and closing the door. It was at that moment that Jacob saw the crumpled piece of paper that had been pushed beneath the bed: the eight-sided star emblazoned with the letters *SCJ*.

His heart grew so heavy, he thought it would burst. His mouth filled with the acrid taste of guilt.

Krupp. Krupp had been here. He'd killed Mickaleen in an effort to hurt Jacob. And Jacob, in turn, had been the unwilling source of Fiona's pain. By embroiling Fiona in his affairs, he had unwittingly drawn her into a pact for revenge made years before.

His fingers tightened in her hair. She wasn't safe. She wouldn't be safe until he got her out of Chicago.

She sobbed, her whole body shaking, and he felt remorse spear through his heart. In one mindless act of vengeance, she had lost her entire family. How could he ever make that up to her?

Scooping her into his arms, he carried her to the door. He didn't know what he should do, he didn't know what *could* be done. But he *would* take her away from this place. From the reminder of all she had lost.

"We need more time! Things have fallen apart on us, and we don't have the luxury of putting them together again!"

Rusty shrugged as Jacob continued to pace the sitting room of the Ambassador Suite. "The governor's assistant has been apprised of the situation, but Carruthers hopes that the attempt to capture Kensington will continue as planned."

Jacob stared at his deputy in amazement. "Has he lost his mind completely? Fiona's father has just been killed. Does Carruthers think that she's going to be able to step onto that train and act as if nothing has happened?"

Rusty held up his hands. "I *told* him, but he wasn't willing to listen. He wants you on that train tomorrow morning. I have a feeling he's hoping that by getting you and Fiona out of the city, the raids by Krupp and his cohorts will ease, giving city officials a chance to track the Star Council down."

"Dammit, man. You and I know—"

"Shh!"

"Shh!"

Alma and Amelia Beasley dodged from the bedroom, closing the door behind them and taking the position of a human wall.

"I must ask you to lower your voices!" Alma whispered vehemently.

Jacob immediately flushed in contrition. "How is she?"

"She's fallen asleep," Amelia whispered, tiptoeing across the room to place an empty cup next to the silver tea service. "I think the rest will do her good, but . . ." she made a *tsk*-ing sound. "Poor dear."

Jacob's gaze bounced from one old woman to the next in pure helplessness. He'd had no experiences in the past to help him react to these situations. He was a man of force, one accustomed to marching into trouble full-steam. He didn't know how to ease a woman's broken heart. He only knew that he had to do *something.*

"Both of you appear tired," he said to the sisters. "Why don't you go get something to eat, take a nap if you wish? I'll watch her this afternoon."

"But—"

Alma placed a restraining hand on her sister's arm. "That would be greatly appreciated, I'm sure."

Nodding, Jacob hesitated for a moment, then moved to the door.

"What should I tell Carruthers?" Rusty asked.

"Tell him . . . tell him . . ." Jacob sighed. "Tell him to go to hell."

He closed himself in the bedroom, leaving Rusty and

the Beasleys to stare awkwardly at one another. Muttering to himself, Rusty stomped from the suite. Alma peered thoughtfully at the door he'd left ajar.

"More tea, Alma?"

Alma barely heard her. Moving slowly, she closed the portal, her forehead creasing.

"Alma?"

"Jacob needs more time. He's so worried about Fiona."

Amelia eyed her open-mouthed, clearly astonished by the abrupt change in conversation.

She pointed in Amelia's direction. "You and I both know that Judge Krupp and his vigilante group are responsible for this."

Amelia set the cup of tea she'd prepared for herself on the table. "You saw it too?"

"The note Jacob was staring at most of the day."

"An eight-pointed star."

"One engraved with the letters *SCJ.*"

Amelia laced her hands together in distress. "That business with the Star Council of Justice was nasty five years ago."

"We both know that Jacob was the one responsible for seeing Stone and Krupp imprisoned."

"Revenge," Amelia whispered.

"Exactly. Those men are trying to trap Jacob in their little schemes, and they've dragged an innocent woman along for the ride."

"So what are we going to do?"

Alma's brow creased in thought. "We've got to find a way to get those two on that tourist train and out of Chicago. I have great faith in the lawmen chasing Krupp. Given a little time, they'll find him."

"But Fiona isn't in any state to get on a train and pose as a genteel gambler."

Alma began to pace, her lips pursing. "She will if we can give her a little time to recover, to gather her props beneath her, as it were."

"Once we explain that Jacob is in danger, she would agree to help."

Alma stared at her sister in surprise.

"Alma, she loves the boy! She would do anything to help him."

"Why, Amelia, I didn't think you'd noticed."

"Not noticed? How can one be ignorant to love?"

"Quite."

The two women strolled to the window, both deep in thought.

"So what we need is some time. If we could only delay the journey."

"Kensington is leaving tomorrow morning. The clerk we asked yesterday evening confirmed that fact."

"Hmm." Alma tapped her fingernail on the window pane. "Then we'll just have to see to it that *he* is delayed as well."

"But how?"

Alma thought for a moment, then straightened her shoulders to military attention. "Get your things, Amelia. I've got an idea."

"Do you think we should?"

"Have we any *other* choice?"

Alma and Amelia Beasley stood on the mud-clumped boardwalk leading to Wilson's Mining Supply Company. Less than a quarter of an hour had passed since they'd eavesdropped on Jacob Grey and decided to lend their own aid.

"Well, no."

"Then I think we should follow our original plan."

"Yes, Sister."

Alma marched down the scarred planks with her usual efficiency of stride, causing Amelia to adopt a near gallop. Once at the door to the office, she stepped inside, shouldering her way through a gaggle of ill-clad, ill-washed men and making her way to the front counter. Somewhere along the way, she lost her younger sister, but she was not about to be dissuaded. Fiery determination filled her veins. She had a mission to perform.

"My good man." She slapped the counter with her parasol, drawing upon her age and her sex, which awarded her certain allowances in a male-dominated environment. One of those was taking her position at the front of the line regardless of the number of people who'd been waiting far longer than she.

The gentleman behind the counter glanced up from his books, his mouth gaping when he saw the elderly woman who waited for his help.

"I wish to buy a stick of dynamite."

"Beg pardon?"

"Have you a problem with your hearing? I *wish* . . . to *buy* . . . a *stick* . . . of *dynamite.*" Each word was punctuated with the rapping of her parasol against the wood.

"Ma'am?"

She plunked her reticule onto the table. "How much?"

"But I can't . . . I mean . . ."

She smiled disarmingly, assuming a congenial tone. "You see, my boy, I am from the country outside of Brandenburg. I'll only be staying in Chicago for a few short days."

"Oh?"

"At home I have a garden."

"Garden?"

"Yes. The thing is infested with gophers."

His eyes widened.

"I intend to *blast* them out!" Her statement was followed by the smack of her parasol, causing the man to jump.

"But ma'am, That would level the place."

"Exactly."

"But—"

"One stick, please," she ordered, withdrawing her coin purse.

"I can't!" he blurted.

She glared at him over her spectacles. "Whyever not?"

"Rules of the management. They won't let you buy the stuff as if it were a beeswax candle."

Alma sighed in genuine irritation. "I can't?"

"No, ma'am."

"Then give me the forms. I'll fill them out now."

"But then there's a waiting period."

"How long?"

"Three days."

She leaned forward. "That is far too long. The gophers will have dined upon *all* my petunias."

The man didn't point out that a blast of dynamite would eradicate all evidence of the flowers as well, but Alma knew he wouldn't dare mention such a thing. One of the benefits of old age. Good manners dictated that the elderly should not have their idiotic ideas criticized in their presence.

Huffing in irritation at the formalities that would completely undermine her plans, Alma snatched up the papers and wove through the press of interested onlookers to the outer door. She spotted her sister and motioned for her to follow.

"Impertinent fool," she stated, marching into the heat.

"He was only following the rules."

"Idiotic rules, which will hamper our goals!"

"Will this help?"

Alma paused when her sister puffed and held up a huge canvas sack.

"What is it?"

"One of the miners left it by the door."

Alma lifted the flap, then slapped a hand on her breast in pure delight. "Oh, Amelia!" she breathed. "You've done it." She caressed one of the cool hard sticks. "You've gotten our dynamite."

Darby Kensington knocked on the door to Krupp's latest hideaway. He felt a twinge of fear as the door cracked open and one gray eye peered out at him.

He wasn't questioned. No one talked to him at all as he

walked into the main room. Although it was crowded with men, none of them spoke. Instead, they stared at him in a way that made his skin crawl.

"Leave us."

The low command eased into the gloom. One by one, the vigilantes, exconvicts, and drifters rose to their feet and filed out. They left only one man: their leader, Judge Krupp.

Kensington stood at near ramrod attention, glaring at the tall, gray-haired gentleman. How he hated Krupp, had grown to hate him more and more with each breath he took. Yet there was a guarded respect as well—for all the man had done, the economic revolt he'd caused with his counterfeiting schemes.

"So, Kensington. You've come for your final instructions."

Kensington noted the silent censure, the scorn, but he steeled himself to it.

"I did what I was told."

"The train—"

"Yes, dammit! I booked passage, bought your supplies, and arranged a half-dozen card games!" He threw his hands into the air. "I'm getting tired of having you and your associates checking up on me like I was an imbecile." Kensington stalked toward him. "I've been your stooge for months now. I've endangered my freedom and my reputation in order to scatter your counterfeit money around the state. But this is the *last* time I do your work, do you hear me?"

"*You* . . . will do as you're told."

When Kensington would have argued, Krupp pinned him with a powerful stare. "You act so greatly put upon, but if you will remember, *I* was the one who located you in that foundling house. *I* was the one who sent you to boarding school, taught you how to keep books, then set you up in your gambling. Without me, you would have been living in the gutter."

Kensington's hands clenched in silent rage, all the

pent-up anger he'd harbored for years bubbling inside him. "If you hadn't—"

"If I hadn't *what?*" Krupp's voice lowered to a menacing tone. "Be careful where you tread, Darby Kensington. *Don't* forget who I am. *Don't* forget what I know. *Don't* forget that with one wrong word, one anonymous tip to the authorities, you could be swinging from the end of a rope as an accomplice to the Star Council of Justice."

"I haven't *done* anything!"

"But will they believe you?"

Kensington eased himself to his full height. His body trembled with rage, but there was nothing he could do to fight against this man. They both knew it.

He whirled toward the door, but Krupp stopped him when he would have stepped outside. "I will have men searching for you at the railway station tomorrow morning. You will do as you're told, board the train, lose heavily, and spend my money. Then, when you are finished, *if* you have pleased me with your efforts . . . I will let you go."

Kensington's hand clenched around the knob and he cursed the day he'd awakened in the orphanage to see a tall, slender gentleman waiting to take him away. He should have run then. He should have made an attempt.

"Do we have an understanding?"

Kensington looked up, into the eyes that were so much like his own. "Yes, Father. I think we understand each other very well."

"How are you feeling?"

Fiona blinked, wondering why a heavy pressure had invaded her chest, her body, making even the simplest movement an effort.

Turning her head, she saw that Jacob had pulled a chair next to the bed. He rested his elbows on his knees, a stance that should have been casual and relaxed, but it only underscored an attitude of waiting.

The memory of all that had occurred that morning flooded into her consciousness slowly, ever so slowly, like ripples on a lake. She shuddered, but allowed no other outward reactions, not wanting him to see her so weak.

"I still feel a little tired."

"That's understandable."

The silence settled around them, awkward in its intensity.

"The governor sends his condolences. Rusty spoke to his aide."

Fiona knew that Jacob expected a spirited remark of some sort, but she just couldn't summon the energy necessary and nodded instead.

"What will you do now?"

She shrugged. "I suppose I could try and get my job at the laundry. As long as you've continued with the rent as promised, I've got my room at the Honeycomb."

"Fiona—"

She held up a hand. "No. Please." She hated the way her voice became husky. "Don't say . . . anything."

He leaned back in his chair, watching her as if he feared that she would fly to pieces. Fiona took great care to appear as calm as she was able.

"Are you hungry?"

"No."

"Is there anything I can—"

She silenced him with a glance. Several minutes passed, then he sighed and said, "I know this is a bad time. I know I'm a bastard for even bringing this up. But I need to know what you plan to do tomorrow."

"Tomorrow?"

"The tourist train."

She placed a hand to her head. She'd forgotten entirely why she and Jacob were together, in this room, this period of time.

"I—"

A knock interrupted them, and Rusty poked his head around the door. Upon seeing Fiona awake and at least coming to terms with her emotions, he smiled tentatively. "Hello, Fiona."

"Rusty."

He stepped hesitantly into the room, mauling his hatbrim in his hands. "I can go away if I'm disturbing you."

Since she'd been put to bed completely dressed except for her shoes, Fiona saw no reason to bar him from entering. Waving her hand, she motioned for him to enter.

Rusty glanced at Jacob, then at her. In the dim evening light, his freckles became more pronounced, his hair an even more fiery red.

"I'm sorry about your father, ma'am."

"Thank you," she said, a stinging pricking at her eyes.

"We took him to a real nice parlor . . . and . . ." He cleared his throat, realizing he was treading on dangerous ground. "Here." Thrusting his hand out, he said, "We found this clenched in his fist. He must have grabbed it when he fell. We figured you'd want it."

Fiona frowned when Rusty dropped a heavy gold watch fob into her palm.

"I don't—"

The words lodged in her mouth as she examined the piece. Hinged like a locket, it would have hung on a man's chain, suspended in the center of his stomach.

Fiona snapped open the casing to stare inside. There was a tiny, blurry photograph of a boy, and inside the lid had been engraved the words: *To Darby. From your father.* Below that, as if it had been crudely carved with the tip of a knife, was a faint, eight-pointed star labeled with the initials *SCJ*. Something about the symbol pricked her consciousness, but she couldn't think what it could mean.

Darby.

Her brow furrowed. Darby. As far as she was aware, her father knew no one by the name of Dar—

A coldness gripped her heart. Her stomach clenched. Kensington? *Kensington?* Was *he* responsible? The moment the thought appeared, she shook it away. It wasn't possible. Kensington was trailed night and day by a host of lawmen. He wouldn't have been able to sneeze without their knowing. The moment he'd made any move toward the Liberty Hotel, Jacob would have been alerted. There was no possible way they would have allowed him to kill two of their own deputies as well as Mickaleen McFee—a man he'd never known, never met.

And yet, he was connected somehow. In some way. Nausea churned in her breast and her breath locked in her body. An uneasiness settled into her very bones. Her father's death had dropped a riddle in the middle of her lap, and the fob was the only piece to the puzzle. Ultimately, she had to confront the man who owned it.

She glanced at Jacob, seeing his concern, knowing instinctively that if he were to see this bit of evidence, he would call off the plan to trap Kensington—he was probably ready to do such a thing anyway, given the state of her emotions. But she couldn't let him. She had to be on the train. She had to meet with Darby Kensington on her own terms.

Her fingers clenched, slamming the lid closed with such pressure the snap of the catch could be heard for several feet.

"Fiona?" Jacob leaned forward, examining her in concern.

"Thank you, Rusty," she said slowly. "Thank you for bringing this to me."

He nodded awkwardly.

Her thumb stroked the warm gold. "Jacob, you may tell the governor that I will keep our bargain. I will be on that train."

"But—"

"The McFees keep their word." She stared sternly in his direction. "I won't be the first to make an exception."

Jacob opened his mouth to question her motives, but an explosion rocked the evening quiet. It was immediately followed by another and another.

"What the hell?"

Jacob rushed toward the window, whipping the draperies aside and peering out. When he saw what appeared like the entire horizon on fire, he swore.

Fiona rose, pushing away the covers and rushing to his side, barely able to believe her eyes. "Sweet Mary and all the Saints," she whispered beside him. "What in heaven's name has happened?"

"The railway station. It's coming from the railway station."

Her mouth gaped ever so slightly. "You can't be serious. But—"

Jacob stared at his deputy. "Only hours ago we were bemoaning the fact that we needed another day. Well, someone has seen to it that we have our extra time."

A pounding began on the main door, and Jacob dodged into the sitting room. Fiona and Rusty followed, in time to see him opening the portal to the young deputy who had served as Fiona's guard.

"Jacob! The train sta—"

"I saw. What in the hell happened?"

"It's too soon to tell, but it appears like an entire section of track has been blown to smitherines, as well as a half-dozen boxcars filled with kerosene barrels. It will take at least forty-eight hours for the mess to be cleaned and repaired."

"Great bloody hell." Jacob gathered his hat and revolver. He was on his way into the corridor when a horrible thought crept into his brain. No. They wouldn't. Would they?

Pausing in his tracks, he slowly turned, surveying the room. "Where are the Beasleys?"

Fiona gestured to the suite across the hall. "They usually take a nap prior to supper."

He took a key from his vest, stormed toward the door, and flung it open. The Beasleys' beds were neatly made, empty.

"I suppose they stepped out for a minute," Fiona stated next to his shoulder.

Jacob barely heard her as he and Rusty exchanged suspicious glances.

"You don't think they're responsible?" Rusty breathed. "Do you?"

"No." The word was firm. Two women in their seventies couldn't possibly cause such utter devastation.

Could they?

15

"LADIES."

The Beasleys started when Jacob spoke. He'd been waiting for nearly an hour, alternating between pacing the narrow hotel chamber and sitting in the single chair, drumming his fingers. In all that time, he'd used every argument he could manufacture to reassure himself that the Beasleys had spent the afternoon shopping. One peek at their soot-blackened faces, however, was all the evidence he needed to the contrary.

"*What* have you done?" he demanded, leaning forward and bracing his arms on his knees.

The women shifted from foot to foot like naughty schoolchildren, their gazes bouncing guiltily.

"Done?"

"The truth."

The room fairly pounded with an uncomfortable silence.

"Now."

Amelia was the first to break, her confession bursting free: "We only meant to bend a little track!"

Alma frowned in disappointment. "Amelia!"

Amelia's face crumpled. "We may as well tell him, Alma. He'll know sooner or later."

"Very true," Jacob concurred. "What happened?"

"Well, first . . ."

"We put a stick of dynamite in a burning trash drum and rolled it under one of the cars," Alma proclaimed proudly.

"Dynamite?"

"We would have used just the dynamite alone—the nice man down at the armory told us how to do it—but we couldn't make it light. Therefore we were forced to develop our own procedure."

Jacob was snagged by the first portion of their explanation. "You *asked* how to detonate it?"

Amelia made a disparaging sound. "We didn't *ask* right out."

"We're not fools."

"We merely embroiled the man in a bit of reminiscing. We thought we could take advantage of what he told us."

"But the fool wasn't quite in touch with reality."

Jacob's hands clenched as he fought for control. "Where did you get the dynamite?"

The two women hesitated.

"We'd rather not say."

"Why did you use it?"

Alma sniffed and stepped around him to lay her reticule on the bed, patting his shoulder as she passed. "Now, now, Jacob. There's no need to snap. We shouldn't have eavesdropped, but we did. You needed help, a little more time. We felt duty-bound to offer our assistance."

"By blowing up the *whole train?"*

"That's a bit of an exaggeration. We damaged—what, Alma?—three cars?"

"Six."

Jacob stared at them in amazement. "You blew up *six* cars? *You?"*

"As I said, we really only intended to bend a little track."

"But the trash drum—"

"—actually, it was an emptied barrel of some sort—"

"—rolled beneath one of the boxcars."

"One filled with kerosene."

"It lit up like fireworks."

"Which set the cars on either side on fire."

"Also of kerosene."

"Which in turn burned two more cars and a caboose."

"Those were *grain* cars, however."

"True."

Jacob's mouth dropped. He couldn't help it. How could the Beasleys have caused so much trouble? All under the guise of trying to help?"

"Please don't chide us, Jacob," Amelia whispered nervously. "We know we went a little too far."

"A little too far? *A little too far!* Ladies, I don't think you understand the ramifications of your actions!"

"We said we were sorry."

"Sorry! Tampering with the railroad is a federal offense!"

"Really?" Amelia gazed at her sister in amazement. "I had no idea. Had you, Sister?"

"We didn't kill anyone."

Amelia blanched. "They'll put us in prison."

Alma sniffed. "Poppycock. No court in the land would convict us."

Probably true. A jury would take one look at their sweet, elderly faces and spun-sugar hair and deem them incapable of any malicious behavior. But they'd trot them off to the nearest asylum without blinking an eye.

As a federal marshal, he'd just heard their confessions. It was his duty, his *job* to see these little old ladies brought to justice. What was he going to do?

Good hell almighty.

"Stay here," he growled, lunging from the chair.

"But—"

"Just *stay* until I come for you."

Jacob had taken little more than three steps into the

hall when Fiona caught his arm and dragged him into her own suite.

"Well?"

"They did it. Good hell, they did it. They admitted as much to me without batting an eyelid."

"What are you going to do?"

"What *can* I do? The Beasleys have committed a crime."

"They thought they were helping you."

"That doesn't excuse the offense."

She glared at him. "Do you mean to tell me that you would turn them in? That you would send two old women to prison?"

"Dammit, Fiona. Don't you think I'm aware of the consequences? Don't you think I'd do anything to avoid this situation—"

"Then—"

"—short of breaking the law myself?"

"Is following the strict letter of the law so important to you that you can't bend the rules a bit?"

"Yes!" He slammed his fist on the door jamb. "I learned through experience the danger of taking such power into my own hands."

She frowned in disbelief. "The high and mighty Jacob Grey once strayed over the lines?"

"Don't mock me, Fiona." He pointed a finger in her direction. "You know nothing about me, nothing about my concerns as a lawman."

She slapped his hand away. "Are you trying to tell me that sending two old ladies to jail is the most pressing worry you have? What about my father's murderer? And that man at the hospital, and—"

"Dammit!" He grasped her elbow, pulling her close, his expression fierce. "Don't you know that's been preying on my mind for hours? Days? Curse Darby Kensington, curse his phony money. I don't care about his petty crimes! Don't you see? The vigilante group I told you about has reorganized. Its leaders, Judge Krupp and Gerald Stone, have ordered the Star Council of Justice to begin a reign of terror. No one's safe—especially not my family and those I associate with. Do you think I give a hoot in hell about the Beasleys and their stray stick of dynamite?"

"The Star Council?" Her brow furrowed. Somewhere she'd heard about such a thing, but the memory was incredibly vague.

He sighed, striding toward the window, watching below, always watching. "Ten years ago, I was approached by fellow lawmen about the growing number of criminals we knew who had broken the law and were abusing the judicial system for their own protection. We decided to . . . take care of them ourselves."

She gasped. "But that's—"

"Illegal."

She sank into a chair. "Never, in all my born days, would I have expected *you* to admit such a thing."

"I was young. Cocky. I thought I knew enough about judicial matters and my companions that the end result would cancel the means."

"What happened?"

"A rash of robberies was sweeping the area, and the Star Council decided that one person was responsible. Although no real proof had been gathered against him, Ethan McGuire was slated for execution."

"Ethan! Lettie's husband?"

He nodded. "They weren't married at the time—in fact, it was Lettie who hid Ethan away so that he couldn't be captured. I was a deputy at the time, and so sure that the Council was doing the right thing. Because of my blind obedience to the group, I nearly sent an innocent man to his death. Luckily, some information was leaked to me implicating my superior, Judge Krupp, his assistant, Gerald Stone, and several other members of the Star Council of Justice for their own crimes. After further investigation, it became apparent that the group was being paid to murder political adversaries and influential businessmen. They wanted Ethan dead because of information he knew about some of their group members. They were even willing to kill Lettie to get to him."

"You were part of this?"

"I'm not proud of the fact."

"But you brought them to justice."

"I sent them to jail. A jail from which they escaped. Since that time, they have made it patently clear that they mean to have their revenge on all of those involved in capturing them."

"Dub Merritt?"

"Krupp had to see to it that the only witness of his escape didn't live."

"My father . . ."

"Somehow, Krupp must have discovered that I had put McFee in the hotel for safekeeping. His death was probably due to no more than an effort to hurt me, though I don't know for sure."

Fiona's hand trembled slightly as she touched her lips. "You *know* the Star Council was responsible for my father's death?"

He regarded her sadly, then withdrew a crumpled sheet of paper from his pocket. "This was found on the floor by his body."

Fiona slowly opened the missive, knowing what she would find, what she would see: an eight-sided star with the letters *SCJ* imprinted inside. Long ago, she'd heard stories of the vigilante group and how Jacob had brought it to justice. The importance of the symbol she saw had been buried in her brain, waiting for the right jog to free it.

"Another similar note was found at the scene of Dub's murder."

"No," she whispered. "No. I—" Horrible thoughts raced through her mind, dangerous conjectures. The fob: The same marking had been etched on the fob. Was Darby somehow connected with this nebulous vigilante group?

"What about Darby?"

"He has nothing to do with the group. I would have known if he was one of the original members."

But what if he had joined up with Krupp and his men in the last little while? She didn't say the thought aloud, but it reverberated in her brain. Dear sweet heaven, what had she and her father fallen into? The more she became embroiled in this assignment, the more intricate became the extent of Kensington's lawbreaking, the more complicated his plots, the more nefarious his contacts.

She opened her mouth, ready to tell Jacob what she knew, then paused. If Jacob had any idea that Darby was connected with the Star Council, he wouldn't let her go. The thought pierced her consciousness like a thunderbolt. If she were to help in uncovering her father's killer—or possible killers—she would have to remain silent, bide her time, and do her own little bit of investigating.

For now.

Fiona stood with her ear pressed to the door, listening as Jacob finished giving instructions to his men.

"We've been ordered by Carruthers to continue with our original plans, despite Krupp's escape. I know some of our own were killed, but it's imperative that we all keep our minds on the matter at hand: capturing Kensington and shutting down his counterfeiting scheme.

"Arthur, Jason. You and your crew take the passenger cars. We need a complete sweep of the occupants every thirty minutes—whether or not the train has stopped. Willis, Jackson, position your men in the boxcars beyond. I want at least six lawmen who can make a roving check at every stop. The railroad has agreed to give us one extra boxcar for arms, horses, and ammunition. We'll put that in position at the very end of the train, by the caboose.

"Be warned: Kensington has to know that his trail is getting hot. You can't be dressed like lawmen. You've got to look like tourists and weary travelers. Understand? Keep him in sight at all times, but subtly."

There were murmurs of agreement, then the group disbanded, one by one, slowly, carefully, some taking the rear stairs, a few the front, while others disappeared into rooms rented on various floors. Fiona had dared one peek and been amazed that a bunch of lawmen—a sort she'd always been taught to distrust—had appeared in her sitting room, wearing an assortment of costumes. Businessmen in tailored suits sat side by side with farmers and shopkeepers and untidy drifters.

Once the door had closed on the last man, Fiona stepped from the bedroom.

Jacob turned, his emotions bare in his eyes: worry, anticipation, pride. "You're sure you want to go through with this?"

"On two conditions."

One of his brows lifted. His lawman's nature seeped into his stance as a kind of wariness.

"Number one, you send the Beasleys home without any sort of prosecution."

"Fiona—"

"Please. Do it for me if for no other reason. Give them *my* pardon."

He touched her cheek. "Fiona, I've bought their tickets home. They'll be leaving the same day we do. However, in order to see them safely tucked away, you'll be left without proper chaperones. There's no time to find someone else. Your reputation could be damaged."

She smiled, tremulously, happily, reading far more into his actions than anyone else might. He was willing to overlook the letter of the law, just this once. He was willing to see the fuzzy gray in between the black and the white.

"I'll gladly suffer the consequences to my supposed reputation if they can leave unfettered."

"What's your second condition?"

She touched his chest, his wrist.

"Make love with me. Show me there is still some tenderness left in a world gone mad, some good, some joy."

"Oh, Fiona." He sighed. "Neither of us knew how far this would go, did we?"

She shook her head.

"I have no regrets." He bent toward her, his eyes kindling deep inside. "No regrets at all."

As they kissed, Fiona sighed, stepping into his embrace, absorbing his strength, his scent, his tenderness. For the rest of her life, she would remember this infinite sensation of being loved.

Loved? Yes. He *did* love her. She hadn't changed her mind in that respect. He might never say the words, he might never admit the fact to himself, but she knew he loved her, and his adoration gave her the courage to go on, to put aside her grief, to work toward justice.

He lifted free, and his broad hands framed her face. "I've never known a woman like you."

"One so frustrating?"

"It only adds to your charm," he teased, then became suddenly serious. "I've grown to depend on you, need you."

It was a powerful statement indeed coming from a man who was generally so implacable, so independent. Fiona could not prevent her sudden smile. Little did he know that with those words, he'd offered her more than she'd ever hoped to receive.

When she didn't speak, he caressed her cheek, her chin. "I don't suppose you have anything you might . . . want to add?"

"Only that you have been the first man to touch my heart."

Her simple answer must have taken him by surprise, for he became still, obviously mulling over the consequences of their shared declarations. The future must not have proved as terrifying as he had earlier supposed, because he grinned, then became sober again.

"Trust me to take care of you."

"I do."

"Trust me to make things right."

"I do."

"Trust me to—"

She placed her fingertips to his lips. "I do."

The blazing light that appeared in his eyes lit an answering fire in Fiona's as well. His shortened breathing affected her own, his obvious yearning matched hers. So when he swept her into his arms, she went gladly. When he divested her of her clothing layer by layer, she surrendered quite willingly. And when he took her, body and soul . . .

She knew she would never love this much again.

16

"You're beautiful."

After all that had happened to Fiona in the last few days, Jacob could scarcely believe how poised and lovely she appeared as she entered the sitting room.

She smiled at the compliment, her head tilting ever so slightly to the side.

"Do you really think so? Enough to capture Kensington's attention?"

"Yes."

Mr. Peebles had clothed her completely in navy blue. How the little man had managed to construct such an elaborate costume—as well as such an extensive wardrobe—in such a short period of time, Jacob had no idea. The tight basque-waisted woolen jacket coated her torso like a thin layer of ink, enhancing her slender arms, the voluptuous swell of her breasts, the wasp-thin span of her waist, and her full hips. From there, a woolen skirt had been draped and puffed, interspersed with strips of velvet and flounces of cool, rich silk that fluttered to the floor and spilled behind her in a slight train. Atop her head, a dainty stovepipe-shaped hat had been balanced over the riotous coiffure of curls. A thin net veiling failed to obscure her face but provided a sense of mystique with its jet-studded web.

"Well, Jacob?" Alma demanded. "Isn't she the most stunning creation you've ever seen?"

"Stunning, just stunning," Amelia echoed.

Jacob couldn't respond to the elderly women. Not without revealing to them how the breath had been knocked from his body and a rampant awareness had begun to pulse through his veins. For the first time since beginning this charade, he knew Fiona had the power to make people believe in her false identity. *Jacob* believed in the vision he saw. He could very well imagine Fiona McFee to be cultured, educated, wealthy.

Spellbinding.

"Let's go." His voice emerged much gruffer than he had intended. Alma and Amelia glanced at him for having failed to comment upon Fiona's attire, and even Mr. Peebles appeared disappointed. But Jacob didn't have time to pander to their whims. They had trains to catch.

A collection of trunks filled with Fiona's extensive wardrobe had been piled in the center of the room. Leaving them there for the host of hotel servants to fetch, Jacob flung open the door and waited for the entourage to pass through.

Fiona paused in the threshold to mutter, "God protects children and the elderly. I hope He—"

"As well as his most perfect creations."

At his words, she met his gaze. In that instant, Jacob knew what he'd said was true and he could no longer hold on to the compliment she so richly deserved to hear.

"You *are* beautiful, Fiona."

Her eyes widened, becoming a dark, slumberous mixture of blue and brown.

"Mr. Peebles made this—"

"Mr. Peebles merely set the frame to the portrait." Unable to help himself, he touched her cheek, remembering her passion, her giving, her devotion. "You are *beautiful,* Fiona. Especially in blue."

With that, he took her hand and laced his fingers between her own. Drawing her slowly behind him, he led her down the stairs. "Let's be on our way. After all, we've a gambler to snare."

Her eyes sparkled in a way that made him suddenly uneasy. "Yes, we've a gambler to snare."

Her skirts lapped over the carpeted treads as she made her way. Jacob remained one step behind, his hand resting on the reassuring length of his pistol partially hidden by his jacket.

Once at the bottom, she joined the Beasley sisters, her carriage regal. "Ladies . . . I believe we all have a train to catch. Shall we?"

She swept from the lobby out of doors, leaving Jacob to make arrangements for the transport of their luggage and the payment of the suite. By the time he'd finished, he discovered that Fiona, her chaperones, and her tailor had hired a carriage and were about to depart.

"We'll meet you at the station, Mr. Grey," she intoned with great dignity, signaling to the driver to pull away from the curb.

Jacob opened his mouth to order her to stay, but he found himself confronting little more than dust. Damn her hide, what was she up to? She *knew* he was supposed to remain with her. Especially now, after all that had happened.

Mounting his own horse, he arrived at the station house mere minutes behind his charge, but Fiona was nowhere to be found.

The fact caused a niggling worry to take root. Jacob was not a man prone to panic. He'd been entangled in situations just as life-threatening and stressful. But after thirty minutes, with the departure of the train imminent and still no sign of Fiona, he felt a measure of dread drop in his stomach like a stone.

Had she changed her mind? Had the death of her father undermined her determination? They'd buried him that morning in a small grassy churchyard on the outskirts of town. Although she'd displayed a quiet grief, there had been no outbursts, no bouts of histrionics.

"We've got to load, Jacob," Rusty murmured at his shoulder.

"Where's Fiona?"

"She isn't in the car?"

"No." He scoured the platform, but amidst the swirl of humanity, he saw no amber curls, no navy suit. "Spread out. Find her!"

Rusty signaled unobtrusively to the many deputies lining the siding. Jacob knew they would be scouring the area like the well-trained experts they were. If she was anywhere nearby, they would find her.

"Jacob, when would you like Fiona to board?"

He whirled to find Alma Beasley standing behind him, her chest puffed out like a pigeon, her eyes glittering with her final duties as Fiona's protector.

"Where in the *hell* have you been?"

"In the ladies' waiting room, of course. Fiona insisted on treating us to a cup of tea."

The ladies' waiting room. He'd never thought Fiona would have even known about such a thing, let alone made use of it.

"Take me to her," he growled.

Alma's brows lifted ever so slightly, but she didn't comment. Indeed, her eyes twinkled in hidden amusement. She made her way through the crowd, into the milling station, and across the scuffed and scarred parquet floor.

"The . . . Widow McFee is a charming woman, Jacob. Absolutely charming." She cast him a quick glance. "I'm pleased to see that you've found yourself a nice young girl."

Jacob meant to refute her statement—he truly did—but at that precise second, he peered across the room to see the moment he had anticipated and dreaded unfolding in front of his very eyes. Fiona stepped from the curtained partition of the ladies' waiting room, followed immediately by the diminutive Miss Amelia. In her hands, Fiona balanced her reticule, an empty bandbox, and a pastry bag. Much to his horror, he saw the way she stepped forward, turned slightly to say something to Mr. Peebles, who'd been sitting on the bench next to the door, and bumped straight into the passing form of Mr. Darby Kensington.

Disregarding Alma Beasley and her resulting comment, Jacob pushed forward, moving as quickly as he could, but his limbs seemed to be mired in quicksand. He saw Fiona's mouth purse in distress, her gaze flick to the person responsible, then her mouth firm and her chin harden. As if moving in a daze, she bent to gather her scattered belongings at the same time the elegant man beside her knelt to help.

Jacob saw Kensington look down. Then the oddest thing occurred. He saw the watch chain draped across her waist, and he stumbled slightly, the blood leaving his cheeks, his hands clenching around his walking cane, but Jacob could see no reason for the reaction.

Closing the distance between them, it was Jacob who helped Fiona to her feet. Jacob who gathered her scattered packages, then swept a proprietary arm around her waist.

"Are you ready, Mrs. McFee? Let's go. Goodbye, ladies, Peebles, thanks for all your help."

Allowing no response, he left Mr. Peebles and the Beasleys to salvage the situation. He dragged her through the station house. The train outside huffed and sputtered. Engineers and porters scrambled over the brick walkway, calling out their final boarding warnings.

Heading straight for the last passenger car, Jacob called orders to Rusty as the man hurried toward him. "I've found her. Get the men on board and tell them to take their positions." Then he pulled Fiona aboard and slammed the door behind him.

* * *

Alma and Amelia Beasley stood open-mouthed on the walkway, watching as Jacob barricaded their charge in the ornate private railway car.

"What do you suppose is wrong?" Amelia asked.

"I think he was irritated that we took time for tea."

"Ahh. What do you suppose he's up to now?"

"Judging by his expression, I doubt it was a bit of kiss and cuddle."

Mr. Peebles stared at them both in amazement.

"Come, Mr. Peebles, don't be so surprised. You must have sensed what was going on," Alma chided. "The two were meant for each other, I—" She broke off suddenly, grasping her sister's arm. "Amelia, look."

By the barest tipping of her head, she motioned down the line of cars to a band of horsemen who had just arrived. In a concerted movement, the doors of one of the boxcars opened, a ramp was shoved into place, and the men boarded. Despite the heat of the morning, they were nearly completely covered in dusters and hats and jackets.

"Alma, what are you staring at?"

"The tall one at the end. Do you see him?"

"I don't—"

"Don't you remember, Amelia? That affair five years ago in Madison?"

Amelia gasped. "Krupp? It couldn't be. It looks like him, and yet . . ." The train puffed and panted, building up steam. "Drat it all, there isn't time to warn Jacob."

"Come along, Amelia. You too, Mr. Peebles. We've got to board one of those cars!"

"But Alma! We haven't any tickets for this excursion! Jacob is sending us home!"

"He can deal with that problem when he finds us."

When Alma began running, Amelia called, "Sister? What are you doing?"

"We've got to get to the baggage cars, Amelia. We've got to be on that train!"

* * *

As the locomotive jerked to a start, Jacob pushed Fiona into an overstuffed settee, bracing his arms on the sides to pin her in. "What in the *hell* were you doing in the waiting room? I told you to go immediately to this car!"

She folded her hands, remaining mulishly silent.

"Answer me!"

"I thought it best to make contact early, so that Kensington would know I was on this train."

"Why was he so rattled when he saw you?"

She shrugged. "I've no idea."

The car pulsed with the *clickity-clack* of the wheels rushing over the track.

"So what do you intend to do now that he's seen you?"

She stood, slipping a jeweled hatpin free. The action should have been completely innocent. Instead, there was something sensual about the way she lifted her arms and drew the slender shaft bit by tantalizing bit from the curls of her hair.

"Nothing."

"Then why approach him?"

She removed her hat and tossed it at his feet, reaching for the buttons of her jacket. "So the man will spend his time thinking of me."

The jet discs came free with exquisite slowness, making him think of anything but a wayward gambler.

"Why?"

"Why not?"

He didn't have an answer for that one. Nor did he have the wherewithal to think of one. She had slipped the garment from her shoulders, exposing a delicate silk blouse beneath. One that was so sheer, he could see each tuck and ruffle of lace stitched to her underthings.

Seeking some measure of control, he jumped to his feet, moving to the sideboard under the window, where he poured himself a drink.

"The Beasleys—"

"Are on the next train to Madison, Jacob. You told me so yourself."

Damn. In the haze of desire beginning to flood his body, he'd forgotten that the women wouldn't be accompanying her. He turned from the sideboard, only to find that she was right behind him. Offering him a smile—a tempting, all-knowing smile—she pushed his jacket from his shoulders, then drew his head down for a frantic kiss. When he would have slowed the nature of the embrace, she broke free, shaking her head.

"No. I need you, Jacob. I *need* you."

Not allowing him to respond, she wrenched at the placket of his shirt, popping the buttons and sending them willy-nilly onto the patterned carpet.

"Fiona?"

She placed her fingers over his lips. "No. Don't talk, don't object. Don't stop."

Object? Stop? Why would he? How could he? Especially when she stepped free to unbutton her skirt, her bustle, and pushed them to the floor. Hastily, urgently, she stripped off her blouse, foundations, and underpinnings, until she stood in front of him in nothing more than a few wisps of China silk. A delicate camisole, split pantaloons, and clocked hose. When she would have removed them as well, he said, "No. Please."

The words were garbled to his own ears, but they caused her to smile. Taking his hand, she led him to the rear of the train, to the dim, shuttered bedchamber draped in maroon velvet. Pushing him onto the bed, she paused long enough to remove his boots, his socks, his trousers. Then, straddling him, she whispered, "We've five hours to the first stop, lawman. I hope you prove up to the test."

Her kiss was fierce. Jacob had never seen her this wild, this needy. It was infinitely arousing, infinitely beguiling. Fiona became the aggressor, the instigator. Her hands roamed his body, searching out the sensitive hollows and secret nerve endings. He gasped, all reason fleeing his body, all thought of gamblers and vigilante groups. There was only her. Fiona.

She shifted, grasping his hardness, rubbing, squeezing, tormenting him no end.

"You want me, lawman."

He could only nod.

"You *want* me."

"Yes."

"Then you will have me, again and again and again." With that, she impaled herself, her head flinging back, her eyes closing, her body shifting in a rhythm as old as time itself. He bucked beneath her, the world spinning away, coalescing into one thought, one searing idea.

Sweet heaven above. How could he ever let this woman go?

17

As the train began to slow, Fiona had the distinct feeling that she was readying herself for battle. She'd washed in the tiny tub in the bathing cubical at the end of the car. Following the regimen the Beasleys had taught her, she'd perfumed, powdered, and coiffed herself, then had dressed, layer by layer, piece by piece. Finally emerging from the bedroom to the sitting area, she paused for effect.

"Well? What do you think?"

Jacob peered over the edge of the newspaper he'd been reading. Fiona could feel the heat of his gaze like a finger, trailing over the black and gold brocade of her hightop shoes, the dull gold underskirt, the heavy black, floor-length jacket edged in swirls of soutache braid and jet beads. Above, her hair had been swept into a bevy of curls on top of her head, and a tiny black bonnet with huge silk sunflowers perched coquettishly over one brow.

When he didn't speak, she smiled. "Stars and garters, Jacob Grey. D'ye mean t' tell me that fer the first time in ages, I've struck ye dumb?"

Fiona felt a pang of surprise when the lilt of her own

brogue sounded odd to her ears. She'd spent so much time eradicating it from her speech that now it felt like it belonged to someone else.

"You're beautiful," he finally managed to utter. "I keep thinking you can't top what you've already done and then . . . you surprise me again." It was not a poetic pronouncement by any means, but a rush of warmth filled her veins nonetheless. The train lurched, then ground to a stop. The time for Fiona's masquerade had begun.

A soft tap at the door to their car brought them both back to the matter at hand. Dropping the newspaper, Jacob eased open the portal, then allowed another gentleman to enter.

The stranger was tall, dark, with startling blue eyes and a boyish smile. He was elegantly attired in a dark frockcoat and bowler, a gold watch chain slung across his flat stomach.

"Fiona, I'd like to introduce Ethan McGuire, the man who has been supplying our bankroll. Ethan, this is Fiona McFee."

"So, Miss McFee. Are you ready for your skirmish with Darby Kensington?"

"Of course."

The smile Fiona flashed Ethan McGuire was a clear mixture of gamin playfulness and coy seduction. It pleased her no end when he blinked and held out his arm to her in something of a daze. Apparently the Beasleys had taught her well.

The heat of the evening hit her the moment she left the railway car. Stepping into the sunshine, she opened her parasol, shielding her face from the worst of the sunlight. Within the next few minutes the die would be cast as to whether or not she'd become "lady" enough to complete this assignment.

Her shoulders drew back ever so slightly and her resolve stiffened. After all that had happened to her father, to her, to Jacob, she would not fail.

Ethan glanced at her questioningly from beneath the

brim of his bowler, but she refused to let even a shred of nervousness show in her stance. "What do you suppose will be on the menu?" she asked idly, tipping her head toward the narrow, brick-front restaurant tucked next to the station house.

Ethan grinned. "Perhaps a little crow for all those who doubted you could pull this off, Fiona."

She tossed him a flirtatious smile. "Perhaps you're right."

Gathering her skirts ever so slightly in one glove-covered hand, she made her way toward the café. Every movement was calculated to cause a bit of a stir. The swish of her skirts, the exaggerated twitch of her bustle, the oh-so-subtle hint of clocked stockings above her brocaded boots. That, combined with her apparent indifference as well as her dashing partner and the evident display of a bodyguard, would inevitably garner more than her share of attention.

They slipped into the cool interior of the railway eating establishment. Most of the passengers who had purchased tourist excursion fares were already seated at the long banks of trestle tables set with linen, china, and crystal. A woman in a black gown and a starched apron approached. When she would have seated them at one of the long benches, Fiona shook her head. Tugging ever so softly on Ethan's sleeve, she forced him to bend down and murmured softly in his ear.

He straightened to say, "The Widow McFee feels . . . uncomfortable sitting at the same table with so many people. She wondered if she might sit . . ."—he scanned the room—"over there." He pointed to a small table in the corner, well away from the light and nearly obscured from the other diners.

The woman appeared surprised but did not demur, leading the way. Fiona deftly took a seat in a place where she would be half hidden from view. Ethan sat directly across from her, while Jacob, the mere "hired help" in this charade, took one of the chairs at the end of the trestle table.

Fiona saw the way his brow lifted ever so slightly, clearly relaying his message: "What in the world are you up to?" He didn't need to say the words, as she knew what he was thinking.

There was no way to explain, no way to relay to him that of all the lessons she'd learned from the Beasleys, this was the most powerful. No man can resist a mystery. She'd already been introduced to Darby Kensington. He knew who she was, what she claimed to be. Soon Ethan McGuire would introduce her into Kensington's gaming circle and she'd be ready to snare him.

She knew the moment he entered the establishment. She could feel it in the prickling at the nape of her neck, but she refused to turn and acknowledge him. She remained calm, unperturbed, reading the hand-lettered parchment with its list of the dishes that would be served that evening.

"He's here," Ethan said, so softly, so casually, he could have been remarking on the food.

"I know."

The meal proved to be delicious in more ways than one. The creamed asparagus soup was hot and spicy, the beef tender, the steamed vegetables divine. But what proved the most tantalizing of all was that Fiona knew she was being watched the entire time. Her quarry had taken the bait.

Dessert was served just as the sun dipped beyond the horizon. A young girl in a crisply ironed gown went about the room, lighting the lamps on the tables, while a pair of boys served melon balls adorned with sprigs of mint.

Fiona shook her head, signaling that she would not take dessert, then dabbed her mouth with her napkin and gathered her parasol and reticule. "I think I'll get a breath of air, Ethan."

He made an effort to rise, but she waved him away. "Stay. Have your melon, a bit of port, and a cigar. Mr.

Grey will accompany me." Standing, she beckoned to Jacob.

Throwing his own napkin to the table, he rose and went to her side, ushering her out of the café with all the diffident respect of an employee.

They began to stroll slowly toward the front of the train, Fiona a half step ahead of her bodyguard.

"I think you've piqued Kensington's curiosity," Jacob said quietly.

As Fiona heard the jingling of the bell attached to the restaurant door, she smiled. "I know."

They paced the length of the train, then turned again, making their way back to their own car. There, not more than three yards away, was Darby Kensington.

Fiona felt Jacob stiffen and knew that his hand had immediately shifted to rest on his revolver. Darby had also seen the instinctive reaction, if the flick of his gaze was anything to go by.

"Come now, Mr. Grey," she drawled in a silky voice, which was just loud enough to carry to the gambler's ears. "We've encountered Mr. Kensington before. Surely you don't consider him a threat."

Kensington offered her a slow grin, one that did not quite reach his eyes. "And here I thought you didn't remember me, Mrs. McFee."

"I make it a point to remember anyone who might prove to be a future opponent, Mr. Kensington."

"You flatter me."

She raised a brow in a haughty manner she'd once seen a shopkeeper employ. "Not at all, Mr. Kensington." The words were said with just the right degree of disdain to assure him that she didn't really care whether or not their paths ever crossed again. Then she walked past him without another glance.

It must have taken him a few seconds to realize that he'd been none too subtly snubbed. She heard the quick clack of bootheels as he hurried to follow her.

"Don't you find it a bit of a coincidence that we're here, together, on the same excursion, Mrs. McFee?"

She paused then, her heart thumping—partly in nervousness, partly in exhilaration, knowing that she would have to guard her tongue against the brogue.

"No, Mr. Kensington. I don't find it a coincidence at all." She paused for effect. "I am accustomed to having men such as you follow me in one way or another." And with that parting remark, she turned and sauntered away, knowing that in Kensington's eyes, she'd just become one of the most irresistible of all types of women. One who felt she could not be obtained.

"Stay close to me, Amelia, Mr. Peebles. We can't chance being seen."

Alma slid open the baggage-car door and attempted to clamber somewhat awkwardly from the edge. Seeing her predicament, Walter Peebles touched her arm. "Allow me."

He jumped to the ground, then turned, holding up his arms to help them alight. Alma looked at Amelia, Amelia at Alma.

"Ooo, such a gentleman," they cooed in unison.

Once they'd managed to find firm footing on the earth again, they tiptoed down the length of the train, using the side that faced away from the platform and the railway station.

"What are we planning to do again, Alma?"

Alma sighed, regretting the fact that Amelia's memory was incredibly short. "Most everyone is still eating at the café. We need to make our way through the train and see if we can't scrounge up something to eat. We'll need something to last us until Kansas, where the first horse-and-buggy excursion is scheduled to take place. You and I both heard Jacob talking to his men about the prison break. *If* the man we saw was Krupp, I doubt he'll show himself before then. He would have to wait for the confusion of a larger station, where there aren't so many railway officials checking everyone's dining tickets. Once we know it's him for certain, we'll warn Jacob."

"What if it wasn't Krupp we saw?"

Alma thought a moment. "Then we'll wait until Denver. That way we'll be too far on the road for Jacob to send us back. We'll just reassume our positions as Fiona's chaperones and head home to Madison at another time."

"Oh."

They crept through the darkness, making their way to the first sitting car. Finding it empty except for an old man at one end who snored, they climbed aboard, creeping down the aisles, peeking into bakery boxes, haversacks, and wicker baskets, stealing an apple here, a biscuit there, and slipping it into their satchels. While they looked, Mr. Peebles kept watch. Only a few minutes had passed before he hissed, "The passengers are starting to come back."

"Rats," Alma muttered under her breath. "Let's go, Amelia."

"But I just—"

"We don't have time to dally!"

"But I found a—"

"Just take whatever it is and let's get out of here!"

Alma grabbed her sister's elbow, tugging her to the rear platform, where Mr. Peebles waited to help them take the steps to the ground. Then they were half walking, half running back to the baggage car.

"Whew!" Alma breathed as she shut the door, closing them all into a thick blackness. "We made it."

Mr. Peebles guffawed, then choked it back, lowering his voice to a whisper. "I can't believe I'm doing this."

Alma flung her hand out into the blackness, patting until she found the rough, woolen fabric of his sleeve. "We're sorry we dragged you into our little set of worries."

"No. No! I'm having the time of my life, I assure you."

There was the rasp of a sulphur-tipped match, and Amelia held the sputtering light aloft. "Alma!" she blurted in shock.

Glancing down, Alma realized she hadn't placed her hand on Mr. Peebles's arm, as she'd supposed. Since all three of them were kneeling on the floor, her aim had been considerably lower.

"My apologies, Mr. Peebles."

"None needed, Miss Alma."

Amelia yelped and blew out the match, as it threatened to singe her fingers. There was a moment of silence, the rustling of her reticule, then she lit another.

"What did you find to eat?" Mr. Peebles asked. "I know it isn't polite to enquire, but I'm famished!"

Alma pried open her carpetbag, revealing a veritable feast inside. "I've two apples, a bag of raisins, three biscuits, a loaf of bread, a wedge of cheese, and a crock of cider. Amelia? What have you got?"

The match puttered out. A beat of silence filled the car.

"Amelia?"

"Well, I—"

"Don't tell me you didn't find anything."

"No, I—"

"Amelia, light another match, for heaven's sake!"

The rasp of the matchstick was followed by the pungent scent of sulphur. Amelia's withered face swam into view, her brow clearly furrowed in distress.

"Amelia?"

"I failed to find any food."

Alma's brow creased in annoyance and she eyed the bulging sides of Amelia's bag. "Then what, pray tell, did you find? A cat?"

"Well, no, I . . ." Sighing, she opened her bag one-handed. "I suppose one of Jacob's deputies brought it with him. The careless man left it alone and unguarded under his seat." She hurriedly added, "It was ours to begin with, so I didn't see why I couldn't take it back!"

"Good heavens, what have you done?" Alma leaned forward to peer into the depths of the carryall. She drew back again, drawing an incredulous breath. "Our dynamite?"

"Um-hmm."

Alma grinned and repeated with great satisfaction. "Our *dynamite!*"

Peebles looked from one woman to the other in disbelief, then looked for himself. Even in the dim light, he paled most noticeably.

"For God's sake, Miss Amelia," he squeaked. "Blow out the match!"

Fiona waited over a day for her next encounter with Darby Kensington. She and Jacob stayed in the railway car, making love, talking, idling their time away—but it was not a comfortable situation. The seriousness of their assignment hung over their heads like a sword until they soon lapsed into silence, Jacob staring out the window, Fiona shuffling cards, playing solitaire, and honing her skills.

During this time, Ethan engaged Kensington in a few lighthearted games of poker. He drank enough to appear a little "loose" and answered a few questions about the mysterious widow.

Kensington was interested, there was no doubt about it. Maybe his pride was partly to blame. After all, she'd boldly stated that she didn't consider him to be her equal in cards. Fiona, however, would have added that she thought his ego was also involved. He'd seen the way she gave little actual attention to Ethan and even less to her bodyguard. He was probably thinking that he alone could snare such an aloof woman. He was accustomed to women flocking to him, she was sure. To have one who remained clearly uninterested in his charm must have irritated him to no end.

Finally, Fiona dressed and readied herself. The train was scheduled to stop in several minutes, and she would encounter Kensington again.

She wore rust for the occasion. The suit was of China silk, puffed and draped and ruffled from the waist down, and so form-fitting above that she could scarcely breathe. Delicate black lace dripped from her neck and wrists like silk cobwebs, while a fragile layer of fringe edged the flounces.

This was her business ensemble. The Beasleys had

chosen it specifically because of its severity—a severity that only served to enhance the womanly curves it cradled.

Lifting her skirt, she tucked the derringer into the top of her garter. Jacob's brows rose.

"Just in case," she murmured.

He didn't object.

With Jacob as her escort, she waited until the next rest stop, then made her way into one of the parlor cars, knowing in an instant that she had captured Kensington's attention. She sat at one of the linen-covered tables, Jacob seated behind her at another table, ever watchful, ever cautious. He spoke softly, looking out the window as if the topic of his dialogue was the weather.

"So far the only currency Darby has used has been real. Ethan has been able to win enough against the man to determine that."

"Is that against his usual pattern?"

Jacob's head shook ever so slightly. "He doesn't seem to use the phony stuff for what he considers 'petty gambling.' He saves that for the 'real' games."

"Then we shall have to see that he has more of a challenge, don't you think?"

Fiona withdrew a new package of cards from her reticule, breaking the seal with the tiny bone-handled knife enclosed in the manicure set the Beasleys had given her as a going-away present. How she missed the old gals, how she . . .

She glanced up, her gaze flicking to the window. She blinked.

"Jacob?"

He didn't look her way. "Is Kensington coming over?"

"No." She tilted her head in order to catch one last glimpse of an elderly pair of women hurrying down the length of the train. In seconds, they were obscured from view. "I thought you said you sent the Beasleys to Madison."

"I did. Why?"

She shook her head. She must have been mistaken. She must have grown so accustomed to their company that now she was associating anyone of advanced age with her friends.

"Good day, Mrs. McFee."

She froze for one split second, the low voice spilling over her with overt cultured charm. Fiona cursed herself. By allowing her attention to be swayed for one instant, Kensington had been able to approach without warning.

She took time in answering. Partly to prevent a bit of Irish from exploding from her lips. Partly to give her heart a chance to drop from her throat to its normal position in her chest.

"Mr. Kensington."

"Playing a bit of solitaire, I see. Such a boring game, don't you think?"

She didn't answer, and he sank uninvited into the chair beside her.

"Where's the challenge, where's the match of wits?"

She finally deigned to meet his gaze. "I take it that you wish to propose an alternate activity."

He offered her a grimace that was meant to show false modesty but that could not hide the greed in his eyes. "Perhaps a light game of poker."

She gathered the cards, tapping them into a neat stack. Her head tipped to one side as she considered the man opposite and determinedly ignored Jacob, who had grown still and tense behind her. The moment had come for Fiona to earn her pardon.

"I think not, Mr. Kensington." The gambler stiffened in affronted dignity, but she continued without a pause, "I never take any sort of card game lightly." She began to shuffle the deck with practiced ease. "If you wish to play with me, the stakes must be truly interesting—if not a bit . . . dangerous. It's the only way I do business, Mr. Kensington."

His lips twitched at the unexpected challenge.

"Very well, Mrs. McFee. Name your game."

"I believe poker would be amusing. Jacob," she called without turning, without taking her eyes from her opponent. "Would you be so kind as to retrieve the satchel with my chips and my gaming money? It seems that Mr. Kensington and I have decided to while away the afternoon matching wits."

"We've got to split up, each of us take one side of the train just in case." Alma ducked behind one of the boxcars, and faced her sister. "The excursion will resume in a quarter-hour. We've *got* to determine if the man we saw was Krupp."

"What makes you think he's going to show himself at *this* stop, Alma?" Amelia inquired, peering cautiously over her shoulder, afraid that Jacob would catch them before they had the proper information to arm themselves.

"Each time the train has taken on water and fuel, we've cracked open our own door and looked down the line. Did we see anything?"

"No."

"Exactly."

Amelia's brows pursed. "Exactly . . . what?"

"Horses."

"Beg pardon?"

"They loaded horses onto the boxcar, correct?"

"Ye-es."

"Well they've got to give them water, don't they? They can bring all the grain and hay they want, but the water would be too awkward and too heavy to bring along for an entire trip. Eventually they've got to run out of whatever emergency supplies they brought and bring their mounts to water." She pointed to the troughs not ten yards away from the boxcar where they believed Krupp was hiding. "Today would be the perfect opportunity."

Amelia brightened. "How clever you are, Sister!"

"Ladies."

The two women jumped, their hands going to their breasts. Alma whirled, glaring at the man who'd crept up behind them.

"Mr. Peebles. Please refrain from sneaking up on us unannounced. We're old women, you know."

"So sorry." He lowered his voice. "I found Jacob and Fiona. They're on one of the parlor cars." His brows waggled significantly. "She's playing cards with Mr. Kensington."

The two women gasped in pleasure. They'd already explained to Mr. Peebles the true nature of Fiona's assignment.

"Good. Good!" Alma took a deep breath. "The sooner they finish with that business, the sooner they can turn their attention to Krupp and—"

The words were jolted from her body when Amelia grasped her arm with a surprisingly vicelike pressure.

"Amelia! Kindly—"

"It's him, Alma!" There was no disguising the true fear in Amelia's tone. "It's him!"

Slowly, Alma turned. They'd been so involved in their conversation, they hadn't heard the boxcar door slide open or the ramp being put into place. But Amelia had noted the first man to pause at the top and survey the scene.

"Dear sweet heaven above," Alma whispered. The years might have hardened him, but there was no mistaking the square jaw, the lean figure.

"Ladies, is it . . ."

"Krupp," Amelia supplied breathlessly. "That man is Judge Krupp."

Ethan left his bag on the railway platform and made his way toward the parlor car. He'd been returning from the midday meal in the railway café, prepared to inform Jacob that Kensington hadn't appeared, when he'd glanced up and caught a peek of their quarry already

251

engaged in conversation with the Widow McFee. It had taken him little more than five minutes to pack and return.

He was just approaching the car when Jacob alighted. Seeing Ethan, he stopped until the man had a chance to catch up.

"She's done it, I do believe," Jacob said proudly. "I've just been sent to gather her chips and her money."

Ethan barely listened to what Jacob said. "I'm off," he stated bluntly.

"What the hell?"

He cocked a thumb at the pair on the train. "You asked me to come, introduce her to the proper climate of people, and whet Kensington's appetite. She's . . . whetted it herself," he said for want of a better word. When Jacob didn't seem to understand the significance of his explanation, he said, "Dammit, man! I've got a wife holed up in Madison about to have a baby at any minute, with the threat of Krupp appearing on her doorstep to exact revenge." As he spoke, he slowly made his way back to where he'd left his valise. "I'm going home."

Jacob opened his mouth as if to argue, then apparently changed his mind. "Take care of Lettie. Take care of them all."

Ethan retrieved his baggage. "You'll be back as soon as you've finished here." It wasn't a question.

Jacob's eyes glowed with an unholy light. "Krupp is far more of a concern for me than that fool," he said, indicating the gambler on the train.

"How's Fiona doing?"

An unwilling grin lit his lips. "It seems I underestimated our dear Fiona McFee. She's more of a lady than I've ever met. And her card skills are incredible. She's been practicing against me for days. I do believe she really can beat the tar out of him."

Ethan nodded in satisfaction. "Then I'll be seeing you soon." He held out his hand. "Good luck. And see that you hold her dear."

At the man's words, Jacob's brow rose questioningly.

"She's a special woman, Jacob. One in a million. And she loves you more than life itself. In my experience, a love like that is more precious than gold." Touching his finger to the brim of his hat in salute, he turned and strode toward the ticket house.

Jacob watched him go. Ethan's parting comment pricked his conscience. He knew the man was right— and if the truth were told, Jacob knew Fiona loved him. As much as he loved her.

The thought was sobering, astounding. It was the first time he'd even allowed himself to think such a thing. But it was true. He loved her. And suddenly he didn't care about the past or possible future repercussions. He only cared about her.

But first they had a gambler to catch.

Jacob quickly made his way to the private railway car, retrieving the bag that he and Fiona had packed so carefully the night before. As befitted her station, Fiona had several stacks of greenbacks and her own set of chips—bright wooden discs that he'd ordered painted with flowers and cherubs, more to annoy Kensington than for any other purpose. He knew it would grate on the man's nerves to play with such feminine frippery.

He turned, about to hurry back, when his eyes caught sight of a gold watch fob lying on the tatted runner of the bureau. His brow furrowed. It was the same piece of jewelry Fiona had been wearing that first day on the train. The same fob that had caused Kensington to react so strangely when he'd seen it.

Jacob paused, setting the case down. He picked up the fob. It was not entirely unusual to look at: oval-shaped, heavy, with an elaborate etching of filigree. It seemed completely out of character for Mickaleen McFee. In fact, Jacob couldn't remember the man ever having a watch. Had he stolen it? If so, why had it caused Kensington to take a second look, let alone stumble out of his usual charming role?

Slipping his thumbnail beneath the edge, Jacob pried it

open. In a single instant, his heart began to beat more quickly, his breathing to become shallow.

To Darby. From your father.

No.

The events of the past few weeks loomed into his consciousness. The way Kensington had always seemed one step ahead of them, Krupp's escape, the murders, the attempts at revenge.

His fingers closed over the fob, squeezing it so tightly that the etchings bit into his skin. Long ago, long before the Star Council had been formed, long before Jacob had become a deputy, there had been rumors. Judge Krupp had tried to run for state office, but a scandal had come to light about an incident in his past. Stories of an illegitimate son had surfaced, then disappeared just as quickly as they'd come. At the time, the people of the district had assumed that the rumors had been nothing more than a political smear campaign.

But what if the tales were true? Dear heaven. What if Darby Kensington was Krupp's son?

Shoving the fob deep in his pocket, Jacob grabbed the case and began to run. He had to get Fiona off the train. Every muscle of his body, every shred of instinct, every cell of his brain shouted a single warning:

Trap!

18

THE TRAIN BEGAN TO HUFF, SPILLING STEAM AND SOOT INTO the late-afternoon air.

"No. No!" The Beasleys looked at one another in horror. They hadn't had time to warn Jacob, and the train was preparing to leave.

"We could run, Alma."

"Neither of us are in any condition to run all the way to the parlor car. Besides"—she gestured as Krupp's men tugged the last of the horses onto the train and slid the ramp inside, slamming the door—"they can't do anything until the next stop. We'll warn him then." She began to hurry to their own car, Mr. Peebles and her sister scurrying behind her. They were nearly there, nearly safe, when Alma made her big mistake. She glanced back, just once, to see if Amelia was able to keep up. Without warning, she ran head-on into someone coming from the opposite direction.

The breath left her body in a whoosh and she fell to the ground in a heap of petticoats and ruffles. Looking up, up, up, up, she gasped in horror when she came face to face with Ethan McGuire.

"What the hell?" he muttered, staring at them all in disbelief.

The train began to shimmy. There wasn't time.

"Get him, Amelia!"

Without hesitation, Amelia swung her bag at the man. The solid thump of the horseshoe she kept inside for protection connected with Ethan's skull, and he wilted.

Alma scrambled to her feet. "Leave him and get on the train. Hurry! If that thing gets going any faster, we'll never be able to jump on!"

The train was already beginning to ease away from the station as Jacob made his way to the parlor car. Dammit! He didn't even have time to warn his men to be on the lookout for Krupp. They'd all assumed that the man was still in Chicago, still wreaking havoc, but Jacob knew right to his bones that the man was somewhere near. He would have to wait until the deputies made their periodic sweeps through the cars. Bit by bit, they could pass the word.

The huge iron wheels began to spin, and Jacob was forced to jog, then run, grabbing the railing of the parlor car and swinging aboard. Pausing for a moment, his back to the painted wood, he closed his eyes, trying to think. It was too late to get Fiona off and whisk her to safety. He would have to play out the charade they'd already started. A little after ten, the excursion would stop again for a late-evening meal. As soon as they'd come to a halt, he would send her home.

Then he'd take Kensington himself and wait for Krupp to appear.

"You play very well, Mrs. McFee."

There was no denying the hard edge to Kensington's voice. For the past hour, he'd been losing. Badly. With each mile, each clack of the train, his composure had slipped, revealing a man who found it difficult to believe that he could be bested by a woman.

Jacob stood up and made his way to the rear of the car, where a sideboard held a collection of cookies and tarts, urns of hot tea and coffee, and a bottle of brandy. One of the porters had just brought the light repast, then left again, heading forward.

"Tea, Mrs. McFee?"

"Thank you, Jacob, I do believe I will."

He heard the rustle of silk as she got up. "Mr. Kensington? Would you care for some tea as well?"

"No. Thank you." His tone was barely civil.

Jacob couldn't miss the twinkle of delight in Fiona's eyes as she joined him.

"He's a bit of a poor sport, isn't he?" she murmured for Jacob's ears alone. She reached for a cup and saucer, holding it out for Jacob to fill. "I'm not sure, but I do believe he started slipping the phony stuff in about an hour ago."

Jacob didn't respond. He found himself staring at Fiona as if he'd never seen her. Dear heaven, what had he done? He'd put this woman in terrible danger. This woman that he . . .

Loved?

No, it couldn't be. He cared for her, yes. He thought of her constantly. But *love?*

A tenderness stole into his soul. A longing. Then, at long last, an acceptance. He loved her. For so long he'd ignored the signs, ignored the increasing worry he'd felt for her safety. He'd thought he'd felt little more than passion, but when she lay in his arms, the emotions he experienced went much deeper than that. Much, much deeper.

"Fiona?" It was a bare breath of sound. He had to tell her, he had to confess his love.

"Jacob, what's wrong? Kensington is staring at you."

In a flash, the significance of his surroundings crashed around him, and all the worries came rushing back. Now wasn't the time for intimate confidences. But soon. Soon.

It was growing dark outside, enough so that his own

reflection stared at him from the window. His and Kensington's. He couldn't miss the way the gambler kept casting furtive glances outside. Why?

"Didn't you hear me?"

"Mmm?"

"I think we've caught him red-handed, Jacob."

"Of course. Good job."

Her brows rose. "You could show a little more enthusiasm for the prospect."

"Fiona." He touched her waist, turning her away from Kensington. "I want you to listen very carefully. In about an hour, the train will . . ." His words petered away when he thought he heard an odd noise coming from outside. He paused, waited. When it didn't occur again, he said, "I want you to—"

Thump, thump-thump-thump-thump.

Jacob's hand tightened automatically. The noise was muted but unmistakable, coming from overhead.

"What—"

"Shh."

His brow creased, trying to pinpoint what could be causing such a commotion. Before his brain could grasp the significance, the door burst open, revealing an armed man. Behind him, two other men were tugging at the hitch.

Kensington stood, bumping the table and sending chips cascading to the floor.

"Come on, Fiona!" Jacob grasped her hand, pulling her toward the rear door, but an abrupt jarring caused them to stumble. The parlor car and the rest of the railway cars behind them had been successfully unhitched from the main portion of the train. Without the impetus of the engine, the wheels began to lose speed.

"Dammit all to hell," Jacob muttered under his breath, glancing out one of the windows. "As soon as we slow down enough, I want you to jump."

She looked out, seeing the rocky banks of the track, the scrub oak and weeds. "I will not."

"Fiona, we haven't got time to argue!"

"He's right, you know," a tall figure said after flinging open the rear door and stepping inside. He spoke again, his low voice silky smooth and filled with menace: "You haven't any time left at all."

Jacob touched Fiona's arm, his fingers digging into her skin, warning her to keep quiet as they confronted the tall, gray-haired man who held them in the sights of his revolver.

Jacob took a deep breath to calm his pounding pulse. "Hello, Krupp." He nodded to a second man standing just behind his nemesis. "Stone."

Krupp's lips tilted in a semblance of a smile, but there was no warmth behind it, only a calculated cruelty. "Why look, Gerald. If it isn't Marshal Jacob Grey. Fancy meeting you here. How many years has it been?" His brows furrowed in open hatred. "How many years since you betrayed me?"

Before Fiona knew what he meant to do, Jacob dodged toward The Judge, but Stone intervened, bludgeoning him over the ear with the hilt of his rifle.

Jacob crumpled to the ground, and Krupp looked at Fiona. "Would you care to try anything as well?"

She shook her head. Her breath came in short pants. Saints above, where were Jacob's men? She knew a fair portion of them had been assigned to the baggage cars and the passenger cars. She'd seen the way they occasionally passed through the parlor car. How had Krupp and his cohorts managed to circumvent their preventive measures?

"If you're waiting for the other deputies to save you, then don't bother to waste your time. We took control of the locomotive just outside of Bennington. Twenty minutes ago, we cut the caboose and the baggage car full of the other deputies loose. As you saw, we then separated you from the rest of the train. Even if the lawmen riding in the passenger cars saw what had occurred, they've no way to get here in time. As for the guards posted to watch you personally . . ." He shrugged. "I'm so sorry to inform you that they won't be warning anyone of anything ever again."

A shiver ran up Fiona's spine. In one bald statement, this man had shown her how cool he could be. How calculated. She stared at him long and hard, wanting to imprint upon her memory the face of the person responsible for the death of her father.

"Tie them up."

Jacob was hauled to his feet. He moaned, weaving. Blood ran from a gash beneath his hair, down his neck, to be soaked up by the fabric of his collar. Fiona had to fight the urge to rush to him, to tend to his wound. Such actions would only result in Krupp's amusement, she was sure. Besides which, she knew that to examine the full extent of Jacob's injuries would unsettle her completely. She had to keep her wits. Jacob was fine—he *had* to be fine. Nothing could happen to him. She wouldn't be able to bear it otherwise.

The wheels squeaked to a slow halt, then shivered as the fractured portion of the train came to a complete stop. After the pulse and pant of the engine and the clacking of the track beneath the iron wheels, the silence was overwhelming.

"Secure them," Krupp ordered again. "I don't want any more outbursts like the last one."

A pair of filthy men who had helped cripple the car stepped forward. Fiona's hands were bound together at her waist, and looking at Jacob, she saw that he'd suffered a similar fate. Then, a rough hand at their spines, they were pushed outside.

Another half-dozen horsemen were assembling in the deserted pasture. They unloaded their mounts from a boxcar toward the end of the string of cars. When they saw Krupp, they gathered close.

"What are you trying to do, Krupp?" Jacob asked when they were surrounded by a circle of Star Council members.

Krupp made a *tsk*-ing noise with his tongue. "Patience, Grey. Patience. It is a quality I was taught all too well in prison. I do believe that you need to learn that some things are worth waiting a lifetime to obtain." He touched Fiona's cheek. "Such as finding one's true love. Securing wealth. Success." His fingers became cruel as they bit into her chin. "And revenge."

Shoving her away, he strode to the horse that had obviously been prepared for his benefit. "Put them on that sway-backed nag."

An old, desperately balking mount was led forward. Except for a bridle, it wore no other tack, not even a blanket. Jacob was pushed onto it first, then Fiona was put behind him. Having her hands bound made it difficult for her to keep her seat, but at least her wrists had been tied in front of her body and not behind, so she was able to tuck her fingers into Jacob's waistband for balance.

Krupp nodded in approval, then inched his own gelding forward so that he was only a scant distance away. Leaning forward, he sneered at Jacob in open disgust. "Over ten years ago, I tried to teach you something, Jacob. I tried to teach you how to be a lawman. I obviously failed. You turned on me. On me and your own kind. Because of that, I think it's time you learned a lesson of another sort: What it's like to be a wanted man."

With that, he slapped the old mare on the rump, causing it to jump, jog a few feet, then prance skittishly in a semicircle.

"Twenty minutes, Jacob. You have twenty minutes to make some sort of escape. Then we'll see how well you like being hunted."

Alma, Amelia, and Mr. Peebles dodged into the baggage car. Pushing the door closed except for a slit, Alma glanced at her companions, trembling with a combination of nerves, exertion, and fear.

261

"What are we going to do?" Amelia was the first to speak. Her normally pale complexion had adopted an even whiter cast.

"We've got to fight back!" Alma proclaimed.

"But how?"

Mr. Peebles cleared his throat. "If I might make a suggestion . . ."

"I doubt there's a gun to be had in all these trunks and satchels."

"Ladies, if I could . . ."

"We'll have to find something."

"There's over a dozen men out there!"

"We've never been one to give up on a fight. Are you going to start now, Amelia?"

"Alma, apologize at—"

"Ladies!"

Mr. Peebles's violent whisper broke into the gathering argument. "We haven't time for bickering."

Amelia blinked and sighed. "Why, Mr. Peebles. How domineering you've become."

Mr. Peebles ignored them. "Where are your things?"

"We left them by the door over there." Amelia pointed to the spot.

"With the dynamite? You haven't thrown it away, have you?"

Alma gave him a withering look. "We might be advanced in years, Mr. Peebles, but we are not fools. Of course we kept it. We *do* have gophers, you know."

He blinked at that odd statement, then waved it away. "Don't you see? We can use the dynamite!"

Alma frowned. "No. There's no way to light the sticks. They are useless, utterly useless without some sort of fuse. We finally put them in a barrel of burning trash and rolled it onto the track."

"Amelia, go get the bag," Mr. Peebles ordered. Then he turned to Alma. "When you blew up the station, was there anything with the sticks? Pieces of fuse, odd sorts of equipment?"

"Well, yes."

"Then we've got all we need, ladies. I'll show you how to set the fuses. All we need are some matches."

"I've got matches!" Amelia volunteered, returning with the bulging bag.

"We are well aware of that," Alma muttered as they hurried to open the carpetbag.

Amelia asked, "Mr. Peebles, how do you know so much about this?"

He grinned in clear delight. "Why ladies, before deciding to work toward my lifelong dream of tailoring, I had another position. That of blasting tunnels for the railroad."

"What are you doing?"

Fiona nudged Jacob when he urged the nag into a brisker walk, all the while turning the animal resolutely toward the train. They'd gone little more than a quarter of a mile, yet he was heading the mare to the point where they'd started.

"They expect us to run, Fiona."

"Let's not disappoint them!"

"If we try to escape we haven't got a ghost of a chance. We have no weapons, no food, no water, no real knowledge of our surroundings. Krupp and his men obviously came into this situation well prepared. Our only defense is to take them by surprise and double back."

"Jacob . . ."

"I know what I'm doing, Fiona."

She frowned at his brusque defense. Didn't he know she was aware of that? Didn't he know that she wasn't afraid for herself but for him? She'd seen the murderous light in Krupp's eyes and the fanaticism to be found in his associates. None of these men would take kindly to having their plans rearranged.

But Jacob refused to reconsider. The mare they rode continued toward the train, sometimes walking, sometimes jogging, never breaking into anything faster than an uncomfortable trot.

"As soon as we reach that ridge up ahead, I want you to get down. Hide there until I—"

"No." Her fingers dug into his skin.

"Fiona, do as I say."

"No. I go with you or neither of us goes."

"Fiona, I won't—"

Whatever he'd been about to say was completely drowned out by a horrible explosion. Jacob immediately dove from the horse, dragging Fiona with him. After a wild snort, the mare reared, then galloped off in the opposite direction, its reins trailing in the dust.

Jacob peered over the ridge as board planks and splintered pieces of iron showered to the ground. Then a second boxcar exploded, lifting from the track before shattering in a hail of fire, smoke, and debris.

"Is Krupp trying to destroy the evidence?" Fiona asked, utterly confused by the turn of events.

"Evidence of what? That he and his men rode on a train? The fact would be painfully obvious to anyone by now, so why blow up the boxcars? It doesn't make sense." He twisted his hands in an attempt to free his bindings, tipping his head to gesture to the members of the Star Council who were trying to control their mounts. Three of the men who'd been too close to the train lay upon the ground, not moving.

Jacob's ropes loosened and he threw them away. When a third boxcar detonated, he ducked, covering Fiona's head with his body as sparks showered the dusty grass.

When he released her, Fiona glanced up, then squinted into the fire-tinted darkness when she thought she saw a shadow, then two.

"Jacob, look." She pointed beyond the tracks, to where a pair of silhouettes were momentarily illuminated against the blaze.

"Good hell almighty, what are the Beasleys doing here? I sent them home."

"On which train?"

"The one . . . after . . . Dammit, they stowed away!"

"Add it to the list of their crimes."

264

He slapped the ground. "And there's Peebles skulking through the smoke."

"Jacob, when you sent the Beasleys back to Madison . . . did you take away their dynamite?"

"Of course I took it away. I gave it to one of my deputies to . . . keep . . ." He glared in the direction of the wreckage. "They stole it! They sneaked onto the train and stole it from him."

"So it would seem."

His lips twitched in a reluctant smile. "I'll be double damned."

He quickly helped to release her hands. Then they watched as Mr. Peebles and his elderly assistants made their way to the next boxcar. When they scuttled away, Jacob ordered, "Stay here."

"But—"

"Just *stay*, Fiona!"

The air reverberated with the horrible thunder of explosives. Jacob dodged into the confusion of screaming horses and shouting men. He disabled two of Krupp's cohorts and returned with three pistols and a rifle.

"I want you to take this." He gave her the rifle.

Her eyes widened. "I've never shot one of these before."

"So wave it around and scare the living hell out of them. I don't care. Just try not to kill me, Peebles, or the Beasleys."

He tucked one of the revolvers in the back waistband of his trousers, then checked the others for bullets. He nodded. "Ready?"

"For what?"

"It's time for a final bit of gambling, Fiona. Isn't that why I hired you?" She had no time to assimilate his words. He turned his attention to the melee below and yelled, "You're completely surrounded, Krupp. Give yourself up." It was a daring lie, but hopefully the confusion would give credit to the claim.

Krupp's horse whirled in agitation as The Judge waved his weapon, searching for a target.

"Dammit, Grey! There's no one here. I dumped most of your men miles away."

"Did you really? Then who do you think caused this mess? A couple of guardian angels?"

Growling, Krupp aimed in the general direction of Jacob's voice. Jacob fired, then flattened himself against the grassy knoll as an answering shot rang out. When Fiona chanced to look at the scene below them, it was to find that Stone had fallen to the ground, clutching his chest.

"Give yourself up, Judge."

Krupp scowled, gesturing for the few uninjured men who remained to assemble. "Never!"

"None of you will be hanged. I'll see to that. You'll merely be returned to prison."

"Like hell. Do you think I believe such a worthless promise?"

"I have connections with the governor. I can—"

"Your so-called connections are nothing compared to my own. Why do you think Carruthers was so adamant that you take this train?"

Jacob swore when he realized Krupp's influence had spread so far, it included one of the governor's aides. The Judge had been very thorough in building his trap. "You can't escape, Krupp."

"I don't give a damn. I *won't* go back."

A stick of dynamite flew into the middle of the fray. The sod heaved. Several men screamed.

"Your associates are being massacred!" Jacob shouted. "Is that what you want to happen?"

"I don't care. I'll see you rot in hell, that's what I'll do."

"How, Krupp? You're surrounded."

Krupp whirled his horse and galloped toward one of the few remaining boxcars. Sliding from the saddle, he yanked open the door. Darby Kensington knelt by the aperture, his eyes wide, his face pale. Pulling him to the ground, Krupp put a pistol to the man's head.

"Let us go. Let us go, or I'll kill him."

"It won't work, Krupp. We already know your connection to Kensington."

"He's a passenger. An innocent bystander."

"He's your son."

Krupp grinned, then threw back his head and chuckled. "I knew you would unravel the clues. I *knew* it!"

"How did you get Darby to help you, Krupp? How did you get him to agree to spread counterfeit money? Did you tell him it was a trap meant to corner me? Or did you promise him it was just a scheme to make a little money?"

Kensington stiffened even more in his father's arms.

"What else did you bother to say to him, Krupp? Did you explain how he'd unwittingly become an accessory to a brutal prison escape and the deaths of several lawmen? Or did you omit those points"—he paused for emphasis—"as well as the fact that you framed him for the murder of Mickaleen McFee?"

Fiona gasped beside him. Krupp grew still, so still, his eyes narrowing.

Slowly, carefully, Jacob rose to his feet and walked toward the man, holding him in his sights. "I'm right, aren't I? You planted his fob at the scene, hoping that I would jump to the obvious conclusion. You wanted to corner me. You wanted to draw me into a situation I couldn't resist. So you began simply at first: a little counterfeiting trouble that would demand my attention, then a tidal wave of phony bills. After I'd begun to investigate, it was only a matter of time before you could begin the final stages of your plot—to free yourself from prison and follow me on Kensington's last voyage."

Krupp grinned. "How very clever, Grey."

"But you didn't count on having Dub survive the breakout."

"He was supposed to die in that prison."

"So when he lived, you used that to your advantage. You arranged his death, leaving a note with the eight-pointed star."

"I knew it would distract you."

"You hoped I would grow careless."

"You must have thought you were so smart. That you knew my motives inside and out. All the while, I was merely leaving a trail of bread crumbs to lead you right to me."

"Hoping that in the process I would grow angry and therefore grow careless."

"I've been jerking you about on a string for months through the use of this fool." He tightened his hold on Kensington, jerking him slightly.

"Damn you!" Kensington wrenched free of Krupp's grasp, tearing the revolver free and pointing it at his father's head. "Damn you all to hell! You *used* me! You set me up as bait, knowing full well that I would be the one to take the fall."

Krupp lifted a calming hand, but Kensington drew the hammer of the pistol, far from pacified.

"I'm your *son*—your *son!* But you never cared about me at all, did you? You retrieved me from the foundling home only after I threatened to become a political embarrassment. You sent me to boarding school, ignored me, abandoned me until I could prove useful again. You *used* me—I thought to spread your counterfeit bills. But now I know the truth. It was to catch *this* man. Then you set *me* up for murder!"

"Shut up, boy."

"No!" He turned away, walking toward Jacob. "I'm surrendering to you. I'll tell you everything he's done from my end of the deal. I'll show records, ticket stubs, and notes I took of the counterfeiting activities he masterminded."

"Shut up, you whelp!" Krupp lunged for the revolver, snatching it from his son's hands. Startled, Kensington began to run. Krupp swore, then pulled the trigger and shot him in the back.

Screaming, Kensington stumbled and fell against Jacob. He gripped the extra pistol tucked into Jacob's trousers. Whirling, he shot once, twice.

Krupp staggered, clutching the scarlet patches that

bloomed on his chest. "Dar . . . by?" He fell to his knees, staring up at his son in genuine amazement. "But—"

The word was only a puff of sound, then Krupp fell to his stomach, his hands curling into the dirt.

Kensington lowered the pistol bit by bit. "You were right, Papa," he declared softly. "Some things *are* worth waiting for." Then he sobbed in pain, sinking to the ground.

The night air was filled with a muted thundering. Acting instinctively, Jacob lifted his weapon in the direction of the noise, then squinted in disbelief. An engine had appeared on the horizon, one pushing the boxcar and caboose that had housed some of his men. As it rolled to a stop, a single man stepped from the locomotive.

"Ethan?" Jacob called in disbelief.

Ethan waved. "I found something of yours abandoned on the tracks and brought it along."

Within seconds, the area was swarming with deputies. Jacob gestured for one of the men to tend to the wounded gambler.

"What the hell brought you here?"

Ethan rubbed at a very noticeable lump on his forehead. "I was ambushed by a pair of old ladies at the last stop."

"The Beasleys?"

He nodded. "When I woke up, I realized something was wrong, something more than just a wish to stow away. The Beasleys never do anything without a very good reason. So I charged into the railway office, bandied your name around a bit, hinted that one of their trains—as well as a few influential passengers—was about to be robbed, and hopped on one of their locomotives."

"Ladies!"

The Beasleys, who had been standing a few feet away, eavesdropping, reluctantly stepped forward.

"Don't be angry, Jacob," Amelia begged.

"We saw Krupp at the station in Chicago."

"But we couldn't be sure it was him."

"There wasn't time to warn you."

"So we stowed away."

"For a time, at least."

Jacob opened his mouth, but they continued.

"Amelia found the dynamite on the train."

Amelia touched his arm. "You really should warn your men about being so careless."

"So when trouble broke out, we had no alternative but to use it."

"Luckily, Mr. Peebles knew what to do."

When the women stopped for breath, he held up a hand. "Enough. Enough! Ladies, I . . . that is, you should have . . ."

But there was nothing to say. He couldn't scold them. They had literally saved his life. His and Fiona's.

"Thank you, ladies."

They beamed, coloring slightly.

"Thank you for all your help—regardless of your rather unorthodox methods."

The next few minutes were spent battling the fires caused by the explosions. Those cars that had not caught fire were pulled free from the others. Then Jacob's men rode in search of the rest of Krupp's cohorts. Most had disappeared into the night, but those that remained were forced to march into the remaining boxcar. An iron padlock from one of Fiona's trunks was threaded through the handle of the door, and Jacob put Mr. Peebles in place as a guard. As Jacob walked away, the man was pacing back and forth in front of the railway car while the Beasleys reviewed the events of the evening and probed him for details of his duties with the railroad.

Not twenty minutes had passed before the deputies from the main portion of the train appeared, led by Rusty. They rode hell-bent over the horizon on mounts they'd borrowed from a farmer ten miles uptrack. After explaining the situation, Jacob sent them out again to hunt down the last few members of the Star Council who had managed to escape.

As a last thought, Jacob called, "Rusty! Get hold of a

telegraph and order the arrest of Carruthers. He's an accessory to all this."

As the noise of their horses disappeared into the darkness, he turned to Fiona. The evening shadows echoed with a thousand thoughts, ideas, imaginings. She could see in his eyes the relief that they had survived, as well as the weariness and the disgust that so many lives had been wasted.

"You should have that gash tended to as soon as possible," she finally said. "It might need to be stitched."

He eyed her strangely, carefully, intently. "I'm horrible with a needle."

"Then maybe you should delegate the job to me."

Taking her hand, he walked with her to the private car where they had spent so much time over the past few days. They stepped into the shadowy interior, where she lit one of the lamps, illuminating the dusky textures of velvet and brocade.

"Sit, please." She gestured to one of the ottomans in front of the settee.

"Fiona, I—"

"Sit." Brooking no refusal, she pushed him down, then gathered water and towels from the bathing room. Upon returning, she set the supplies on the small reading table at his elbow.

"You are a very tricky man, Jacob Grey. You should have told me that you'd found the fob."

Jacob caught her hand. "I only found it today. I saw it on the bureau. All the little details suddenly seemed to fall into place. It didn't make sense. Why would Kensington kill your father? He didn't know anything about him. And why would he keep his appointment with that train if he knew we were following him? If there's one thing I've learned about the man, it's that he's a bit of a coward. He's not opposed to making a little money, skirting the edge of the law. But he doesn't have what it takes to commit cold-blooded murder. I began to stew over the details of this assignment like a desperate man. Not because of all that had occurred. Not because of the threat Krupp presented. But because I was suddenly struck like a thunderbolt with an idea that seemed totally incredible."

His hand spread over her spine, testing the fragile line that—in the last few days—he had become accustomed to finding enshrouded in steel and canvas and silk. "Suddenly I broke out in an icy sweat. I went running to the parlor car, intent on dragging you off and sending you to safety. All because I'd finally admitted to myself that I've been a stubborn fool."

"Oh?"

"I've allowed myself to be blinded to one of the basic realities of life." His fingers crept up to tangle in her tousled hair. "Man was not meant to spend his life alone. Especially once he has found the other half of his heart."

She blinked at him in disbelief.

"I couldn't bear to think that anything could happen to you. I had to protect you at all costs. Because I love you, Fiona McFee," he stated more clearly.

To his surprise, she didn't throw her arms around his neck or melt into his embrace. She jumped to her feet and began pacing the length of the car.

"So what do we do now?"

He stared at her in astonishment. "I thought a church wedding might be in order, then a house of some sort, and maybe a couple of kids, if you don't mind."

Her eyes gleamed with unshed tears. "Jacob, we've already had this conversation. A relationship between us is impossible."

"Why? You love me too. I know you do."

"Yes, Jacob. I love you. But nothing has changed. You're still a lawman. I'm still a woman with a past."

"Dammit, Fiona!" An increased commotion from outside signaled the return of the bulk of his men. Jacob stood up and took her wrist. "Come with me."

Allowing her no opportunity to protest, he dragged her to the landing outside the main door. As soon as they'd both stepped outside, he held his fingers to his teeth and whistled. Immediately, the deputies turned, some of them in the midst of leading their prisoners to the temporary holding cell made from the only surviving boxcar.

"Men, I intend to marry this woman."

They offered no more reaction than if he'd announced the state of the weather.

"She's a criminal, you know. Soon to be pardoned by the governor, but a criminal nonetheless."

"Kiss her quick and get out here and help us!" one man shouted. The rest turned away to tend to their duties.

Jacob gently pushed Fiona against the railing, bracing his hands on either side of her hips. "Satisfied? It may have taken overly long for *me* to recognize the fact, but no one cares about your past, Fiona. Heaven knows, I don't."

At that, she did throw her arms around his neck to hug him tight. "Ye'd better not be forgettin' yer promises, lawman," she warned.

"Your ribald ways will never be mentioned again."

"That's not what I'm referrin' to. Ye can mention me past as much as ye want. I'm not ashamed of what I am, what I've done. It's the house I'm referrin' to."

He laughed, hauling her close for a passionate kiss, one that displayed his delight and his adoration, his love and his total commitment. When he finally withdrew, there was the soft sound of applause from the opposite side of the track. Peering around the corner of the car, they saw the Beasley sisters grinning and waggling their fingers in greeting.

"I thought I ordered you to go home," Jacob called out.

"We knew you'd be needing our help."

"So I did, ladies."

They blushed becomingly, demonstrating the coquettishness of a pair of young girls.

"I told you he had an affection for her, Amelia."

"No, Sister, *I* told *you*."

Alma sighed. "It matters little who told whom."

"They are adorable together."

"They'll have beautiful children."

Fiona laughed, burying her face in Jacob's chest in embarrassment. "Well, Jacob, I suppose there's only one more question to be addressed."

"What's that?"

"It's obvious who my bridesmaids will be. But which of the Beasleys should walk in first during the church processional?"

Epilogue

JACOB GREY SWUNG FROM HIS HORSE AND TOOK A MOMENT TO stop, close his eyes, and breathe deeply.

A hint of fall tinged the air, although it was only mid-September. Somewhere, in the midst of the breeze, he sensed baking bread and something more—probably cookies or sweetbreads. He heard the high-pitched squeals of Jake and Celie running through the garden, Lettie's calls of caution, Ethan's murmured replies.

His eyes opened and he stared up at the Grey family boarding house where he had been born, where he had grown up. So much had happened, he could scarcely credit how much his life had changed. After dealing with Krupp and his men, Jacob had brought Fiona here, to his birthplace, the little town of Madison, Illinois. They'd joined Lettie, arriving just in time for the birth of her third child. Then, within days, there had been a wedding.

His and Fiona's.

He looped the reins of his mount around the hitching post, smiling in pleasure as the sun glinted on the gold band he wore on his left hand. Yes, so much had changed. All for the better.

Walking up the cracked brick walk, he climbed the

steps to the stoop, ignoring the front door and following the whitewashed boards of the porch to the side of the house, where a screened enclosure looked out toward the creek. He slipped inside, slowly, quietly, not wanting to startle the woman who sat in a rocking chair, crooning an Irish lullaby to the baby in her arms.

"What did they say, Jacob?"

He smiled, realizing that he needn't have bothered to tiptoe. Fiona had known the moment he'd arrived.

"They grumbled a bit, hemmed and hawed, but they finally accepted my resignation as U.S. marshal."

She glanced up from the bundle in her arms, little Phebe Fiona McGuire, her namesake and godchild. "I suppose that means you're officially unemployed?"

He grinned, shaking his head. "Not really. It seems that Madison's sheriff intends to move to Kentucky to be closer to his family. They've offered the position to me."

She smiled in genuine delight. "So we'll be staying here?"

"We'll be staying here." He walked toward her, kneeling on the floor to stroke the baby's cheek, then glance into his wife's beautiful face.

"You've kept your promises, Jacob."

His brow furrowed in confusion.

"A church wedding," she reminded him softly. "A house . . . All that remains . . ."

He stared at her thoughtfully, before finishing, "Is a couple of kids." He glanced down at the baby in her arms, feeling the potent hunger that it be his child, his son or daughter. "We've only been married a short time. You'll probably want to wait a bit."

"No." She leaned close to whisper, "If my suspicions are confirmed, there will be no waiting for us, Jacob Grey."

Jacob stared at her in disbelief, then laughed, hugging her tightly against him, baby and all. Phebe squirmed and snuffled, and he was forced to draw back.

"Really?"

"It's a little soon to say, but I think so."

"Are you all right? Are you ill? Heavens! You shouldn't be out in the heat like this! I'd—"

She placed a finger over his lips. "I love you, Jacob."

The protestations, the worry drained free beneath a tidal wave of wonder. Staring at her, he wondered what he had done so right in his life that the Fates would offer him this woman, this gem, this prize. He had no illusions that their life together would be filled with honeysuckle and roses—they were both far too stubborn and independent for that. But he did know that the future would never be dull, never be lonely. They had survived gunfire, murder, and mayhem.

Now they only had to wait and watch the silken promises of the past unfold, blossom, and grow into the reality of a beautiful future.

"Let's go inside."

"Whatever you say."

He helped her stand, drawing her into the cool shadows of the house. Only after their footsteps had disappeared did two blue-tinted heads pop up from the edge of the stoop.

"Do you think they knew we were eavesdropping?" Amelia asked in concern.

Alma snorted. "Doubt it. They're far too wrapped up in themselves for that."

The women sat down again on the bench from which they'd heard the entire conversation unobserved.

"How long do you suppose before the baby will come?"

"It will be a spring baby, I'd say."

"Ooo. How lovely! Just when the flowers are coming out."

Alma opened her mouth to say something, paused, then stared at her sister in anxiety. "We must ready the garden immediately, Amelia."

"Plant extra bulbs."

"Daffodils, tulips . . . yes! We'll have this yard blooming to beat the band for that dear child."

Amelia's hand flew to her lips. "Oh, no."

"What?"

"The gophers! We've had such an infestation this past year. They'll eat all our bulbs."

Alma took as deep a breath as her corset would allow, then stood up and began marching determinedly toward their own rooms in the back portion of the house. "Come along, Amelia."

"Where are we going?"

"To get the dynamite. Those gophers *will not* spoil our surprise for that baby. You get the sticks, I'll get the fuses, then we'll drop them down the holes and blast those little varmints to kingdom come!"